The Misadventures of the
Laundry Hag:

Swept Under the Rug

Jennifer L. Hart

Contents

The Misadventures of the Laundry Hag:

Swept Under the Rug

Crime and grime are everywhere, at least in Maggie Phillips' opinion. Deep in the throes of a New England winter, Maggie's still adjusting to her new role as confidential informant for the Hudson Police Department. When a suspicious fax is sent to one of her new clients, Maggie is sure she's unearthed a conspiracy. With no crime to investigate, however, the Hudson P.D. can do nothing-that is until a wealthy trophy wife disappears and the FBI is called in to the hunt.

On the home front, her twelve-year-old son is growing up way too fast, while her brother is back with a few surprises destined to wreak havoc on the household. To frost the whole crappy cake, her best friend's marriage is falling apart, which leaves Maggie worrying over her own. All of the family drama is put into perspective, however, when Maggie is arrested for kidnapping and blackmail.

Between economic woes and a now tarnished reputation, Maggie is in way over her head. Yet out of the ashes of frustration and failure, something great might emerge. If she survives the birthing process that is....

Prologue

"**I** need to speak with Detective Capri, ASAP!" No doubt I looked like a lunatic rushing in off the streets, my hair a wind-blown rat's nest and reeking of Murphy oil soap. Somewhere in my mad dash from the Valentino estate to my Mini Cooper, I'd lost my pony-tail holder and trashed the knee on my favorite pair of cleaning jeans. No matter though, I still clutched the evidence to my chest, gripping the photocopied paper with all my adrenalin-charged strength.

The blond mountain of a uniformed officer behind the battered check-in desk didn't quite roll his eyes, but I could tell he'd stifled the impulse. "She's in a meeting, Ms. Phillips—"

"*Mrs.* Phillips." I corrected out of habit. God alone knew why the officers at the Hudson Police Department couldn't seem to get it through their heads that I was married. Probably because no man in his right mind would lay claim to the over-zealous Laundry Hag.

Too bad for Neil, he'd been stuck with me long before I'd become the bane of Hudson's finest.

"Mrs. Phillips," The burley blond guy tried to stare me down, but I wasn't about to back off. I had two pre-teens at home and if this stegosaurus descendent wanted a battle of wills, I'd kick his Big & Tall butt.

"Look Bub, I'm working with Detective Capri and she needs this information, stat!" Cripes, I needed to lay off the primetime medical dramas.

He rose to his full height, which practically brushed the hanging lamp behind the desk. Thunderclouds gathered along his eyebrows and I wondered whether the bub or the stat had torqued him up.

"It's all right, Stan, I'm here." Detective Capri hustled down the corridor from the bowels of the precinct. Either she had stellar timing or someone tipped her off that her favorite visitor was making another scene.

Capri dressed like a man, walked like a man and from what little I'd seen of her in

8

action, she fought like a man. I had no idea what her first name was, but I called her Butch since no man could be more so.

Capri wore pantsuits a la the Hillary for Prez collection; always with the juxtaposition military issue combat boots. Today's suit came in a navy blue with a crisp white button-up and her only accessory was a scowl. "If you'll follow me Ma'am." She didn't make it a question, just whirled on her size nine shit-kicker and trundled off.

I cast a smug glance to the blond menace before scurrying after her.

Capri led me to her office, a small cubbyhole littered with polyurethane coffee cups and reams of random papers in varying colors. My inner neat-freak itched to tidy the stacks and dispose of the garbage, but from previous conversations, I'd gleaned some insight into the detective. Capri liked her mess and wouldn't allow me to monkey with her system.

"What do you have for me?" Small talk was not one of Capri's strengths, but I appreciated that she didn't roll her eyes or lace her tone with sarcasm. I may not possess much pride, but the Hudson P.D. did a number on it with every visit.

"Here," I snapped the photocopy open and handed the paper over with a flourish. "I was cleaning at the Valentinos'—"

"Do you mean Markus Valentino, the electronics mogul?" Capri cut me with a sharp glance.

"Yes, he owns a place on the outskirts of town with trophy wife number three, a former

Miss Texas. She hired me on right after Christmas, and today I happened to be dusting the den when a fax came in."

Capri studied the photocopy, her mouth set in a grim line. "'The Phoenix is rising; you're gonna get burned'," she read aloud. "Where's the original?"

"I put it back in the fax machine for Valentino to find." Capri shook her head and I scowled, wondering what was on her mind.

"I meant what number did the fax come from? If you had the number we could trace it back to the source."

Oh. Well, shoot. I shrugged helplessly and felt like a twit for not paying attention to such an important detail.

Capri shuffled some papers and actually found a clear spot on her desk. She set my evidence down and spun the paper to face me. "These letters appear to be cut and pasted out of magazines. See how the type is different? Of course, without seeing the original, I have no way of knowing if this is in color, if the letters came from different papers or not. Some word programs can create this particular effect. You sure it was a fax, not a photocopy? Most people have the two-in-one machines."

I nodded; encouraged because she hadn't brushed my find aside. "No one else was in that wing of the house and the machine made a weird ring-buzz noise combo before the paper came out. What do you think it means?"

"Honestly? It's probably a prop in some role-playing sex game. The fax had to come from someone privy to the fax number, hence someone who is acquainted with Mister or Mrs.

10

Valentino. The Phoenix may very well be a pet name for Valentino's Johnson."

Shit on a stick. "Yeah, that's what Neil thought, too." Oops. Did I say the words aloud?

"Maggie," Capri growled and I winced. Oh Magoo, you've done it again! The detective only called me Maggie when she was preparing a lecture. Silence hung in the air and just like the pause between an infant's cries, the longer the breath, the louder the complaint.

"You are supposed to be one of my confidential informants. Do you need me to define 'confidential' to you again?"

Unthinkingly, I squirmed in my seat. "I just thought—"

"No, you didn't think. Your husband does *not* need to be brought into the loop, especially since he has no connection with the law. Isn't it bad enough everyone at the station has a pretty clear idea of why you show up here thrice weekly? Most C.I.'s bring in bogus tips to collect a fee. But you're not after the money; you're looking to bring down the bad guys. Problem is; that's my job. Here's how the position works. You bring me a tip, I investigate the tip. The more information you give me, the more time I invest in following up on your leads. So far, we've got diddly-squat. Take a stab at how many man-hours I've put into following up on your tips?"

I threw my shoulders back, straightening my spine. "Hey, I'm new to this cloak and dagger scene and can I help it if I don't know what I'm looking for?"

"Trust your instincts." Her matter-of-fact statement stabbed me in the gut, but I hid

11

my reaction quickly. No need to flaunt my vulnerability to Capri, since I wasn't sure I could trust *her* yet.

Since the last detective I'd put my faith in had tried to shoot me, I was a smidge gun shy.

"Go home, Mrs. Phillips and don't contact me again until you have information on an actual crime."

I'd been dismissed. Again. Battling my temper, I stuck my nose in the air and sashayed out of Capri's office, feigning confidence I didn't feel. I'm a big believer in the fake it 'til you make it school of thought. Unfortunately, I bumped into the water cooler, and sent the ten-gallon jug crashing to the floor where it glugged its contents onto the linoleum.

Let me tell you, it's hard to maintain a dignified air when you constantly need to seek out a mop in order to clean up after yourself and everyone around you. At least I enjoy my work.

One

"**M**aggie, I think it's clean enough." Sylvia stood with her hands on her hips, a scowl marring her classic features. In that pose, wearing a purple leotard and turquoise tights, she could have petitioned for membership to the *Justice League*. Work-out Woman, battling the bulge one frumpy housewife at a time.

"You're supposed to be toning with the abdominal machine, not rubbing it down for the night."

"Can I help it if it's dusty?" I swiped at the pulley system with my paper towel, obviously the first to do so in quite a while.

"You want me to be comfortable doing the reps, then let me get to know the machine first."

Sylvia snorted. "This isn't a date, even though there will be a bit of skin-to-vinyl contact."

"Exactly! And how many other patrons have indulged in the same? Hairy, sweaty pimply-assed patrons." I squinted at the crunch machine. "You're the whore of the fitness world."

Sylvia let out a bark of laughter. "You're terrible; stalling because you don't want to do the exercises."

Well, give the woman a cigar! I wondered what tipped her off, my sloth-like movements or whining like a seven-year-old girl in Toys-R-Us's Barbie section. Usually, my bevy of complaints was enough to convince Sylvia to hang at the juice bar and gab, but for some unknown reason, she'd decided to stick to her guns.

"I can't believe you bring your own bottle of cleanser. The gym provides plenty of anti-fungal, anti-bacterial spray solutions for people to use."

I snorted and scrubbed the levers under the seat. "Yeah, I've been watching and I have yet to see anyone replace the liquid in those spray bottles. Besides, have you taken a look at the unsavory sorts who frequent this dive?"

"Like your husband?" Sylvia smirked. "Maggie, you need to get a grip. You're becoming a paranoid recluse and it's not doing a thing for your figure."

I ignored her brutal observation, mostly because she was right. This obsessive creature

14

I'd become wasn't fit or fun, but I couldn't keep from indulging my fears; I'd seen too many horrors and looked evil in the eye.

Sylvia nabbed my cleanser and pointed to the seat. "Sit and crunch, now."

Fine, but I didn't have to like it. I sat and lowered the shoulder harness, before gripping the handles. Struggling, I tried to contract my abdominal muscles and make the motion to rock my upper body toward my lap, but couldn't do it. "What weight is this thing set for?"

Sylvia glanced over me and the corner of her mouth kicked up. "You're only pulling ten pounds in addition to your own body weight. Still want to argue about your state of physical fitness?"

Or lack thereof. Damn, she was right, I was a mess. Fervently, I tried again and managed to lift the weight about three quarters of an inch, before gravity bested me. I released the handles, huffing at the indignity and the exertion.

"Great job, now just do fourteen more reps, take a breather then two more sets."

"You're joking, right?"

"If you want to tone, you need lower weight, higher reps. Of course if you want to build muscle I could always add some more weight."

"Sylvie, at this rate, we'll be here all night! And I want to get home in time for *House*."

She pinched the bridge of her nose. "I'm getting a headache. How about you do your scrub-n-scour routine, while I run out to my car and see if I have any ibuprofen? I'll meet you in the ball room in five, but you're gonna do the exercises."

I'd never heard Sylvia this agitated before and it unnerved me. Usually she radiated inner calm, a self-possessed rock to my sea of turbulent emotion. "Do you wanna talk about it?"

Sylvia shook her head and took what she referred to as a cleansing breath. Since she wasn't huffing Lysol, I was clueless as to the cleansing part. "Maybe another day, I'm a little tired."

And I wasn't helping, acting like a petulant five-year-old. The purplish smudges under her eyes matched her leotard, but I doubted she'd set out to make that fashion statement. Maybe this work-out was more for her benefit than mine. Guilt flayed me and I made a silent vow to keep the pithy commentary to a minimum.

"I'm here if you need to vent," I offered and spritzed the seat of the crunch machine.

"I know, and thanks. Ball room in five." She turned and made her way around various weight machines towards the lobby.

Crud muffins. I really didn't want to do calisthenics. A stroll on the treadmill or even the Stairmaster I could deal with, but calisthenics were akin to self-imposed torture. Worse even than the weight machines, since other patrons wanted a shot at those and there was a time limit. Using one's own body for resistance could go on until the end of time. And given my state of physical fitness and Sylvia's do or die mood, it just might.

16

Disheartened, I gave the crunch machine a final swipe and trundled in the direction of the ball room. The ball room was really a storage studio located in the far corner of the fitness area. Staff and members alike stored a cache of various free weights, balance balls and yoga mats while some of the personal trainers took their clients there for one-on-one instruction, but it usually remained empty. Light shone from beneath the door, and I deduced that the staff hadn't locked it up for the night. So much for my feeble hope.

Quit your griping. You need this exercise. My inner critic scolded and I knew it was right. As a hopeless klutz, I had no equal and I'd been avoiding any kind of obvious exercise for longer than I could remember. But I'd crossed the hill to the far side of thirty and was losing muscle tone as well as dealing with a slower metabolism. People already wondered how I'd snagged a prize stud like Neil—who at almost thirty-seven, looked more like a male underwear model then when I'd married him a decade ago. I didn't need to add my flabby abs and saggy buns to the grisly picture.

Resolve firmly duct-taped to the sticking place, I opened the door to the ball room and almost tripped over my own feet.

Why did this keep happening to me?

The room was occupied, all right. The man had his mesh gym shorts tangled around his ankles and all of the bits normally covered were blocked by a big-haired brunette on her knees in front of him. They were making a surprising amount of noise—a soundtrack I

17

would take with me to the grave—and hadn't noticed my arrival.

I would have backed away quietly, but froze when I finally caught a glimpse of the man's features. (Hey, next time you see a bottom-less man see if his face is the first place *you* look.)

Even though I didn't make a move, the lunatic in my head was running in circles, flapping her arms like a crazed Henny Penny and chanting "The sky is falling, the sky is falling!"

"Hey, I brought the radio from my studio I thought...." I'll never know what Sylvia thought in that final moment before the sky clobbered her, because she'd caught sight of her husband being serviced in the ball room.

Eric and his partner picked up the pace, their rhythm striving for the ultimate crescendo and I wanted to nudge Sylvia into action. If it were me in her shoes, I'd make damn sure he never got to finish, before I started the ritualistic disembowelment. But this was her crisis to deal with as she saw fit.

Apparently, she needed more time, because she tugged me out the door and closed it soundlessly behind her.

"Sylvie...," I started, but any words I offered her would be cold comfort at best.

"Why isn't he in his office?" Sylvia's asked in an even tone. Her perfect blond eyebrows met at the bridge of her straight nose. "He has an office on the second floor since he made assistant manager. Why the ball room?"

"Does it matter?" I asked quietly, enraged both for my friend and with her. Why

18

the hell wasn't she confronting the faithless S.O.B? I had her back, if she needed moral support, or a wingman for the take down. I may not be fit, but I could definitely tackle Eric from behind and keep him pinned while she gelded him. Or rip the tramp's hair out of her feather-headed scalp.

Sylvia shook her head and stared at the ground. No doubt she was processing, making plans, deciding on the best way to handle the philandering scum-sucking cretin.

I might have been a tiny bit miffed over the situation, but sometimes going with one's gut was the best course of action. No amount of consideration would prevent Eric from getting his rocks off, but an accurately thrown ten pound barbell....

Then, it was too late. Eric opened the door and I caught a glimpse of the dark haired woman stuffing her megaboobs back into her jog bra and casting him a disbelieving look for his obvious consideration.

Eric brushed past me without acknowledging my presence, but stopped dead when his gaze took in a pale-faced Sylvia. She'd wrapped her arms around herself and wouldn't meet his stare. Her posture radiated hurt in staggering waves, combating with the righteous anger I threw off on her behalf.

"Sylvie, I...." He trailed off, searching for a cover story and she looked at him hopefully as if whatever came out of his mouth would erase the last five minutes.

"We were just—"

"Having a little oral sex." The woman finished for him. Hell hath no fury indeed. This

19

broad had taken in the scene, realized Eric had walked into a cauldron of hot water, and tossed a load of kindling on the fire. "Sorry Hon, he told me he wasn't seeing anybody."

"This is his wife!" I yelled in outrage. Damn it all, someone needed to shout.

The brunette blanched and I shot a scud-missile at her with my eyes. "What the hell is wrong with you that you perform sexual favors in a public place with a guy you barely know? Don't you value yourself? Aren't you worth more than a quickie on the sly with a lying pig? What would your mother think?"

She opened and closed her mouth like a fish.

"Maggie," Sylvia pleaded, but I wasn't done. Some things need attention in the here and now. I whirled on Eric.

"And you! I actually thought you had a few brain cells to rub together. What kind of insensitive ass-Muppet betrays his gorgeous wife for a five second orgasm with an overly-teased piece of fluff?"

"You don't know what the hell you're talking about. Why don't you stay out of my business?" A warning threaded through Eric's tone.

Sylvia hadn't said a word other than my name and continued to tug half-heartedly on my arm. Other people had ceased their workouts to watch the spectacle. Poor Sylvia. And I had to don my crazy hat bringing more attention to the situation. The mortification written across her face convinced me.

"That's a mighty fine idea." I whirled on my heel and marched off to the front desk. "I

want to cancel my membership," I announced
to the tanned Adonis manning the phones.

"Uh...well, there's a form you need to fill
out and—"

I waved a hand, practically bonking him
on the beak. "Whatever. Just as long as I can
register a complaint with the owner."

"A complaint about what?"

"Unsanitary conditions in the ball
room."

* * * *

I asked Sylvia to come to my house for a
bit, but deep down I knew she craved alone
time, and wasn't surprised when she refused.
With any luck, she'd bounce back and set her
life straight by changing the locks on her front
door before Eric came home. I'd already
offered to send Neil to the local hardware store
on her behalf.

"Hey gang, Mom's home!" Neil stood
and stretched his back as I staggered over the
threshold of our humble abode. As was custom,
two backpacks, three baskets of unfolded linens
and a pile of mail awaited my attention in the
miniscule entryway which doubled as our
foyer. The new coat of sage paint I'd applied a
few days earlier still smelled fresh and Neil had
finally hung the family pictures I'd been
hounding him about.

"Good workout?" Neil dropped a kiss on
the top of my head and I stifled the urge to fall
into his arms and sob. Two adrenaline spikes
and more surprises and self-doubt than I'd
wanted to count in the past ten hours made

stringing a sentence together damn near impossible.

"Mom, Josh is in the bathroom and he won't come out!" Kenny's words were punctuated with violent pounding. "Come on, dweeb, I gotta go!"

"Kenny, use ours for the love of Pete!" Neil's voice was tinged with exasperation.

"How long has he been in there?"

Neil glanced at the mantel clock below his big screen T.V., where he'd paused an episode of *Deadliest Catch*. "Almost an hour."

"Is he sick? Vomiting? Have you called the doctor yet? I heard there's a stomach bug going around—"

I cut myself off and headed for the kitchen where the emergency phone numbers resided, but Neil tugged me back by the shirt.

"Maggie, he's not sick, he's twelve. *Twel*-ve, as in adolescent, pre-pubescent twelve."

I blinked a few times and Neil chucked me under the chin then locked his gaze with mine in silent communion. I stared into the hazel depths and the light dawned.

"Cripes, not yet." I sagged onto my ugly yet practical barstools and the urgency to do something fled. "I'm not ready for this."

"Really Uncle Scrooge, this is nothing you need to do anything about." Neil stood behind me and massaged the tension from my neck and shoulders." He's getting older, he has a girlfriend—"

"No he doesn't." I shook my head and shrugged out from under his hold.

"That girl who was here at Thanksgiving, Olivia."

"There's nothing official, they just chat online sometimes."

Neil cocked his head to the side and narrowed his eyes at me. "Kids don't meet at a sock hop, then share a root beer float at the local soda shop anymore, Maggs. Communicating online is dating to the next generation."

"I was born in the seventies, Neil. And my first date tried to sell me stolen lawn gnomes he'd filched from the church rummage sale."

He stared at me for a beat, then doubled over in laughter. I'm pretty sure he believed I'd made that up. I sighed. Truth can be stranger than fiction.

Once Neil got control of himself, he resumed the shoulder rub in silence. Obviously, he thought I was a few yachts shy of a boat show. He just didn't get the mother-to-adopted son dynamic. It seemed like a few days ago, Josh had been a solemn, wide-eyed toddler in need of a mother's unconditional love. And now he was growing up, in the bathroom....

I winced and derailed that train of thought. Neil was right, as usual. This had nothing to do with me and everything to do with Mother Nature, the selfish cow.

"They've been fighting more lately, over space and privacy. It's probably time to give Josh his own room." Apparently Neil decided to keep the bombs falling before I could fully regroup. My life was changing too fast and I didn't cotton to change very well. Upheaval was one guaranteed ingredient to turn the mild-mannered Laundry Hag into a belligerent, frothing beast.

My wrath focused on Neil, the calm eye in the center of my category five turmoil. The man didn't get worked up about anything and while this usually provided a good balance in our marriage, right now he was pissing me off.

I blanked my expression. "If that's what you think is best."

His eyebrows drew together to form a dark V. "Don't do this, Maggie."

Tapping my inner southern Belle, I smiled absently and patted his arm. "You always know what to do, so I'll defer to your superior intellect."

He groaned and dropped his chin to his chest. Take that, hot stuff!

Neil hated when I didn't fight back almost as much as I hated losing every argument we had. Granted, sometimes we'd fight, he'd win and then I'd go my merry way, doing as I pleased. Typically though, I wanted to please him before myself so arguing was always a win-win scenario for Neil. Not arguing, however childish it may seem, gave me a bit of a boost. My husband is not the type of man to yell at a woman, especially a non-confrontational woman. I always stopped short of bringing tears into the game, but every so often I needed an edge, a way to make him understand my level of frustration.

The patronizing tone took all the fight out of Neil. His shoulders rounded and he leaned back against the counter. He didn't say anything and I got up to fetch a glass of water, just to give myself something to do.

"I set up an appointment with a marriage counselor for tomorrow."

The water slid down the wrong pipe and I choked. "Are you serious?" I wheezed at his profile.

He didn't answer me, just stared at the school calendar on the fridge. Neil had mentioned going to a marriage counselor a few months back, but I thought the idea went extinct after the holidays. Granted, we had problems and miscommunications, but to actually go to therapy like our relationship was falling apart....

Unbidden, the image of Eric and his bimbo in the ball room flashed and I cringed. No doubt, I'd been born with some sort of fornicator locator, because I always seem to walk in on people having sex. As if that isn't enough, it was always people having sex who *shouldn't* be having sex, at least with each other. I studied my handsome husband and flinched at the stress lines around his eyes. Guilt flayed me for my self-centeredness. He deserved more from me. A few hours out of my crazy life might not be a bad thing and deep down, I was afraid if I didn't acquiesce to this, one day my fornicator locator might steer me to Neil. My heart couldn't take that kind of beating.

"Okay, I'll be sure to clear my schedule."

Two

"Maggie, dear, it's Laura."

Despite the widespread induction of caller ID, my mother-in-law always insists on identifying herself to me when she phones. As if the sound of her voice wasn't enough to whip up a healthy dose of dread in my bowels.

She'd never once invited me to call her Mom. Never made the effort to nurture any kind of relationship with her only daughter-in-law, no matter how far I went out of my way to please her. I dealt with her because I had to, for

26

Neil and the boys. Family obligations really stinks sometimes.

"How are you, Laura?" I strove to keep a distant and polite note in my voice, but I'm not big on hiding my emotions. Holding stuff in gives people ulcers.

I'd picked up the phone on the way to the mailbox and the winter air stole the breath from my lungs. The second week in February and at least another month of daytime highs slightly above freezing. I really missed Virginia Beach.

"I've been better, what with this new partner at the firm driving me to distraction. They get younger every year and the inexperience shows. Holding a sweaty hand and telling the newest pimple-faced hire that it'll all be just fine is *not* how I foresaw spending my golden years."

I couldn't picture my mother-in-law holding anyone's hand unless it was to keep him still while she latched onto his jugular.

"However, that's another matter. The reason I'm calling is to invite you to a luncheon downtown on Thursday."

I held the phone away from my ear and scowled at it. No way did I hear that right. "Come again?"

"It'll be a decent-size event for a friend of mine who is retiring. Right down the street from Beacon Hill."

"You want me to go to a luncheon? With you?" The questions sounded even more stupid than I'd imagined, but in my defense, my mother-in-law brings out the worst in me. The last time she'd introduced me to friends of

27

hers, I'd been detained by the police after some yahoo off-ed a man and dumped his body in my wheelbarrow. Even if I wasn't a devoted stay-at-home-mom and a cleaning lady to boot, I figured Laura wouldn't show me off. Must be the bumpkin stamp on my forehead.

"Yes dear.... A luncheon." The answer came slowly, as if Laura was communicating with the squirrelly village idiot. She said dear the way some people say dumb-ass.

Scowling, I rolled my head around on my shoulders, as if understanding would fall into place with enough centripetal force.

"I will email you the time and address. You can come early and pick me up at the house. Be sure to wear something appropriate, none of your flashier get-ups."

I blinked, but didn't respond. Neil once said his mother issued more orders than all the BUD/s instructors he'd had during training to become a SEAL. While her words might have been camouflaged as a request, there was no doubt in my mind that I'd been appointed for the task.

"I'll have to check my schedule before I can commit to anything," I hedged, but there was no way I'd agree to her whims until I figured out the why of it. "Neil and I have some stuff going on and I promised—"

"What sort of 'stuff'?" Suspicion coated her tone.

For an instant, my inner smart-aleck wanted to retort 'wild monkey sex,' but I came to my senses in time. Laura made it blatantly obvious that she didn't appreciate my sense of

28

humor. Her loss. I was simply glad Neil hadn't inherited her superiority complex.

"Oh you know, some post-holiday shopping, a few appointments we've been putting off, things like that." I purposefully kept my answer vague because I didn't want Laura's take on our seeing a marriage counselor. Of course, she'd see it as my fault and do her best to make me feel like a steaming pile of manure.

"I see. Well, I would hate to hold you up from your busy social life." The frost in her voice chilled me more than the Massachusetts's winter. The phone clicked in my ear. Another lesson on how to win friends and influence in-laws brought to you by Maggie Phillips.

The snow had melted a bit on our driveway, but more was predicted for the next day. How did Yankees deal with this every stinking year?

I scuttled inside and wrapped a blanket around my shoulders. Flipped through the mail, sorted bills from junk and left Neil's *Men's Fitness* magazine on his end table.

Another fight had ensued when Neil realized I'd cancelled all of our memberships to the gym. Now he was stuck running at the high school track and working out with free weights in our garage to keep fit and he wasn't happy about it.

Depressed, I sat down at the computer and checked my email. Several requests had come in for my cleaning services. I sent the auto response Josh had created for me, letting the client know my rates had changed. When I'd first been lured into this cleaning business,

I'd worked for way too little and consequently, became the Hag everyone wanted to hire. By charging more, I'd turned off some potential clients, but also made a bit of money last month. I still had to turn people down because I had yet to hire a new cleaning partner.

Now what? Neil was at work, picking up some overtime before our 1:00 session with the marriage guru and the boys wouldn't be back from school for hours. I'd knocked on Sylvia's door twice already and she either wasn't home or refused to answer. Eric's SUV hadn't been parked in the driveway, so I gathered he was lying low like the snake he resembled.

Ruminating on Eric and Sylvia's marriage was not a healthy way to spend my time. After a few moments, I decided to take a page out of Neil's book and exercise my troubles away.

Every pair of sweats I owned had at least two bleach stains on them, so I snagged a pair of my husband's track pants, rolling them at the waist a few times so I wouldn't trip over the cuffs. Donning crappy sneakers and an extra sweatshirt, gloves and Neil's SEAL cap, I checked out my appearance then wished I'd resisted. I looked like the Stay-Puff marshmallow man. Hopefully Bill Murray wouldn't show up and zap me into another dimension.

Grabbing my keys and cell phone, I locked the house then hit the streets. Our neighborhood is built on a series of rolling hills and the bright sun sparkled off the snow covered rooftops below. Mid-morning on a weekday, no neighbors were out and about

30

since I'm the only stay-at-home mom in the community. Just as well, since I didn't particularly want any witnesses as I stumbled/ran.

Jogging has never been my forte and I lasted maybe a minute before I decreased my unsteady lope to a brisk walk. My mother had always said I was one of those girls who couldn't do two things at once, and bless her skeptical soul, she was right. Neither my irascible brother nor I could walk and chew gum, let alone jog and think. Since I didn't want to think about Josh locking himself in the bathroom, Eric getting serviced by the Fran Dresher look-alike or my husband thinking our marriage needed an intervention, I picked up my pace again. My muscles were strong, built from years of vigorous cleaning and frenetic mothering, but I couldn't seem to get my breathing under control.

Stumble, step, wheeze, stumble, step, wheeze. I focused on inhaling through my nose, shoving oxygen down into my lungs by force of will. After another indeterminable amount of time— maybe forty seconds— I slowed again and gasped for breath. This was ridiculous, my husband could run a five minute mile and he was pushing forty! Granted, he had the benefit of BUD/s training, the hardcore physical conditioning required for a man to become a Navy SEAL, but Neil was a natural athlete and made his health a priority.

As I struggled for air, my gaze landed on the Kline mansion situated on top of the hill. Last I knew, Mr. Kline had put the house up for sale and was off being strange in some other neighborhood. He was a decent, if wacky man, but I wished I'd never met him. My life had spiraled out of control the moment I'd set foot in his house and I wanted it back.

Determination burned in the pit of my stomach and I started off again. I was tired of my pity party, tired of being the laughingstock of the Hudson P.D. Tired of fretting about my family and friends, tired of jumping every time a door slammed or a car backfired. That sick S.O.B had already taken enough in his quest for vengeance, and he couldn't hurt me anymore. I needed to get some control over my life. Neil had told me the men who made it all the way through the zealous training and into the SEAL teams shared one common trait, absolute resolve. They saw the trident pin at the end and unflinchingly worked to attain it.

Well, I wanted to be fit and fabulous, or at least be able to run a freaking mile if I wanted. My cell phone rang and I praised the Lord and slowed to retrieve it from my pants pocket. Rome wasn't built in a day after all.

"Hello?" I rasped into the phone. Crap, one would think I'd been having a smoking contest with the Marlboro Man.

"Maggie my love, where are you?" Leo sang into the phone. Ever upbeat and energetic, Leo is a housekeeper for my in-laws and my best bud, after Neil, for close to a decade. He's worked for Laura for almost as long and is the only person I know who calls her a gorgon to her face. Why she hasn't fired him is still a mystery, but I suspect it has something to do with his triple chocolate cake. Gorgons need to eat, too.

"You're in a good mood." I observed.

"Why talk when you can sing? Why walk when you can dance?" Leo sighed dreamily and it clicked into place.

"Uh oh, you met someone. Where and what's he like? Come on Leo, dish."

"Perhaps I'm happy just because the sun is shining and here I have a few minutes to talk to my very best friend. Does everything in the world need to be about a man?"

"Yes," we answered at the same time and laughed.

"So come on, get to the juicy stuff. What does he look like?" No man would ever be good enough for my pal, not only is he a total peach on a fast track for sainthood, he looks a bit like a mature Jude Law, only less broody. Chances were good that I'd feel the same way about both Kenny and Josh when they started dating, so smothering Leo was good practice.

"Where are you?" Leo asked again.

"Where are you?" I shot back and moved over to the side of the road to let a car pass. Instead, the vehicle slowed and the window rolled down to reveal a grinning Leo.

"Want some candy, little girl?"

"You're a sick, sick man. How did you find me?" I shut my phone and climbed into the car.

"I went to your house first and when no one answered, I called you. The wheezing tipped me off. Thought you could use a ride home. Or an oxygen tank."

"Quit picking on me and spill."

Leo loved to tell drawn-out stories and he was quite good at painting a picture. "Since

33

it was my night off, I went to a party in South Boston with a few of my friends. Do you remember Dillon?"

"The angel who made me those slipcovers?" Without consulting me, my mother-in-law had purchased a sofa and matching love-seat for us for Christmas. It may have been a nice gesture, if made out of kindness instead of mortification. Or if the furniture was scotch-guarded to protect the gleaming white upholstery.

"That's him. Anywho, he bought this fab mini-mansion, which he just finished renovating. Total Greco-Roman masterpiece, sculpted columns, authentic wall treatments throughout. He had the idea he'd do a restore and flip, but with the market cooling off, he got stuck with it."

"Yikes, makes me glad we unloaded our house in Virginia Beach when we did." I'd been following the housing bubble story online and some of the tales curled my hair. My own personal nightmare is to be penniless and at the whim of the universe. It'd happened before and I'd survived, but the thought of losing everything, of being so poor I couldn't buy food for my family gave me palpitations.

"Well, he rented out the upstairs half for a song so he could keep up with mortgage payments." Leo was like a little kid saving his favorite piece of candy 'til last.

"And...," I prompted as Leo pulled up to my house.

"Do you have any good coffee? Not that generic brand swill, but fresh-off-the-Columbian-mule coffee?"

34

"I swear; you are such a drama queen."

"Hello kettle, this is the pot calling and I'm sorry to say it, but you're black."

"Fine, I'll make you some real coffee." I lunged from the car, and slammed the door. So what if I was proving his point?

My freezer was stocked for a Leo visit and I retrieved a bag of whole bean medium-dark and tossed it at his head. "You make the coffee. I need a shower."

"Work on my day off? You must be joking."

"You brought it on yourself, pal. Besides, you make better coffee."

"True, true. It's such a burden being me." Leo knew where I kept everything and he already had the filter in place by the time I left the kitchen.

I have showering down to a science, as long as I don't have to look good afterwards. I can go from mud wrestler filthy to sparkling clean in under two minutes. The low-maintenance look, or as close as I get to it without resembling an alpaca. Neil appreciates this about me and I usually ignore my dormant and understated pride, except when I want to make an impact. Then it takes over an hour to get myself whipped together.

Leo didn't need me to impress him, so after I garbed my frame in a faded sweatshirt and a pair of decent jeans; I traipsed in the kitchen and poured myself the first cup. "Enough of the stall tactics, I want the juicy tid-bits."

"Where was I?" Leo tapped his chin in mock forgetfulness. The man has a brain like a steel drum, he has to in order to run Ralph and Laura's household so smoothly. I circled my hand, indicating he should move it along. "Dillon and his masterpiece."

"Right, so we had a small get together there last weekend—"

"For the Super Bowl?" I interrupted, smiling behind the rim of my mug.

Leo quirked an eyebrow. "As a matter of fact, yes Miss Sassy-pants."

I gagged on my coffee. "Seriously?" The mental picture of Leo and his Bostonian pals hanging around munching chips and staring at a big screen wouldn't gel. They were more the Oscar-party types.

"We each dressed up in our favorite player's team colors and I brought these little spinach-stuffed puff pastries, absolutely delish! I'll shoot you the recipe."

"Of course," I murmured, getting a better angle on the image. "So get to the entrée already."

"Well, he's a Raider's fan—"

"They didn't make it to the Super Bowl."

Leo shot me a withering glance. "Your point being...?"

I smiled and promised myself I wouldn't cut him off anymore.

"So he had the snazzy little black and silver outfit; I swear he looked just like a young Tom Jones. As soon as I saw him, I got heart palpitations and made for the kitchen. He came in to get a glass of white wine and comment on the pastries. It was Kismet. And he asked me out for tonight. I keep waiting to wake up, you know?"

36

I nodded and patted his hand. He had gone through a painful break-up a few years back, the guy decimated his heart and drained his bank account, and Leo's confidence was still in recovery. Having Calamity Jane as a best friend was helping with the problem. It's hard to feel down when you're laughing your ass off and he got to go to sleep at night with the thought, *life could always be worse, I could be Maggie.*

Though Maggie got to sleep with Neil, and that made up for a great deal, humiliation-wise. Ah, life's little balms.

"You're starting to drool, what on Earth are you thinking about?"

"Nothing," I mumbled and flushed to the roots of my hair. The Baptist in me hated getting caught thinking about sex.

Leo gave me a once over, then smiled in comprehension. "You two are so darn cute, like puppies." He sighed. "*That's* what I want from a partner, you know? That total, I think about you all day long, can't wait to come home at night kind of relationship."

"You'll find it." I reassured him.

"Well, it's too soon to tell with Richard." The light of hope in his eyes contradicted his down-to-Earth words.

"Where are you boys going tonight?"

"The theatre, I think. There's a new play opening and I mentioned it a few dozen times to Richard."

"So dish," I hopped off the stool and scrounged in the pantry for a snack. I came up with a box of butterfly crackers and the ingredients for cucumber dip. "What does

Richard do? What's his last name?" I was so focused on him, that I poured too much dip mix into the sour cream.

"Shoot."

Leo hip-checked me out of the way and took over. He's lucky I don't have control issues.

"He and a family member are renting the upstairs living space while waiting for their new house to close. Do you have any cream cheese to cut this with?"

"In the dairy drawer. A family member?"

Leo cleared his throat and muttered something incomprehensible under his breath.

"What was that?"

"His mother."

Eek! "Please tell me he's not one of those...,"

Leo gave me the squinty-eyed glare of death. "One of those whats?"

"Mama's boys."

Leo puffed his chest out like a blowfish. "Is it wrong that a man will help his mother during a time of transition? I happen to think it's sweet."

Rain on his parade, why don't ya. "Leo...I didn't mean anything by it." I stomped my judgmental harpy back into her snarky box and pasted a docile expression on my face. "So what's his last name?"

"Head," Leo didn't make eye contact as he stirred the dip. All that exercise must have shorted my brain because it took me the pace of five heartbeats to put it together.

"You're going out with a man named Richard Head," I stated slowly to make sure.

"I knew you'd be like this!" Leo slammed the serving spoon onto the counter and stormed out of the house. Sour cream and dip mix had been catapulted into my coffee and I watched the disgusting little white blobs congeal for a moment, wondering what just happened.

Three

"**Is** this really necessary?" I whined at Neil from the passenger's seat. We were on our way to meet with Dr. Robert Ludlum PH.D, the marriage counselor. This was worse than facing the sit-up machine at the gym. Having never sought psychological help before, I had no idea what to expect and was freaking out, though I hid it well.

My handsome husband didn't bat an eye. "You tell me, Maggie."

Uh oh. He'd Maggie-ed me; this was some serious stuff all right. "Marriage counseling is for couples who fight all the time. We hardly ever fight."

He snorted.

"We don't." I insisted. "Yelling is just how I communicate. No one hears me otherwise."

Neil pulled into an angled parking slot and shut off the engine, but made no move to exit the car. "Are you happy?"

"Do you mean right at this moment, or in the grand scheme of things?" I stalled for time, wondering what had gotten into him. Typically he oozed confidence, but now that I thought back on it, he'd been kinda weird ever since my brush with death.

Neil scowled at me and opened his door, and I sat, wondering if this downhill crap-fest would ever end. I wanted to take a nap and pray that when I woke up everyone would be back to normal. Before I sunk into a catatonic state, Neil opened my door and extended his hand to me. His gentlemanly streak must have overridden his irritation. If I were in his shoes, I probably would have kicked me out of the car six miles ago. Did I really need some PH.D to look me in the eye and say "You're damn lucky he puts up with you?" No new info there.

The building that housed Dr. Ludlum's office was a red brick behemoth, at least by Hudson's standards. Unlike some of the charming brick buildings typical of small town New England, this beastie held no architectural appeal. Institutionalized windows sat evenly spaced on the first through third floors, looking like ominous eyes waiting for unsuspecting prey to venture close enough....

Or I could just be a nut. Maybe I needed to spend more time in buildings like this, reclining on some PhD's battered sofa, figuring out exactly what was wrong with me.

"What's wrong, Maggie?" Neil stopped halfway up the steps, turning to face me. "Are you hyperventilating?"

Crap. My breathing sounded worse than when I tried to jog and I did an about face and sat down hard on the steps. A warm hand settled on my neck forcing my head between my knees. The roaring ocean in my mind crashed over my auditory sense and I felt more than heard Neil whispering soothing sounds against my hair.

As ridiculous as the position appeared, it helped. The freezing concrete beneath the seat of my jeans, the bite of the north wind and Neil's solid reassuring presence, all settled down the screaming monkeys banging their cymbals between my ears. I stayed put with my patient husband, greedily enjoying his total attention while annoyed by my own weakness. What kind of a monster gleaned perverse enjoyment from another's worry?

"You're right," I told him, keeping my head perpendicular to my legs, so I could avoid eye contact. "I'm totally screwed up. It's not your fault though Neil, so please stop thinking that you did or didn't do something, okay?"

Neil pulled me up by the collar of my jacket and secured me against him with one steel arm. "Stop that. These histrionics are not going to get you out of the meeting, so suck it up."

Was he deaf? "Hey, I'm giving you a free pass here, pal. No guilt, no regret. Not your fault, *capiche*?"

"I heard you and I even believe that *you* believe that, at least most of the time. But the choice I made to stay with the SEAL teams, it affected you. Maybe you never complained, but you did get used to making the tough calls on your own. You didn't... need me."

I opened my mouth to refute his ridiculous assessment but Neil scowled at me. That was not an easy thing for him to say, no matter how frigging ludicrous the notion might be, and he needed to get this out in the open. My mouth shut with a tooth-jarring click.

"And you're still operating that way, like I'm not there for you to bounce ideas around with. Yes, you ask me about the trivial stuff, what should we have for dinner or what color to paint the goddamn foyer. But the big calls, like the thing with the gym, accepting the C.I. position, the meetings at the school..., I'm surplus in your life Maggie."

I stared at him while mentally chanting, *don't call him a dumb-ass; don't call him a dumb-ass.* "You dumb-ass," I announced. Following directions never had been my strong suit. "Fine, we both need to get in there and have our heads shrunk, but that is the most asinine statement I've ever heard. Surplus, my lily-white hide." I pulled myself to a standing position, brushing gray snow off the back of my parka. Neil stood too, and turned away, but not before I caught sight of his twitching lips. What was so funny...?

"You manipulative bastard!" I shrieked and swung at him with my left hand. The layers of his coat and my glove protected him from the extremely wimpy force behind my enraged

43

blow which landed on his good shoulder with a soft *whumpff*. "You are *soooo* your mother's son! I can't believe you freaking *played* me!"

He was outright laughing by this point, his face flushed and happy. "Sorry, Uncle Scrooge," he gasped, the chuckles ruining the sincerity behind his words. Hearing him laugh like that, it suddenly occurred to me how long it had been since we had last had fun, laughed for the sake of it. "I wasn't about to let you do the pity-party spiel and get all mopey and self-deprecating. It's ineffective and we've had enough of that lately, don't ya think?"

"Well, now I'm pissed-off instead. That work for you, Dr. Evil?" I still couldn't believe he duped me. If I had one weakness, it was Neil's insecurities. I guarded his heart like a griffin hoarding precious treasure and he knew it.

"I see you, even behind all the B.S. posturing, you know that, right?" The way his green eyes seemed to drink in my features, made me feel like the most desirable woman alive. Sure, somewhere in my head I knew my apple cheeks were bright pink from the cold, my lips chapped and my hair a fly-away mess. But I also knew Neil saw beyond all that. He was hatless, despite the freezing temperatures and the vicious wind tussled his golden-brown locks.

"Yes, I do know that. But I'm still gonna beat you down when you least suspect."

Neil kissed my cheek and took my gloved hand, leading us into the maw of the building. "Sounds like a date to me."

44

* * * *

Doctor Robert Ludlum, "call me Bob," greeted me with a wimpy handshake reminiscent of a dead herring which he followed with a pointed glance at the office wall clock. True, we were a few minutes late, but the outer office stood empty. Neil shucked his coat and helped me doff my battered parka while introductions were made. An awkward silence ensued, broken only by the ticking of his Walmart plastic clock. I'd seen it on sale last week for $9.99 and was relieved, in retrospect, to have bypassed the deal.

A quick glance around revealed a few ladder-backed chairs and a worn copy of the DSM IV on an elegant coffee table. The reception desk was empty, save for an appointment book and a few pens. No computer or telephone, but since it was the portable digital age, perhaps his assistant carried a laptop and cell phone to lunch with her.

Useless prattling is my forte and I turned to the psychiatrist. "So Bob—"

"That's Dr. Bob," The marriage counselor chided and pushed his taped glasses further up the bridge of his pointy beak. Sporting a navy sweater-vest over a powder blue button-down shirt, pleated khaki's and penny loafers, he looked like Fred Rogers's long lost brother. Though I couldn't see his socks I would have bet my car that they were paisley.

"Dr. Bob," I smiled and stifled the urge to crack my knuckles. If I'd invested the requisite time in earning a PH.D I'd probably insist on being called Doctor, too. "Are we ready to start, or what?"

Neil covered his chuckle with a cough. Waiting doesn't bother Neil. He'd told me he'd once spent four days still as a statue, waiting for a terrorist guerilla group to move on. He and one of his SEAL teammates had been pinned down and after running out of MRE's—meals ready to eat which isn't exactly gourmet dining, were forced to live off the native insects that happened to crawl within grabbing reach. They used hand signals to communicate with each other. Neil had the market cornered in patience.

Dr. Bob scowled at me. "Are you in a hurry Mrs. Phillips?"

"No, I just thought—"

"Highways are not built overnight, Mrs. Phillips. The same is true for thoroughfares of communication. Rushing either is a waste of time and resources."

I cringed a bit. Waste is a four letter word to me, something to be avoided at all costs. Still, standing here engaging in a staring contest didn't seem especially productive either, but no doubt Dr. Bob had already picked me out as the troublemaker so I kept my mouth shut.

Dr. Bob cleared his throat. "I like to start all my sessions with new couples with some one-on-one time. It's important for me know you as individuals first before we can begin working on your relationship. After all, a person in a marriage is only as content as the least happy person in the relationship. Since

I've spoken with Mr. Phillips over the phone, I think we should start with Mrs. Phillips."

Yippie. I suppressed my heel clicking and followed Dr. Bob into his inner sanctum.

"Please close the door Mrs. Phillips. This is a confidential session."

I glanced out into the waiting area but Neil had whipped out his cell phone and settled back on one of the chairs, so he missed my grimace. Sighing softly, I closed the door with a final sounding click.

"Tell me about yourself, please Mrs. Phillips." Dr. Bob sat behind his desk, fingers steepled in front of him.

"Well Neil and I have been married for ten years—" My voice cut off at his raised hand.

"You, Mrs. Phillips. I'm sure you have an identity away from your husband."

Did he just smirk at me? I studied him intently, but his face was neutral, giving away nothing.

"Okay, well, I'm thirty-two and I just started up my own business last year—"

Dr. Bob shook his head and sighed. "You're going to be a challenge, aren't you?"

"I'm not trying to be difficult. It's just that after Neil and the boys and my cleaning business, there isn't much time for anything else."

"So you blame Neil and his children for your lack of identity." He nodded his head and scribbled something on a yellow legal pad.

"I didn't say that!"

He squinted at me out of one eye and wrote something else, probably having to do with my volatile temper. I took a deep breath

47

and retrenched. "How about you tell me about yourself Dr. Bob?"

Leaning back in his chair, Dr. Bob cocked his head to the side. "I've been a marriage counselor for fifteen years—"

"Ah ha!" I interrupted. "You can't do it, either."

He blinked owlishly. "Do what?"

"Introduce yourself without leaning on your job."

His lips compressed into a thin line of disapproval. "Mrs. Phillips, it's *my job* to help you. Nothing else about me is relevant to our time here."

Damn. I had to concede the point. "Okay, well where were we?"

"How's your sex life?"

My accent might label me a genteel southern woman by birth, but I'd been a Navy wife for several years. Our lives were surrounded by raunchy men who oftentimes forgot I was in the room. Or got drunk and didn't care. If he was attempting to unnerve me, he needed to try harder than that. "Just ducky, how about you?"

He blew out a sigh. "I know your husband is concerned about your relationship, Mrs. Phillips. If you aren't going to take these sessions seriously, we're all just wasting our time."

Double hit for the good doctor. Preying on my guilt over Neil's concerns and throwing "W" word into the ring. I was way out of my comfort zone.

"Sorry," I apologized. "I'll shelve the pithy retorts."

He bared his teeth in what might have been a smile and wrote something down on his notepad.

My cell phone rang and I sagged in relief. Bless the kind soul who thought to call me at this particular moment.

Dr. Bob gave me his evil eye as I dug in my bag for my cell. Positive I would eventually receive a lecture on distractions and time wasting, I turn forty-five degrees in the chair for pseudo privacy.

"Laundry Hag cleaning services, Maggie speaking," My cell phone caught all of my business calls since Kenny hadn't quite figured out how to take a proper message on the land line.

"Maggie, this is Candie Valentino,"

Ah the former Ms. Texas. I really liked her, as opposed to some of the other socialites that I took on as clients. Candie always greeted me by name when I cleaned their vast estate. "What can I help you with Mrs. Valentino?"

There was a slight pause. "Um, Maggie, did you send something here?"

"Something?" My eyebrows met just above my nose. "No, why do you ask?"

"We received a package and it came in a box with your logo on it?" Her voice went up at the end phrasing a fact like a question.

I frowned. My logo was a freebie Neil had found online and I'd ordered a few shirts and hats as well as a bunch of business cards for promotional purposes. The site had offered boxes, but I saw no need for them. "Does the box say Laundry Hag on it anywhere?"

"No, it's just the picture on the side. It's like one of those bakery boxes you know?"

Something prickled the hair along the back of my neck. "Candie, what came in the box?"

"A dead bird."

"Gross!" I said before I thought better of it. Dr. Bob stared at me quizzically, but I ignored his protest as I rose from the armchair. "Did you report it?"

"To who?" Candie asked as I opened the door to the waiting area. Neil took one look at my face and was up out of his chair.

"The police, the CDC. It might be infected with avian bird flu."

"Oh God, I didn't even think of that." Candie's tone was laced with panic.

"What's going on?" Neil asked.

I covered the speaker with my palm. "We have to go to the Valentino house. I'll explain on the way."

Dr. Bob sputtered from the doorway, "But your session—"

Neil turned back to deal with the doctor and I focused on my phone. "Candie, you need to report this. Call the Hudson police department and ask to speak with Detective Capri. I'll be there as soon as I can and whatever you do, don't touch that box!"

Candie didn't respond, but the sound of violent retching was answer enough.

Four

We parked in front of the Valentino's house. The brick and stone behemoth, flanked by leafless deciduous trees, sat at the end of a private drive. While the house was gated, the gate stood open, probably in expectation of the police. Lights blazed from every window and reflected off the brilliant snow and the sight took my breath for a minute. The mansion did have a Currier and Ives look to it, even the snow seemed whiter than in my middle-class neighborhood.

"Tell me again why we're here." Neil scowled at me and shifted in the driver's seat, bashing his knee into the gearshift. Whoever had designed the Mini Cooper didn't have six foot, two inch retired Navy SEAL's in mind.

"Mrs. Valentino called me, thinking I had something to do with the dead bird. My logo was on the delivery box. Therefore, I have a vested interest in getting to the bottom of this."

He winced as he rubbed his abused knee. "Only in your mind, Uncle Scrooge. Do they know you intercepted that fax the other day?"

I rolled my eyes. "What do I look like, a complete doofus? I made a copy of the fax before I beat feet outta there. The original I left precisely where I found it."

"I still say you're sticking your nose into somebody's kinky sex life," He grinned and met my gaze. "That's always entertaining, at least."

I thought of Sylvia's stricken face. "Not so much from my angle. Besides, you ever heard of anyone with a dead fowl fetish?"

"No, but that doesn't mean it doesn't exist. I'm a sheltered sort, you know."

I snorted and unbuckled my seatbelt. "Yeah, Neil the Pure with his lily-white sensibilities. How about the thing you did to me last week in the shower? What bedtime story featured that particular move?"

"My favorite." He glanced around. "You sure she called the police? I'm not seeing any lights yet and we've been sitting here for five minutes on top of the twenty minute drive."

"I told her to call, but she was a little busy doing the Technicolor yawn and then my phone went dead. And you left yours at Dr. Boob's. I mean Bob's."

He opened his door. "Might as well knock and see what's up."

The air hit me as soon as I straightened from the car, whipping my hair into my face. Neil grasped my gloved hand and pulled me to the relative shelter of the porch. He rang the doorbell and we waited.

"Maybe she took the package directly to the police station. Or animal control." Neil guessed.

I opened my mouth to respond, but a black Jaguar slid to an abrupt stop in front of the house and Mr. Valentino emerged. He sprinted up the porch steps and brushed by us without a word, inserting his key in the door. It swung open and he didn't bother to shut it so Neil tugged me inside.

"Candace?" Mr. V called out stomping through the foyer. "I can't just show up whenever you're in the mood to...."

Neil cleared his throat and gave me a knowing smirk. Valentino spun on his heel and scowled at us, his gaze focused on my husband. "Who the hell are you?"

Neil dropped my hand and extended his own. "Neil Phillips, sir. Your wife called mine."

"Phillips, Phillips," Mr. V pursed his lips. "Why does that name sound familiar?"

"Your wife hired me to clean twice a week. I'm Maggie Phillips from the Laundry Hag cleaning services." I informed him. Though I'd been on the job for almost a month, this was the first time I'd seen Valentino up close. Jet black hair cut fashionably short and GQ worthy stubble only emphasized his high cheekbones and pale complexion. His eyes, almost a neon shade of blue, stole attention from his extra-large nose, an almost beaklike

53

appendage which announced his Greek heritage. He appeared the perfect masculine foil for Candie's petite blonde beauty, but some instinct told me theirs wasn't a love match.

"Well, get to it then," Markus Valentino dismissed me with a wave of his hand and continued his hunt for his wife.

Before I could get my back up, Neil called to his retreating form. "We're here about the bird."

Valentino stopped in mid-stride, like his feet had been super-glued in place. It was almost comical, like a Wile E. Coyote signature move before he fell off a cliff.

"What bird?" Mr. V's tone held suspicion, and as he turned back around to face us, I noted a brief flicker in his eyes. Fear perhaps?

"Oh, Markus!" Candie rushed down the stairs and flung herself at her husband. Beneath her tan, she was sickly pale and trembling. "It's awful, just plain terrible."

"What is?" Valentino held her an arm's length away. "I get this message from Sierra that you need me here, but no explanation. Just what is going on?"

Candie looked as if he had slapped her. With visible effort she pulled back and composed herself. "It's in the kitchen." Without another word she led the way, Valentino hot on her heels.

"What a tool," Neil murmured almost inaudibly. I heard him though and grinned. He'd read my mind.

We followed the footsteps into the kitchen. A large white box, like a bakery container sat open on the granite island. Candie had been right, it was the little caricature from my business logo, the sprightly little woman with a pink kerchief wrapped around her head and matching vacuum. Candie stood in the corner next to the gourmet refrigerator, arms wrapped around her upper body. Valentino loomed over the box then pulled away in disgust, yanking a handkerchief to his face. I shuffled past Neil and stood on my tip toes to get a better look. The carcass did resemble a large bird, one that had been barbecued. The stench invaded my nostrils and I stepped back.

"If I had to guess, I'd say it was some sort of hawk, maybe a falcon," Neil moved closer, seemingly oblivious of the putrid smell. "Did you phone the police?"

"What for? It's obviously a prank." Valentino scoffed, the tone losing some impact delivered as it was through the hanky.

"If it's a prank, I'm missing the punch line. Dead fowl in a bakery box, how is that funny?" Neil asked his tone mild. "Looks more like a message to me."

"Just who the hell are you?" Valentino seethed.

"A concerned husband. Whoever sent this didn't do it by certified mail. The smell alone insures that. And the box has my wife's logo on it, which means the perp wants to shift attention to her."

"Why wouldn't he go all the way though?" I asked "If he ripped off my caricature, he could have put my business

55

name on there too, made the connection even more obvious."

"Who gives a shit?" Valentino thundered, closing the lid with his hanky-free hand. "It's just some freak playing a game. Not worth all this fuss and bother."

Out of the three of us, Markus Valentino was the only one who appeared remotely riled. The stress brought out his Texas accent and a vein bulged in his forehead. Neil stood like the calm eye in the center of a shit storm and both Candie and I were green around the gills.

"I recommend you report this to the police. Mrs. Valentino has our number and we'll be happy to answer any questions they might have." Neil inclined his head toward Candie and then led me to the front door by my arm.

"We can't just leave—" I protested as he propelled me forward.

"There's nothing else we can do." Neil replied. "We can't force him to call the cops and your connection is shaky at best."

"Why do you think my logo was on the box but not my name?" I repeated my earlier question. Neil didn't answer until we were both secure in the car and heading towards the main road.

"Someone is messing with Valentino. Did you see him freeze when we mentioned the bird? I think whoever sent that box has been watching them and snagged your logo to cast suspicion on you. Maybe they didn't want it to be obvious that it was you, or maybe the site that I ordered your stuff from has copyright protection for its consumer's company names. I'll look into that when we get home."

I wanted to ask why me, but didn't bother as it sounded too whiney and Neil had put up with enough from me today. "Do you think Valentino knows who is behind this?" I asked instead.

Neil cut his gaze to me briefly. "I'd bet my left nut on it."

****

"Why is there a camper in front of our house?" Neil squinted at said vehicle through the grimy windshield of my Mini.

"I have no idea. Maybe one of the neighbors is having company from out of town?" I suggested as Neil parked behind the vehicle which blocked most of our driveway.

"Maggie, this is Massachusetts. People go south during the winter, since you'd have to be a kook to visit in February."

He had a point. I sure as hell wouldn't load up a gas-guzzling RV and hit the road for Hudson to play chicken with a Nor'easter during the winter.

Neil exited the car as I stepped into a giant pile of slush, soaking my left foot as the muck spilled over the top of my ankle high boot. The gray sky held the threat of more snow, with heavily pregnant clouds looking ready to pop.

"I'm going to ask around and see who this thing belongs to and request the owner move it so we can park in our driveway." Neil was already heading across the street.

57

I squished my way to the front porch and then let out a groan as I realized Neil had my key ring. Crap, now what? I couldn't call Neil since my cell was dead and I really didn't want to wait for frostbite to set in. The thermometer was reading in the single digits. I dug in my black shoulder bag, hoping to unearth a spare when my front door swung open.

"Marty!" I squealed and threw my arms around my brother's neck. I hadn't heard from him since before the holidays and I'd lost quite a bit of sleep worrying about him. I should have known better. Marty, like an oil slick, always managed to ooze his way to the surface.

"What's up Laundry Hag?" My younger brother returned my hug with interest.

"Same old, same old. How about you?" I shucked my parka and leaned against the door, forcing my numb fingers to unlace the saturated boot.

"Well, a lot actually," Marty grinned and chucked his thumb toward the camper. "Did you check out my new wheels?"

The boot resisted and I used my other foot to toe it off with a slurping sound. "You're kidding, right? Sprout, are you out of your mind?"

Marty immediately went on the defensive. "It was a sound investment. I bought it off this guy who'd inherited it last summer. Got it for a sweet deal, Maggs, and I needed the room."

"For your collection of skin flicks and beer caps?" I asked, feeling my blood pressure heading for a new high. Damn, Neil was going

58

to be pissed about the camper. And about Marty's return. My brother had a nasty habit of popping up at the worst of times, mooching his little heart out, wreaking general havoc in my house and leaving at the height of the chaos. Neil put up with him for the same reason I dealt with his mother, because we loved each other and therefore had no other option.

Marty got large, filling up the doorway to my living room with his imposing girth. "Get off your high-horse. You don't know the first thing about my situation."

"Of course I don't. You don't freaking talk to me! The only time you show up on my doorstep is when you're in over your head and you need me to fix something!" Exasperated, I skidded on the wet parquet floor and headed for the bathroom. A hot shower was in order if I was in for Neil vs. Marty, the cage match.

"Maggie, wait!" Marty shouted but I held up a hand, not wanting to deal at the moment. I turned the door knob and pushed open the bathroom door.

A woman was seated in my bathtub, neck deep in bubbles. Her eyes were closed and she had ear buds in, so she didn't turn at my startled cry. Peony pink toes tapped on the faucet of the garden tub in time to the music.

I stared for a minute, wondering if my mind had snapped like a dry twig. Who was she and why was she in my tub and, by the scent of things, helping herself to my lilac bubble bath? Marty pounded on the door and I reached behind my back for the handle. Whoever she was, she deserved privacy and I had just turned the knob when she rose from the bubbles and all of my thoughts derailed.

"Hey there," Uncaring of her nudity and my open-mouthed gape she stepped from the tub and reached for a towel, which refused to meet ends over her hugely pregnant belly. "You must be Maggie." Her voice held the thick syrup of the South.

Water cascaded down her figure from her wet hair, and she plucked a second towel from the rack to swath her head in, turban-style.

"Yeah, I'm Maggie. I'll, uh, wait out there." Offering a wan smile I slipped out into the hall where my brother stood. Marty wouldn't meet my eyes. So I got in his face.

"Care to explain?" I huffed, mortified and out of patience. Neil was gonna shit monkeys.

"This isn't how I planned this, you know," Marty's tone was belligerent, but laced with guilt. "Penny was tired after the drive and I tried to call your cell, but it kept going to voicemail. So I figured she could clean up while we waited."

My temper was at the boiling point and I dragged Marty down the hall to my bedroom so Penny wouldn't hear me erupt. I needn't have worried as the drone of the hairdryer filtered into the room.

"She's pregnant, Marty! At least five months along! Correct me if I'm wrong but five months ago, you were still living with Dee in the Bronx!"

"I know that!" Marty huffed and ran a hand thru his hair.

60

"Were you cheating on Dee? Is that why you two broke up?" Dee was a zoologist at the Bronx Zoo, and she had been great for Marty. At least until wanderlust had taken hold of him yet again.

For a moment, Marty looked hurt, much like the sixteen year old boy I had raised after our parents' deaths. I squelched the nurture impulse; he was a grown man now and needed to be aware of the consequences of his actions. "I've never cheated on a woman in my life, Maggie. Dee wanted someone steady and dependable."

I pointed sharply in the direction of the bathroom. "And this girl doesn't? Cripes Marty, in a few months she's gonna have a baby!"
"I'm great with kids. Kenny and Josh love me."

"It's not the same. You're the favorite playmate, but you get to give them back at the end of the day."

My brother raised his chin in a gesture of stubborn defiance. "I can learn how to be a parent, just like you did. It's not like any of those shmoes crapping out kids right, left and sideways gets an owner's manual or how to for dummies."

The drier cut off and I lowered my voice to a menacing whisper. "This isn't a game you can walk away from when you get bored, Sprout. Babies especially depend on you for everything. You don't get vacation or sick days."

He opened his mouth to respond but I held up a hand as the front door slammed. I closed my eyes, searching for the right words to

61

explain the situation to Neil. Unfortunately, I took too long.

"No luck with the camper, Uncle Scrooge. You in here?" His soft footsteps stopped outside of the bathroom. I heard the hinges squeak ominously.

Oh hell, no. I shoved Marty aside and flung open the door. Neil was struggling to get his T shirt over his head, probably intent on taking a shower, just as I had been. Penny's towel had been shucked and I caught her reflection in the mirror as she eyeballed the broad expanse of my husband's chest.

Neil's shirt gave way and he took a breath, as if to continue but let it out in a whoosh when he realized he was being ogled by a pregnant stranger.

"Helllooo handsome," Penny drawled.

I shot Marty a death glare and sprinted to close the bathroom door.

Five

"**S**ylvie, come on. Open the door." I stood outside my friend's house and begged. Neil had gone to pick up the boys from school and I couldn't stand to be in my house with Marty and Penny for another minute. Everything about Marty's Baby's Mama annoyed the daylights out of me. Her favorite song was *Redneck Woman,* which I had actually kind of enjoyed until she played it for the thirty seventh time on our stereo. Penny's hair, which had dried to a curly mass of coppery beauty, made me tug self-consciously on my own gray-streaked brown locks. Her accent made my eyelid spasm, which, I admitted to myself, was kind of hypocritical. Technically, I grew up south of the Mason-

Dixon Line, but I've been told by numerous sources that I talk more like a trucker on the Jersey turnpike than a Southern Belle. And the way she praised every fool notion to pass my brother's lips was beyond ridiculous.

Despite Marty's protests, both Neil and I agreed there was no way on God's green Earth that we would let a pregnant woman sleep in the RV in sub-zero temperatures. I'd pulled Neil aside and offered to send them away, for the sake of his sanity, but he'd just sighed and gone about filling the air mattress where *we* would sleep until the weather improved. Or Penny went into labor, whatever came first.

"Please, Sylvia. It's frigging cold as a witch's britches out here and I've had a bear of a day and I won't be able to sleep on my ancient air mattress tonight till I see for myself that you're all right."

The door opened a crack and I sighed in relief. Stepping inside, I hugged Sylvia before my brain registered what I'd seen. Her blond locks were pulled back in a sloppy pony-tail, highlighting her gauntness. She wore a grubby T-shirt covered by humongous overalls and a determined expression that I'd never seen on her typically serene features. After shutting out the cold she turned to face me, hands on hips, but made no move to invite me in further

"I'm kind of in the middle of something right now. This isn't a good time to visit." Sylvia's right foot tapped and she practically vibrated with nervous energy.

"What are you doing and how can I help?" I shucked my jacket and rolled up my sleeves in a gesture of solidarity. I'd pooched

64

the encounter with Eric and possibly made things much worse for her, and I was prepared to make amends.

Sylvia sighed and dropped her chin to her chest. "Maggie, go home."

"Not until you let me apologize." I stated stubbornly. "I was going to make you my classic I'm sorry casserole, but it's got sausage in it and I know you wouldn't eat it." Sylvia was a vegan and card carrying member of PETA.

"While I appreciate the half-assed gesture, you don't have anything to apologize for. You weren't screwing Eric in the ball room."

"No, but I made a scene and I figured I'd brought more attention to your situation than you wanted, especially at your place of employment."

Sylvia didn't say anything, just stared down at her paint-spattered boots.

"Are you remodeling?"

Her ponytail bobbed as she shook her head. "I'm applying the principles of Feng Shui to the house."

"Didn't you already have it all Feng Shui-ed?" I asked.

Her gaze darted to mine for a moment then out the window. "That was for mine and Eric's home. Now it's just my house and I need positive energy to improve my Chi."

I had no idea what to say. I'd been prepared to be a shoulder to cry on or share a drink and rail about cheating bastards but Chi was out of my realm of understanding.

"So, put me to work. You want to move a sofa or dresser? Marty's in town and Neil will be back soon—"

"Maggie, stop." Sylvia held up her hand in a hold-it-right-there gesture. "I just want to be alone for a little while, okay?"

Stung, I nodded and donned my coat again. "Please call me if you need *anything*."

"I will," Sylvia offered me a ghost of her usual smile and I left before I started to cry. What a screwed-up day.

Deflated, I headed back to my house. Thoughts buzzed like pissed-off bees inside my skull, nattering on about what a lousy friend/wife/sister I had become. Was it my curse to disappoint the people I loved time and again?

"Shut up," I growled at myself. Mental flagellation didn't accomplish anything. What I needed was to form a proactive plan. Set a goal and strive for it as well as prioritize my life.

When I started thinking about it that way, the task didn't seem so daunting. Neil and my marriage came first. Dr. Bob may be a tool, but he might be a useful tool, if applied correctly. My course set, I huddled in the relative shelter of the garage and dialed my freshly charged cell phone. Dr. Bob answered his own phone on the first ring.

"This is Maggie Phillips. I was wondering if I could maybe come back in at some point this week to continue our session?"

Silence reigned for the span of several heartbeats. "What for?" Dr. Bob asked, bewilderment cutting through the static on my end of the line.

Spit it out and move on with life. My mother's voice comes to me every so often, usually when I've hit an emotional wall. I've made it a habit to listen to her as she always protects my interests. "I've done some thinking and I realize that I need to treat my marriage as a priority."

"Mrs. Phillips, I'm going to be blunt here. While you may seem sincere now, I predict that every session will be a battle and frankly, there are easier ways to spend my days."

What, my money wasn't green enough for him? I took a deep breath, sucking frigid oxygen all the way down to my toes. "Neil wants this and I want Neil to be happy and I'm willing to do anything to get us there."

"Fine," Dr. Bob snapped. "I'll pencil you in for 10 AM tomorrow."

I flipped through my mental to-do list. "Oh, no Dr. Bob I have a—"

"10 AM if you're serious, Mrs. Phillips. If you don't show up, I'll know otherwise." A distinctive click had me gaping at the phone.

What a control freak! Doubts surfaced about my resolution but I shoved them to the dark recess of my brain. I'd made a decision and would stick with it, no matter what.

Okay, next on the priority list came Marty, but I didn't feel up to another round. While my cell phone was out I scrolled through the contact list, feeling a bit like Earl, trying to improve my Karma by righting my many wrongs.

"This is Leo, leave me a quickie and I'll tap you back." I giggled at the tinny recording and cleared my throat before the beep.

"I'm sorry, Leo. I was being a twit. What I *should* have said is that I'm very happy for you and Richard. There, I'm going to shut up before I stick my foot back down my gullet. Love you. Oh this is Maggie, by the way."

There. Despite the frostbite, I was starting to feel better. Undoubtedly, Sylvia would come around and Leo would forgive me. I still had no idea what, if anything, to do about the dead bird, but there was no frigging way I would drag Detective Capri into it without an okay from the Valentinos.

Neil's truck pulled to a stop in our driveway—Marty had moved the RV up enough so we could park off the street—and Kenny scrambled out, followed by a more somber Josh.

"Hey you guys!" I greeted them. "You wanna help mom with some self-improvement?"

Kenny eyeballed me, a wary expression in his green gaze. "You're not gonna make us eat bean curd again are you?"

Sylvia had given me a Vegan cookbook for Christmas which really is an oxymoron; since from what I'd seen, the Vegans don't really cook so much as prepare various greens. Dutifully, I'd invited Sylvie and Eric over to sample the result. I shuddered at the memory. After they left, Neil had picked up a pizza.

"Not in this lifetime, Sport. I wanna start an exercise regime. You guys are all fit and I need some pointers."

68

Now Neil was shooting me a squinty-eyed glare. "What gives?"

"I'm just trying to make my health a priority is all." I huffed.

Josh laughed. "Dad said you don't like Uncle Marty's new girlfriend."

"We just met," I hedged. "I don't know her well enough to decide if I like her or not." Though I was strongly leaning towards or not.

We trudged up the front steps. Neil grinned, probably at the astuteness of our oldest son. "What kind of exercise are you thinking about Uncle Scrooge?"

"Well I tried jogging the other day, but I didn't make it very far." Understatement of the year.

"You have to get a rhythm going for jogging." Neil knocked his boots against the doorframe in an effort to shake loose some of the crusted-on salt and grime. Kenny and Josh didn't bother, just kicked their shoes on the runner. "That's why military formations always chant as they run. Maybe you could try listening to music while you exercise."

"You can borrow my iPod if you want." Josh volunteered. "I have an armband carrier you could wear. I'll even make you a Playlist."

I shucked my jacket. "Thanks Scamp, but I doubt I'll like your music." Josh listened to rap, which was not my cup of tea.

"No, I meant a Playlist with your music. Dad had me transfer all of your CD's into iTunes, so it'll just be a matter of picking songs with the right tempo."

"Uh...," I had no idea what he meant or even how to work an iPod. I was just a few years past the technologically savvy generation.

"I'll show you how to work it." Neil whispered a smile in his voice. Of course, Neil was older than me but much more in tune with the times. Technology didn't intimidate Navy SEALs who were trained to disarm a nuclear warhead as well as rebuild an engine. An iPod wasn't even a blip on Neil's radar.

Kenny dumped his backpack on top of his coat and boots and padded down the hall to the fridge. "You got to remember to stretch both before and after you exercise so you don't injure yourself. And if you really want to get in shape, you need to add some weight-lifting to your routine, too, maybe three times a week. Cardio only burns calories for a few hours, but strength-training burns for up to two days after."

I gaped at him as he opened the refrigerator door. "Where did you learn all this?"

Kenny shrugged, or at least I think he did. It was hard to tell with his head MIA, scrounging for an after school snack. "From Dad."

Neil caught my gaze and while he didn't quite smirk, his expression gloated, *see my boys listen to me.*

Of course. The better question was why didn't I know any of this? To me, physical exertion should have a reward for all the effort. Like baking a cake or scrubbing out the tub. Exercise for the sake of exercise hadn't appealed to me. And most of the exercise Neil

70

and I engaged in together was not for fitness purposes.

"How y'all doing?" Penny glided from the hallway, greeting Kenny and Josh with a warm smile. She turned up the heat for Neil and I clenched my molars together.

Be nice. My mother's voice cautioned. But still, this tart was eyeing my husband, *again* and I didn't like it at all, especially when she was supposed to be with my brother.

"Where's Marty?" I stepped in front of Neil and Penny shifted her focus to me.

"Out in the garage, looking for something he needs to fix the shower in the camper."

"Excuse me," Neil practically shoved me aside in an effort to keep Marty from rearranging his entire tool chest.

After clearing my throat, I introduced Kenny and Josh to Penny, and then asked the room what they'd like for dinner. Josh shrugged and Kenny murmured an "I dunno." Typical, so I shuffled over to the pantry to search its contents.

"Can I do anythin'?" Penny drawled from behind me. The g was lost in her accent.

I closed my eyes; face still buried between the minute rice and Quaker oats. "Just have a seat and keep me company." I gestured over my shoulder toward the counter and my ugly barstools.

The boys may not have an opinion about dinner, but I needed comfort food. Meatloaf, my Grandma Irma's recipe, Mac-n-Cheese and broccoli, to help move all that

71

cholesterol through the body, seemed to be the ticket.

I grabbed the breadcrumbs and a box of Rotini, which actually holds the cheese sauce better than elbows, and turned around and bumped into Penny. I dropped my armload in an effort to catch her, but she took a graceful step back, absorbing the impact as well as avoiding the mess of breadcrumbs on the floor.

"Sorry," I muttered. "I thought you were going to sit down."

"I've been sitting for days on the drive up here. I wanna move around a bit."

"How 'bout fetching a broom, then?" Shit, *my* accent was deepening the longer I talked with her. I'd made an effort to lose the southern since most native New Englanders would talk slowly around me after they'd picked up on the accent. At this rate, I'd be y'all-ing by bedtime.

Penny smiled and asked me where I kept the broom. I pointed to the laundry alcove where my Laundry Hag Commandments plaque hung above the washing machine.

Neil had outdone himself with the new sign. Before I started my business, Neil and the boys had called me the Laundry Goddess and lived in constant fear of my wrath should they try to pirate a load of wash. After one particularly memorable rant, where I'd dubbed myself the Laundry Hag, Neil had immediately gone to work on a new sign, this one hand painted on a huge slab of slate. Penny handed me the broom, but returned to read the sign out loud.

1. Thou shall separate thy whites (i.e. socks, undergarments) from thy colored clothes.

2. Thou shall not mix thy sheets with thy towels.

3. Honor thy (my) lint screen and keep it free of crud.

4. Thy workout clothes must be washed with thy towels not my new white top.

5. Empty thy pockets of gum, Chapstick, baseball cards, wallets, keys, candy, Swiss army knives, and all other pocket flotsam or thou will evoke the wrath of the Laundry Hag.

6. Thou shall not mess with the water temperature settings without my permission.

7. Thou must remove clothes from the washing machine in a timely manner, i.e. before the plague of mildew sets in.

8 .If thou are confused about liquid vs. powdered detergent, ASK!"

"Cute, if a bit blasphemous." Penny smiled at me, her hands propping up her lower back in classic pregnant woman repose.

I swept the breadcrumbs into my dustpan. "I'm pretty sure God has a sense of humor. How else could you explain Yanni?"

"Gotcha," Penny grinned and I felt the first tentative string of friendship tether us together. Maybe this wouldn't, as Josh liked to say, totally bite.

"When's dinner?" Neil emerged from the garage and asked.

I sighed as I dumped the remainder of the breadcrumbs into the trash. "Gonna be late. I need to run to the store and buy more breadcrumbs for meatloaf."

Neil groaned. "They're predicting six to eight inches of snow tonight. The stores are going to be mobbed. You *might* get back here by breakfast."

"You got any bread? That's what I use in my meatloaf recipe."

Neil's eyes lit up. "Yeah, why don't you try that Maggie? We never did have lunch and I'm starving."

But it won't be the same as Grandma Irma's, I wanted to whine. I held my tongue though, since Neil's missing lunch was due to my need to investigate the dead bird and my brother's appearance.

"It's good to try new things." My face felt stiff as I said the words.

"How 'bout I cook and you take a break?" Penny said and my spine stiffened. There were three things in life that I was proprietary about to the point of hoarding. My husband, my romance novels and my kitchen. Leo was the only person I allowed to cook in my kitchen because he respected my system.

"Sounds like a plan," Neil said and smiled at Penny, who smiled back. I looked at my brother's pregnant girlfriend and felt our string of friendship snap like worn out dental floss.

74

Six

The ringing telephone jarred me awake the next morning. I rolled off the air mattress and my knees hit the living room carpet eight inches below. Neil groaned, as the motion had jostled the bed, and then rolled over. It had been a lousy night for both of us. I'd been in a mood before dinner and the fact that Penny's meatloaf was truly fabulous, only soured it further. Josh, the little wisenheimer, had indeed made me a Playlist for my exercise regime, dubbed Mom's Old Fogy Music. *Dire Straits* is not fogy music.

I scrambled for the kitchen and picked up in the middle of the third ring. The clock on the stove read 5:58. "Hello?"

"Mrs. Phillips?" This is Mrs. O'Toole. We're calling in the phone tree, for a two hour delay." Mrs. O'Toole seemed as perturbed by the early hour as I did. The Superintendent of our district was a nut, afraid that Big Brother was watching his every move and refused to upgrade to an automated emergency system. So we had to do the phone tree thing in alphabetical order every stinking time there was a snow delay. To top it off, he always put us on a two hour delay first, even if Rudolph was needed to see through the soup, so we had to do it twice.

"Do you know who your contact person is?" Mrs. O'Toole grumped.

"I've got the Prescott's number memorized." And on speed dial number four in case, like this morning, I didn't have my coffee yet.

"Talk to you at eight." Mrs. O'Toole hung up.

I called the Prescott residence, relayed the message and shuffled down to the boys' room to turn off their alarm clocks.

Kenny, a very light sleeper, blinked up at me as I clicked his radio off. "Wha...?"

"Go back to sleep, pal." I murmured and backed out of the room.

I yawned and headed toward the coffee maker, stopping short to see my husband already filling the pot.

"What are you doing up?" Since it was Wednesday, Neil didn't need to be in until two for his four hour shift.

"Thought I'd head to work early, see if I could catch a little more overtime this week."

"Oh," I said. While his explanation made sense, I hated any extra time Neil spent at work. We'd missed out on a great deal of together time while he was career navy and though his current job was less demanding, I still felt cheated when he wasn't around.

"What's on your agenda for the day?" He asked while scooping grounds into the coffee filter.

Not wanting to mention the make-up Dr. Bob visit, I struggled for something else to tell him. "I have a cleaning job at noon. New client over on Rosewood lane." I hastened to add at his scowl.

His expression cleared a bit. "Do me a favor and beg off any more jobs at the Valentino's for a bit, okay? That bird was a warning for them and the whole situation gives me a chill."

"Me too," I agreed, hoping he wouldn't notice that I hadn't promised anything. While I never lied to Neil, I did sometimes leave out information, for his own peace of mind, of course. I wasn't due back at the Valentino's 'til Friday afternoon anyhow.

"Are you still looking for a new cleaning partner?" Neil queried as he retrieved the Frosted Flakes from the pantry. I swear the man eats like an eight year old.

"I'm not sure," I answered as I watched him dump *four tablespoons of sugar* on his ½ cup of cereal. And the crazy part was he'd never had a cavity in his life. "I'm only working about twenty hours a week at this point and the schedule is erratic. It's hard to find an employee who'll put up with that."

"Why don't you ask Penny? She might help you out." Neil dumped milk over his tooth-decay-in-a-bowl.

Was he serious? "If you'll recall, I've tried the pregnant cleaning partner route before and it didn't turn out very well." I poured my coffee and took the first bracing sip.

Neil shrugged and ate his cereal. "It was only a suggestion. She seems nice, kind of reminds me of you."

Coffee went down my windpipe and I choked, tears welling in my eyes. "What do you mean?" I wheezed.

Neil shook his head and rinsed his empty bowl. "Nothing, I guess it's the accent."

Grrrr.

"I'm going to take a shower. Wanna conserve water and share?" The heat in his green eyes was unmistakable. Chances were good that until Marty and Penny moved on, the only private time we could claim would be in the shower.

I opened my mouth to reply, but Penny glided into the room. No waddling for this pregnant Southern Belle. "Morning ya'll. That sure is one comfy bed, much better than the fold out in the camper."

"I'm happy you slept well." I stretched to alleviate the stiffness in my back. Neil gave Penny a wink and headed off to the bathroom. Alone, I sighed and poured more coffee.

"So, Penny, have you thought of any baby names yet?" It struck me as I observed her silhouette that I was going to be an auntie. I loved babies and babies that I could cuddle and spoil on a regular basis were the best.

"Not really," Penny said mildly as she poured a glass of milk. "I guess we'll just see what she looks like."

"So it's a girl?"

"I don't know." I waited for her to continue, but she just drank her milk.

"Well, have you had an ultrasound yet?" I probed.

"Nope."

A nasty thought took root. "You have been to an obstetrician, right?"

"Nu uh."

"A midwife then," I grasped. No reply. I blinked, then blinked again. "Penny you have to get prenatal care. You should be on vitamins, and have tests—"

78

"Relax, Maggie. Women have been having babies since the dawn of time. It's a natural process."

"Yeah and women *died* having babies without proper medical treatment. Do you have medical insurance?" But I already knew what the answer would be before she shook her head.

Frickin' perfect. My brother had no job and no insurance and apparently neither did Penny. With a baby on the way and no place to live except an ancient death trap on wheels. Lord, have mercy.

"If you'll excuse me a minute," I shot her a wan smile then marched to my bedroom. Marty lay sprawled on top of the covers, bare ass exposed to the world. I swiped a sneaker from the floor and flung it at the full moon.

"What the—" Marty launched out of bed.

"Get your hide in gear. You're coming cleaning with me."

"Now?" Marty asked with a glance at the alarm clock.

"No, later. Now, you're going to get on the computer and do a little research into insurance plans and OB/GYN's for your pregnant girlfriend. Did you know she hasn't been to a doctor yet?" I hissed.

"Well, that's really her call—"

"Not while she's carrying my niece or nephew and sleeping in my bed it isn't. This family has endured enough tragedy and I refuse to sit by and do nothing while you two endanger a child."

"Calm down, Maggs. We're on top of it."

79

"The only thing you were on top of is my duvet. Now you have a choice. Either be a grown up and earn your keep or get out."

Marty took a step back, eyes going wide. "You don't mean that."

"The hell I don't." I understood his disbelief. Even before Neil and I had married, my home had always been Marty's safe haven, a place to weather any shit storm he'd stirred up. Time and again, he'd put strain on our home life and my relationship with Neil. But expecting to mooch and act like a runaway from juvie hall wasn't gonna happen this time.

Marty opened and closed his mouth a few times like a large mouth Bass. Really though what could he say? I stepped closer and lowered my voice. "You're better than what you've become Sprout. I want to be proud of you, I do. You have to earn it, though. So get to work."

"Anything else, boss?" though his tone was snide, I answered him seriously.

"Yeah, put on some pants for Chrissakes."

* * * *

"Hello?" The obnoxious clock in Dr. Bob's waiting room read ten minutes to ten when I answered my cell. There was still no sign of a receptionist and no voices carried from behind his closed door. True to my prediction, the schools were closed due to inclement weather. I'd left Penny in charge of the house almost half an hour before, not wanting to be late to my therapy session.

Somehow, I doubted Dr. Bob would accept the weather as a suitable excuse for tardiness.

"Hey there laundry hag," Leo's voice carried over the phone and I sighed in relief to hear his voice.

"I'm so sorry," I began, though I still wasn't sure why he'd been so upset the day before. We'd known each other for a decade and this wasn't the first time I'd behaved like an insensitive buffoon.

"Water under the bridge, Maggie, really. Can I ask you a favor though?"

"Sure Leo, anything. Ask away."

"I was wondering if you were still seeking a cleaning partner."

"Oh my God," I breathed. "Leo did you get fired?" I couldn't imagine it, my in-laws without Leo. I'd have lost my spy in the enemy camp. *It's not always about you, Margaret.* My mother's voice scolded, but then again she'd never met Laura.

"No, no you silly goose." Leo laughed and I closed my eyes in thanksgiving. "I'm asking for Richard, not myself."

Ah yes, the notorious Richard Head. Seriously, what had his mother been thinking? Maybe, *if I name my baby Richard Head, he'll never have a relationship and take care of me in my dotage.* Seemed like her plan was working, too.

"Richard wants a cleaning job?" I asked, keeping my gaze on the ticking clock. I didn't want Dr. Bob coming out and catching me on the phone, though I wasn't sure why it mattered.

"Yeah, he just told me last night that he lost his job at the bank, he'd been a loan officer you know and I guess he made one too many bad calls with lending. Anyhow, now everyone is tightening up their belt buckles and he's SOL. So, I talked him into trying something new."

"By coming to clean with me? Leo, I just hired Marty, who is in a mess of his own and I just don't have enough jobs...."

"So take on a few more." Leo suggested.

"Well, like you said, with the economy, people are looking to scale back. There aren't that many more jobs to be had, Leo."

"You should think bigger. How about cleaning for businesses? Like doctor's offices or a law firm."

That's what I love about Leo. America's in the throes of financial crisis and he makes it sound like I'd be an idiot not to expand my business.

It was two minutes to ten. "All right Leo, I'll look into it on one condition."

"What's that?" His tone was wary.

"I'll need two teams of two and you have to pair with Marty or I might throttle him."

"Oh goodie," Leo said with relish. Unlike me, Leo intimidated Marty, not in a homophobic way as much as in an *I don't get you, man* way. I knew Leo would not only moonlight as my team two point man, but get some actual work out of my brother. Plus the likelihood of Marty's death-by-strangulation went down considerably.

"I'll check into it and get back to you." I said and shut my phone as Dr. Bob's office door swung inwards.

"Mrs. Phillips," Dr. Bob made a sweeping gesture indicating that I should enter his private domain.

"How are you, Dr. Bob?" I asked politely, forcing a smile. Possibly, I was more nervous than I'd been the day before. He ignored my attempt at pleasantry.

"So Maggie," Dr. Bob began as I sat on the edge of the chair. "Did you and your husband have sex last night?"

So much for chit chat. "No," I answered honestly, though why I felt a pang of guilt was a mystery.

"I see." Dr. Bob scribbled something on his pad that looked suspiciously like the word frigid. "Do you make your desires known to him, Maggie?"

No one had ever accused me of being subtle. "Always," I stated.

"And how would you rate your sex drive, on a scale of one to ten."

Hell, he was asking me to do math? I thought I'd been done with math after scraping by the accounting class requirement for my business degree several years ago. "I'm not sure—"

"How about Neil's then? What would you rank his desire for sexual intercourse as being on that same scale?"

"Um, I'm not sure—"

"Is his higher or lower than yours?"

"Higher," He is a man, after all.

"How much higher? One point, two, five?" Dr. Bob dug like a bloodhound sniffing out a meaty ham hock

"I'd say he's about three points higher, but that's normal, isn't it?"

He didn't answer, just scribbled away on that damn pad again.

Do not get huffy or defensive. I counseled myself. Not like anyone else was going to see the notes he was making about my sex life.

"In any relationship, communication is essential. When I say communication, I'm referring to both verbal and nonverbal. In a romantic relationship, sex is a big part of nonverbal communication. You must be open to all forms of communication from your spouse. Do you make yourself available, Maggie?"

I thought back to this morning when Neil wanted me to shower with him. "I try, but sometimes life gets in the way."

Dr. Bob slammed his pen down. "That is just an excuse and a pretty lousy one. Right up there with the classic "Not tonight dear, I have a headache." He made his voice all breathy and effeminate which was hysterical. I laughed until I caught his scowl. Whoops.

"Do not make the mistake of getting hung up on what's normal, Maggie. While sex once a week is a rich bounty for some couples, others might go insane without for more than thirty-six hours."

For once I didn't have a witty response on my lips. "Do you mean some couples or some men?"

"Sex is an elemental need, like food or shelter. Think of it this way; if one well dries up, does a man just roll over and die? Or will he venture down a new path to find another well?

Seven

Was *the entire world obsessed with sex?* I wondered as I perused the homework assignment given to me by Dr. Bob. Just how was I supposed to accomplish *that* with Marty and his pregnant girlfriend in my bed, Josh locked in the bathroom for a healthy portion of the day and Neil at work to get away from the chaos. Not that I blamed him. I'd tried to reason with Dr. Bob, told him that a house full of relatives was not conducive to one orgasm— let alone the baker's dozen called for on this piece of paper—but he'd hustled me out through the empty reception area.

Maybe we should just leave my brother in charge for a week and take this to-do list and hit the Caribbean. Yeah, no snow *or* torched birds, the idea held merit. Of course, Child

Protective Services would be camped out on our doorstep within twenty-four hours and how would I concentrate with that mental picture? And concentration was essential, as well as some time and perhaps a few scented candles....

Shoot, I really was an old fogy.

Swathing myself in my scarf, hat, earmuffs, gloves and heavy parka, I'd taken my first step toward my car when I remembered about Neil's phone. Not wanting to bother Dr. Bob, I scoured the waiting room, but only the DSMV IV on the coffee table was smaller than a breadbox. Maybe he hadn't left it here? On my hands and knees, I checked under the sofa and was about to concede defeat when I heard the door creak open.

"Mrs. Phillips?" The doctor's tone was flat, no inflection whatsoever for the sight of my hind end in the air. I scrambled up, bashing my elbow on the table in my haste.

"Sorry, I was just looking for Neil's phone." I rubbed my elbow and smiled sheepishly.

"Your husband retrieved his phone yesterday afternoon," He informed me. "He was quite relieved to have it back."

I'd started to nod, but stopped mid-motion and scowled. Neil hadn't told me he'd come back here. And what was with the doctor's word choice. Relieved? That seemed a bit over the top. He'd known he left his cell here, noticed it missing in the car on our way to the Valentino's, after my battery had crapped out.

87

Why hadn't he told me he'd picked it up? Neil told me everything, at least everything that wasn't classified. Honesty was the cornerstone of our relationship. True, I hadn't told him I was coming back here today, but that was different, damn it. And now Dr. Bob knew Neil had withheld information from me, no matter how insignificant.

Mountain out of a mosquito bite. I told myself. It doesn't mean anything. Hiding my real thoughts was a challenge, but I somehow blanked my expression. "Of course, it probably just slipped his mind. Thanks again, I'll see you next week."

I hustled out of there, not wanting his insight into the matter. Dr. Bob had done enough damage to my psyche for one day.

So what if Neil had gone out of his way yesterday, before picking up the boys, to retrieve his phone? He wanted it back, just in case. *In case of what?* My inner skeptic surfaced and smirked at me. *What call would have been so important that he refused to go one night without his phone? Anyone could reach him at the house, right?*

Unless *anyone* didn't have the house number, because Neil didn't want *anyone* talking to me? Maybe for the same reason Neil didn't want me picking up his phone, having an opportunity to scroll through the incoming and outgoing calls—

"Stop it!" I shrieked at my runaway thoughts, the sound doubly loud inside my tiny car. Damn Dr. Bob and his well metaphor and Eric and even Marty for cheating and watering this ugly seed of doubt.

Needing to hear Neil's voice, I plucked my cell phone out of my bag and hit speed dial number one. His phone must have been off because my call went straight to voicemail. I didn't bother leaving a message, just hit speed dial number two, and waited while the line rang at his desk. Five rings later I was about to hang up when an unfamiliar male voice answered.

"Um, hi, I'm looking for Neil Phillips?"

"Sorry, lady, he ain't in yet." The guy who'd answered replied.

My queasy stomach flipped over. My dashboard clock read 11:08. Neil had left the house shortly after seven. "I thought he'd be at his desk, you know, trying to pick up some overtime?"

The guy with the south Boston accent laughed. "Didn't you hear? The company shelved all overtime, due to the economy. Why pay us hardworking stiffs extra when third party can do it for less?"

"No overtime," I echoed; my voice hollow in my ears.

"Nah, but he'll be in for his regular shift at two. Or you could try him at home, if you've got the number."

"I have the number, thanks." Not like he'd answer that line either.

How many times had Neil left the house claiming he was going to pick up a little overtime? Just since the holidays, at least two dozen I could call to mind. How had I missed this?

Shoving all of my emotions away, I turned on the car and pointed it toward home.

I'd made it about a block when I pulled over at a Cumberland Farms, hopped out and stuffed Dr. Bob's homework in the trash. I had cleaning to do and an unwilling partner to light a fire under; homework was just not going to happen this week.

Breezing into the house on the prow of the North Wind, I slammed the door and bee-lined to my war pantry. The new customer, a divorced man new homeowner, had been utterly clueless about what kind of cleaning he'd needed. "Can't you just come over and clean?" He'd whined.

That was exactly what I planned to do. Exhaust myself, not thinking about Neil, his movements, his phone or any other depressing thoughts. Just clean and make some money, little Mary flipping Sunshine with a Swiffer.

"Is everything all right?" Penny's flat vowels and lack of g's grated on my last nerve.

"No, every *thang* is NOT *all rite*. Did you get an appointment with an obstetrician yet?"

Penny nodded and glanced away, but not before I saw the hurt in her eyes. Damn, what was I thinking? Mocking a pregnant woman, when had I become a bully?

I exhaled between clenched teeth. "I'm sorry, Penny. Please ignore ninety-five percent of what comes out of my mouth. I'm not upset with you, okay?"

She nodded, but I knew it wasn't okay. Was it the girl's fault that I was used to being queen bee around here and had taken serious umbrage to being displaced by the pregnant princess? And she was a girl, barley out of her teens, if I was any judge. "How old are you, Penny?" I asked.

"I'll be twenty-two in April." Her chin jutted out and I smiled.

"That's about how old I was when I took over caring for Josh and Kenny."

"Good for you." Penny spun on her bare heel and marched off to the bedroom. Apparently, I had some serious fence mending to do there.

"Marty!" I bellowed. No answering shout. After stuffing every spray, foam and squirt bottle I could think of into my carrier, I opened the garage door. Marty and the boys were in the middle of weight bench reps. I waited for Josh to finish a set before speaking. "Hey Marty, we need to leave in ten."

Kenny traded with Josh and Marty moved to the spotter's position. "I'll be ready as soon as we finish here." He waved me off.

Loading my supplies only took a minute. Restless, I stomped to the den and flicked on the computer. Neil had promised to look into the property rights for the advertising site, but I didn't want to think about what Neil had or hadn't done right then.

The website was still saved under my favorites and after a quick scan, I didn't pick up any copyright protection on company names or slogans. So why hadn't the dead bird sender just snagged my entire name instead of just the logo? Could it just be a weird coincidence?

I surfed to Google and typed in *Phoenix, bird* just to see what would surface. First was the Wikipedia page, which I ignored, 'cause any Joe Schmoe could add stuff on there. The next

91

was a link about the mythology around the Phoenix, which symbolized immortality, resurrection and life after death. Fascinated, I began to read.

* * * *

"Maggs, I think it's clean enough." Marty gestured at the innocent stainless steel sink I'd scrubbed with a vengeance. My new client, Lucas Sloan, was nowhere to be found, but his brother had let us in to "do our thing." The old ranch home, a similar layout to my own abode, was in desperate need of some TLC. Other than a massive T.V. and beat-up recliner, the place held only cardboard boxes. And about two years' worth of grime.

"I'm doing shiny sink, 101." I answered my brother as I scoured the last of the Comet from the basin. "I've already bleached it to remove set-in stains and all that's left is to Windex it to a shine. This should be done every six months."

Marty leaned against the counter. "Fascinating, truly." I caught his eye roll in my peripheral vision.

"Did you finish vacuuming?" I asked, while I spritzed the basin.

"Yup and I even used the attachments for the corners and whatnot."

"How about the master bedroom?" I wiped down the swan neck faucet.

"Done, as much as I could. Looks like the guy's living out of a suitcase. There weren't any hangers in the closet or pharmaceuticals in the medicine cabinet."

Being a snoop, I'd already noted the lack of medicine. "It's a rental. Ben, the guy who let us in, says that Sloan is in a custody battle and he wants the place spic-n-span before the court sends someone out here to evaluate."

"Poor bastard," Marty shook his head. "Bad enough his marriage broke up but now he's gotta live under a microscope just to spend time with his kids. How come the wife always gets custody?"

Ignoring Marty's stall tactics, I pointed at the Swiffer duster. "See if you can reach that light fixture in the foyer. Oh and the ceiling fan in the den." Lucas Sloan's personal life was none of our business, and while that usually didn't stop me from sticking my nose in, I just didn't have the fortitude at the moment.

Leo had once charged me with having a "bad case of the shoulds." As in, one should organize a library by author *and* by genre and Kenny, you should have thought of that before we left the house. He claimed it was part of my control-freak personality and asked how I benefited from knowing how something should be done. I'd taken his musings as a rhetorical question.

Marty grumbled and skulked out of the kitchen. I studied the sink, confident that my labor had helped. While the 1970's era kitchen didn't exactly sparkle, it did appear tidy and nothing pointed to a salmonella outbreak. My work was done.

Lugging my Rubbermaid bin of cleaning supplies towards the door, I noticed an envelope stuffed under the phone base. The

93

logo on the upper left hand corner caught my gaze. Safari Power Solutions with the slogan, *Go on Safari while we do the work.* I was pretty sure it was a subsidiary company owned by one Markus Valentino. Neil had also dropped the name a few times in reference to some project or other at his job.

Peeking around the corner to note Marty's whereabouts, I set my bin down and picked up the envelope. It was open and empty, but a phone number had been scribbled on the back. For no apparent reason, I keyed the number into my cell phone but before I could hit send, the front door opened.

"You all done in here?" Ben Sloan called out, not coming all the way into the house. From his vantage point, he could only see the hallway leading to the bedrooms and the living room. Luck on my side, I slid the envelope back under the phone and hefted my bin.

"Just about," I smiled and he grunted in response. If this euphoric personality was a family trait, I could understand why Sloan's marriage had tanked. "We still have to pack up our supplies. Here's one of my cards, could you give it to your brother for me?"

Ben nodded and pocketed my card. I called to Marty and humped my load of cleaning paraphernalia to the Mini Cooper.

Hot on my heels, Marty dumped the duster and Vacuum unceremoniously into the back, making the car dip and bounce. What had I been thinking, buying this clown car to haul all of my crap? While I'd watched a video where the car held fifteen bags of quick dry cement, it could only do it with the rear seats down and my vacuum was an industrial strength model, AKA BIG. On a normal day, I had to drop my cleaning stuff at home before I could pick up the kids. Ah, who was I kidding? I loved that car.

While Marty loaded the rest of our gear, I filled out an invoice and walked it over to Ben. He took one look at the total and sucked in a breath. "You're kidding, right?"

"Um, no." My prices were very reasonable and I'd never had any complaints about my results. Sometimes being a neat freak was a benefit.

"Shit, Lucas can't afford this. He still owes me fifty bucks."

"Mr. Sloan asked me to clean the entire house, which I did. He knew what my hourly rates were before I showed up today." I made an effort not to sound defensive, but Ben's scowl told me it didn't work.

"Whatever lady, I'm just saying this is more than I make for two and a half hours of real work."

Dickhead. I could have gone into the whole breakdown of supplies, insurance, my partner's fee—which I would set aside in a secret account for him until after the baby arrived—but why bother? "Have a nice day." I said instead and hurried back to the car.

"What was that all about?" My brother asked as I turned the engine over.

"Another satisfied customer." I sighed and glanced over to Marty. He had a bit of fuzz stuck in his short hair and he hadn't bothered to shave. "The guy balked at the bill. Fortunately, he's not the one who's supposed to pay us." We cruised around the Cul-de-sac and headed back to the main road.

"He didn't pay you?" Marty fidgeted with the temperature controls and I slapped his hand.

"Just give it a sec, it'll warm up. It wasn't his house, Marty. Don't worry; I have an arrangement with the other Mr. Sloan. "

"You should get the money upfront."

I sighed. "Sprout, no one is going to pay their cleaning service upfront, especially not a new client who has yet to inspect the job."

"But what happens if that guy tries to talk his brother into stiffing you?" Marty would not let the subject drop. "I mean, what would you do then?"

My first impulse was to answer that I'd send Neil over to persuade the guy to change his mind. I flinched, my thoughts skirting away from Neil as they had done all afternoon. "Probably threaten to take him to small claims court." I said instead. "After what the guy has been through with a divorce and a child custody battle, he'd probably rather cough up the money than have another reason to go to court."

"I still say it's risky. One of these days, you're gonna get burned."

I slammed on the brakes and we jerked to a stop six feet before the stop sign. Marty's words had reminded me of the cut and paste fax. "The Phoenix is rising, you're gonna get burned," I muttered.

"What?" Marty asked.

"Never mind." After the reading I'd done on the myth of the Phoenix, I knew the

96

bird symbolized rebirth and eternal life. The Greeks and Ancient Egyptians also believed it was connected to the sun god, who enjoyed its song and unique status, for there could only be one alive at any given time. According to myth, the bird lived from anywhere from 500 to over 1000 years and that when it felt the breath of Death hovering, it would build its own funeral pyre and be swallowed by the flames. A new Phoenix would then rise from the ashes of the blaze to start the cycle all over again.

Although everyone else believed the note was some type of kinky foreplay, I'd seen fear on both of the Valentinos' faces. Discounting that theory, *the Phoenix is rising* would probably refer to the rebirth part of the myth. The *you're gonna get burned,* however, made no sense. Other than in the X-Men comics, the Phoenix was not portrayed as violent or vengeful. Several of the articles I'd uncovered had even stated that the bird possessed healing powers. And there was still no explanation for the charred hawk.

"We're gonna make a quick trip to the police station." I told my brother and made an illegal U-Turn at the next light.

Eight

"**M**aggie," Detective Capri's expression was pained. "I've yet to reach either of the Valentinos. They haven't filed a report, so I'm without evidence to pursue."

Same old song and dance. "There is something going on with them, I can feel it. First the fax about the Phoenix and then the charred bird."

"You could notify P.E.T.A about the bird, maybe they can do something, but if Mr. Valentino wants the matter dropped. My hands are tied."

I blew air between my lips, attempting to get my hair out of my face. "You told me to trust my instincts. Well, they're screaming that all is not well here. Somebody used my logo to deliver a nasty message, bringing me into the fray."

"Maggie, I'm telling you to back off. If Valentino finds out you're making a stink about this, he might sue you for slander."

Crap, I hadn't thought about that possibility. Bad enough Marty had me fretting over being stiffed by new clients. To top that off, it was getting into tax season and since I was self-employed, I'd have to pay for my earnings, pitiful though they may have been last year. I really couldn't afford a lawsuit.

"Fine," I said. "I'll let it go, but I swear to you something is going on with them."

Capri offered me a stiff smile. "Noted. Now, I think you'd better get going if you want to be on time to pick up your kids."

"No school today, due to the snow," But I took the hint anyway.

Marty was seated by the check-in desk and I noticed the Stegosaurus from calamity's past smirked at me as I collected my brother.

"Can we stop at the store?" Marty asked as I pushed my way out into the frigid afternoon air.

"Which store and what are you after?" Knowing his agenda ahead of time solved many problems since there was a history of Marty realizing he'd misplaced his wallet while we held up the check-out line. .

"I was thinking Walmart, I need to get Penny some gloves and warm socks."

I sighed. My day was crappy enough without adding a trip to Walmart into the mix. In its inception, Walmart was a great idea, the first real buy anything at any time store.

Unfortunately, the hunt for a great deal brought out the viciousness in people and buying a pack of toilet tissue usually resulted in several bruises on my person as well as raised blood pressure. "She can borrow anything of mine that she needs." I told Marty even as I merged with traffic migrating toward the superstore.

"How about underwear?" Marty raised an eyebrow.

"Yeah, that's not going to happen. Besides, I should restock some of my cleaning supplies."

"Thanks, sis." Marty grinned at me.

"Do me a favor and call the house. Ask if anyone needs anything, since we're going." Some jack-ass in a Sienna barreled through the red light at the intersection and I simultaneously slammed on my brakes and pounded the horn. "What's your problem, pal!" I shouted, even though it was fourteen degrees outside and my windows were rolled up. The vehicle kept moving at its bat-outta-hell speed. Where were Hudson's finest when you needed 'em?

I proceeded through the light to the cadence of annoyed horns from every direction. Superb day, all around.

Marty spoke to whoever had answered on the house phone. I couldn't help but note we were on Broad Street traveling South past Forestvale Cemetery and would soon be approaching Technology Drive, which wound uphill to Intel. Part of me wanted to cruise the parking lot in hopes of spotting Neil's truck, and had I been alone I might have succumbed

100

to the impulse. However, with Marty in the car to witness my actions, the notion lost its appeal. I merged onto 85 South and wound my way into a parking space.

Marty snapped my phone closed. "Nobody needs anything."

Of course not. Nobody would need anything from the store until five minutes after I'd unpacked the purchases. Then, I'd be hit with a bevy of, "Hey Mom why didn't you get more....?

The Hudson Walmart was not a Supercenter, which meant I'd have to make another stop for groceries. "Make it fast, Sprout and remember whatever you buy we have to fit into the car."

Marty nodded and was off. Having left my coupon book at home, I decided to forgo the cleaning supplies on this trip. Instead, I browsed a display of coolers and outdoor furniture, (jumping the seasonal gun a bit weren't they?) but my thoughts were on Neil. With a bit of distance, I realized there could be a perfectly acceptable reason why he had lied to me about the overtime. In retrospect, I should have picked up on the lack of extra money in our account, since I was the financial guru in our house, even if I did have to do some math. That I didn't notice must mean something, but damned if I knew what.

"Hey, Maggie," I turned around and blinked when I saw Eric. I opened my mouth, but what could I say to him? Making a scene in the gym after he'd been caught in the act was one thing, but I was not about to start screaming at the scum-sucking dickweed in the middle of Walmart. Low though they may be, a girl has to have standards. I compressed my lips together and shot daggers at him with my gaze instead.

"I, um, wanted to apologize for the unpleasantness at the gym the other day and wanted to make sure you knew we valued your family's membership."

"Message received." I turned away in dismissal, but Eric caught my arm.

"The owner fired Sylvia."

"What?!" I shrieked in outrage. "Why?"

Eric shuffled his feet, unwilling to look me in the eye. "Well, membership has dropped off, what with the economy and all.... And her classes have been less than half full since December. After the incident, he said one of us had to go."

"So even though the *incident* was your fault, you let her take the fall?" The man was lower than a snake's belly.

Eric huffed his indignation. "I'm the assistant manager and a full-time employee. It made good financial sense to—"

I held up a hand in his face. "Save it for someone who gives a rat's ass."

He hung his head. "She won't return my phone calls or let me into the house."

"Can you fault her, really?"

"Get off your high horse, Maggie. Sylvia isn't perfect and she wasn't carrying her weight in our marriage. It would have ended sooner or later."

I blinked. "Are you trying to foist the blame on *her*?" Unbelievable.

102

Eric studied me a moment before he shook his head. "I see this isn't getting me anywhere. I'll leave you alone." He walked off without a backwards glance.

"Miserable piece of crap," I muttered and headed for maternity wear, eager to claim Marty and go home. Walmart was just not good for my mental health.

* * * *

"Mom, Grandma called. She said to remind you about lunch tomorrow." Josh didn't bother looking up from the computer screen as he relayed the information. I blinked, wondering what lunch he was referring to, before it struck me. "You mean the luncheon?" Dang, Laura's invitation/order to appear at a society luncheon had completely slipped my mind. Maybe on purpose, but now I was stuck. Laura would chain me in the basement if I cancelled on her without twenty-four hours' notice. Our HMO was more understanding.

Flipping through my day planner, I noted my next cleaning job was the Valentino's on Friday morning. No work excuse for me. Maybe Neil would have an idea how I could get out.... Well, maybe not. Neil and I had bigger issues than his mother commandeering me for a society event.

Penny poked her head around the corner. "I hope you don't mind, but I made a casserole for dinner, since y'all didn't have plans." Her tone belied that she didn't give a flipping fig if I minded or not. Not that I blamed her, I'd been a bitch-on-wheels ever since she'd arrived. Granted the circumstances

103

were less than ideal, but where was my innate Southern hospitality?

"Sounds great, Penny. When's your first doctor's appointment?" Marty had indeed found a decent health plan, which would cover the majority of Penny's medical bills. We'd set the plan into motion, but the policy had to be reviewed and approved by several faceless pencil-pushers before it went into effect. Of course, I was picking up the tab for it as his current employer, but it was a small price to pay for my niece or nephew's wellbeing.

"Next Wednesday at 10 AM." Penny responded as crisply as her honeyed accent would allow.

No excuse there, either. Maybe Marty would run me over with his RV....

"Oh and your friend from next door stopped by." Penny tossed over her shoulder as she maneuvered her way to the kitchen. I followed, my eyebrows meeting at the bridge of my nose.

"Sylvia stopped by? What did she say?"

Penny shrugged and removed a Caffeine-Free Diet Coke that had somehow made its way into my refrigerator. Extracting a Caffeine-Full Non-Diet Coke, I stared at her, willing her to talk to me.

"Yes, she came by. I don't recall exactly what she said, other than asking you to come over when you had the chance."

Part of me wanted to leap for the door and find out what was up with my poor, unemployed and soon-to-be-divorced friend. But I shelved the urge, knowing I had something else to do first.

"About before, Penny—"

"Nothin' doin'," Penny turned and peeked into the oven checking on her casserole. "Do your boys like tuna? I made a tuna-noodle dish."

"They'll eat anything." I answered, and then tagged on, "Unless it's Vegan fare."

Penny closed the oven door and scowled at me. "What about you?"

Truthfully, I loathed fish in any form and the smell of baking tuna had my gag reflex acting up. I'd eat it though, along with a slice of humble pie.

"I appreciate your cooking for us; you don't need to put yourself out like this."

Penny didn't say anything, just stared at the linoleum. "Not a problem. I like to cook, especially for people who like to eat."

Her statement explained a great deal about her relationship with Marty. The Sampson siblings loved to eat, as our mother had been a blue-ribbon winner in any baking contest she'd ever entered. Food equaled love through our formative years. "Have you ever worked in food service?" I asked her.

"No," Penny answered, and turned around so suddenly I knew she was lying.

"Ok-ay," I dragged the word out, grasping for something else to say to her. The situation was beyond uncomfortable and I wanted to kick my brother for tossing it in my lap. Stupid, selfish, thoughtless Marty and stupid, selfish, doormat, Maggie. The Sampson progeny had more than a love of food in common. "Well, I'm going over to Sylvia's for a bit. Send one of the boys over if you need anything."

"Sure," Penny answered and took a sip of her soda, still avoiding eye contact.

After relaying my plans to Marty and the boys, I squished myself into the requisite winter gear, boots, coat, mittens and hat, for the thirty yard walk to Sylvia's front door. I didn't want to catch a chill in the sub-Artic night.

I pressed the doorbell and shivered while I waited. Crap, I should have called her first so she knew it was me and not that toad Eric. My cell phone was in my jacket pocket, but I'd have to remove at least one glove to dial. There was no way I could key in the right sequence on my puny keypad with thick wool mittens on my paws.

Frustrated at my own lack of foresight I kicked the door and, to my surprise, it swung open. *That is not good,* I thought even as I called out for Sylvia. Though twilight had settled in the blue-black winter's sky, Sylvia's house was totally dark, no light visible from where I lurked.

"Sylvie?" I called out again and heard a muffled sob from the direction of the master bedroom. Okay, that needed some attention. First, though, I made sure the door was shut and locked before following the sound. Good God, the house felt like a frigging meat locker. I shuddered at the thought and did my best to ignore the herd of butterflies-on-crack bouncing around in my stomach.

Taking a moment to allow my eyes to adjust, I scanned the living room and office.

106

T.V, DVR, Computer and Sylvie's laptop were all accounted for, so I gleaned she hadn't been burgled. My electricity was on and thrumming, so it wasn't a power outage. I tried a light switch, to see if the darkness was voluntary. Still no light.

The pitiful sound repeated and I made my way toward the bedroom. For a moment, my imagination took hold. What if there was an intruder, one more interested in Sylvia than her electronics? Shit, what if he had her at gunpoint? Should I call the police?

Before I'd made a decision, Sylvia started to laugh and I exhaled in relief. True, her giggles had a slightly hysterical note to them, but at least she wasn't gagged and tied to her bed.

"Sylvia?" Peeking around her open door, I blinked at the sight. There was some light in Sylvia's house after all, candlelight. Rows of candles, divided into groups of three, were tiered by size until they looked like flaming bleachers on her dresser. The room was a mess, clothes, books, CDs, DVDs tossed about haphazardly and left wherever they'd fallen. Sylvia sat crossed-legged on the floor in the middle of the heap, a big bottle of Absolute Vodka cradled between her folded legs. Her left hand was wrapped around what looked like a cluster of twigs.

"Um, Sylvie," I knocked softly on the door, hoping I wouldn't startle her. Her hair was unkempt and in the flickering candlelight, I thought she might be wearing flannel pajamas. When she looked up, the wild emotion on her face almost made me take a step back. Happiness, confusion, fear, relief, it was all there, in the span of one heartbeat.

"Maggie!" She smiled, and raised the bottle to her lips in a half-assed toast to my presence. "You got a light?"

I glanced at the burning tapers. "No, I don't."

"Damn. I really need a light." Her deliberate tone and enunciation pointed at heavy intoxication.

I kicked a pile of stuff off to one side and sat down next to her. "Why's it so cold and dark in here?"

She giggled and took another slug from her bottle. "I got fired."

Unsure of whether I should bring up my meeting with Eric, I said nothing, just nodded.

"My husband was cheating on me at our mutual place of employment and I get fired. Where's the frigging cosmic balance in that?" Sylvia snarled and sloshed the liquid around in her bottle in time to her wild gesticulations.

"Um..., there isn't any?" I guessed. I'd never seen her drink as much as a sip of champagne, her body being a temple and all. Now, drunk off her ass and disheveled, she reminded me of, well, me.

She pointed at me and laughed. "You called it, Maggie. Mag-gie, hag-gie, the Laundry Hag." More giggling.

"What's with the sticks?" I gestured at her handful and she blinked as though she'd forgotten what she held.

"It's Sage, not sticks. I planned on smudging the house, particularly the bedroom."

108

"What's smudging?" Where did she come across all this stuff?

"Spiritual house cleansing," She answered. "To exorcise Eric from the room and purify the house."

"Sylvia, why is the power turned off?" I took the bottle from her so she couldn't hide behind it. She'd only been fired a few days ago, so I was pretty sure she wasn't destitute. Yet.

"No one paid the bill. I thought Eric paid it, like he always does. And I guess he was gone before I saw it with my own eyes." The eyes in question filled with tears. "It wasn't the first time."

I sat up straighter. "What do you mean?"

"Once a cheater, always a cheater," Sylvia's voice sing-songed as she waggled her finger at me. "They're all alike, Maggie. Every Y-chromosome carrier, deep down at a molecular level. Doesn't matter what you do for 'em, how much you give, they still have that roving eye."

I swallowed. "I don't believe that, Sylvie."

Sylvia snatched her bottle back. "Some things are true no matter what you believe.

Nine

"**W**hy is Sylvia sleeping on our air mattress?" I jumped at Neil's question, bashing my funny bone on the open medicine cabinet as I spun around. The running water in the bathtub had masked the sound of his approach.

"Lord, you scared ten years off my life." As I caught my breath, I studied my husband, wondering where he'd been this morning. He didn't appear any different than he had last night, other than the fatigue lines around his deep-set green eyes. Arms folded across his chest, he stared me down and I turned to shut off the water in the tub.

"How was your day?" I asked, glancing at him out of the corner of my eye.

"Shitty. We had more problems than the engineers anticipated and I have to be back in at six tomorrow. Now, I'm tired and I want nothing more than six hours of uninterrupted sleep, but it seems that your girlfriend is camped out on the living room floor."

Passed out was more like it. I swallowed at the news he was going to disappear again and knowing he wasn't going to be at work, that he'd just lied to my face, got my back up.

"It's only for one night. Eric didn't pay the bills on time and Sylvia's without power and heat until she can settle her accounts during business hours tomorrow. I'll get her straightened out first thing."

"And where did you plan on us sleeping tonight?"

"Marty's camper," I hefted my chin defiantly. "I already hooked up the portable space heater so if you wanna go crash, be my guest."

Neil stared at me for a beat. "Are you telling me that I can't sleep in my own house?"

"For one damn night, Neil. Suck it up."

He crowded me against the bathroom sink, a dangerous light in his eyes. "Suck it up?" He repeated, leaning in so I was trapped between his body and the counter.

"You were a SEAL, for the love of grief. Aren't you accustomed to roughing it?" For a second, I thought he was going to lose it and shout the house down, waking its various occupants. Then, something shifted; he cocked his head to the side, and studied me.

"Maggie, what's going on? Did something happen?" Concern was written clearly across his features and threaded through his deep voice. Oh, God, I was going to cave. This was not the time. I needed him furious, ready to tear my head off because he had to sleep in the world's crappiest RV, not compassionate. I had no defense against Neil's sympathy and how wrong would it be to melt into his arms for the night?

Very wrong, at least until I knew what was going on with him. Neil had never lied to me before, at least not to my knowledge, and Dr. Bob's well metaphor, along with Sylvia's conviction that men were designed to stray, had taken root. My rational mind went over the facts, time and again, but the truth wouldn't be denied. Neil lied to me and I'd caught him. Even if he wasn't cheating, he'd still betrayed my trust.

"Yes and no. I don't want to get into it now, all right?" I ducked his arm and leaned over the tub, checking the water temperature. Tired and heartsick, part of me cried out to grab hold of my husband and sob until these horrible feelings went away. The reprieve would come at a price though, which I'd pay come the morning when Neil disappeared again. And I wasn't willing to barter my self-respect for the illusion of comfort.

Ask him, my mother's voice echoed in my head, but I pushed her advice away. There was no guarantee he wouldn't lie to me again. Some things needed to be witnessed firsthand.

"Penny cooked again. I saved you some casserole. It's in the fridge; just nuke it for two minutes." I could feel his gaze on my back and turned to face him. "Give me a few minutes, please. Between Penny and Josh, the bathroom has been like Grand Central all day."

Neil opened his mouth to say something, but then thought better of it. "I'll leave you alone." The door shut with a final sounding click.

I stared at the bath, lacking the energy to shed my clothes and slither into the water until I was immersed in bubbles. Like a soak in the tub would make everything all right? No matter how long I stalled, I still had to get out eventually and join Neil in the camper. He'd poke and prod until I told him everything. Dr. Bob and his stupid highways of communication could kiss my butt.

"Maggie," Neil tapped on the door and I closed my eyes.

"What is it?"

"Phone for you."

Huh, that was odd. It was after ten and almost everyone I knew was under our roof. "Who is it?"

"Detective Capri." There was a pause, and then Neil opened the bathroom door. He looked pointedly at the undisturbed bathwater, but refused to comment. "She wants to know when you last spoke with Mrs. Valentino."

I held out my hand for the phone. "What's going on, Detective?

Capri's clipped Bostonian accent came over the line. "When was your last contact with Candie Valentino?"

I stared at Neil who leaned against the sink, shamelessly eavesdropping. "Yesterday, after the to-do with the dead bird. Why?"

113

Capri ignored the question. "You didn't speak with her over the phone, maybe try to convince her to talk to me, or leave her husband?"

I scowled at my cordless. "No, I told you. I've been busy today. Has something happened to Candie?"

Capri exhaled a sound like a gale force wind over the phone line. "I don't know for sure. Her husband thinks she's been abducted."

"Like by aliens?" I scoffed at the notion.

"No, as in kidnapped." The detective corrected me.

"Kidnapped?" I squeaked and over by the mirror, Neil's posture went on full alert.

"There was a note, another cut and paste deal, like you stumbled across. Standard kidnapper fare, I'm afraid."

"Oh, God." I'd been right, I'd been right all along and now I was going to be sick. Then something occurred to me. "Wait, why are you telling me all this?"

Capri cleared her throat. "Valentino called the FBI. Kidnapping is their territory. This is over my head now, but I want you to be careful and to warn you that you're going to be called in for questioning."

"When?" My knuckles were white as I gripped the cordless phone. I stared at Neil and he stared back, panic flowing on an open current between us.

The doorbell rang.

"Now," Capri said and disconnected.

* * * *

114

The two federal special agents who had come to interview me were ushered into the kitchen. Neil had answered the door while I put on a pot of coffee. Introductions were made and then I shut the door to the living room, where Sylvia's soft snores remained undisturbed. I puttered around, refilling the sugar bowl and setting out steaming mugs, which neither Special Agent Salazar nor Special Agent Feist touched. I downed my first cup and waited.

"Have a seat Mrs. Phillips." Special Agent Salazar indicated my ugly barstool with a motion of his dark skinned hand. I refilled my mug and sat. Neil stood behind me, his hands on my shoulders, in an obvious show of support.

The questions began and I answered as best I could. Yes, I knew Candie Valentino, no not well. My cleaning services had been referred to her by a mutual acquaintance. No, I didn't know Markus Valentino well; I'd only met him for the first time the day before.

"So, why then did Mrs. Valentino phone you when she received the package?" Special Agent Feist asked. His tone implied I was hiding some sort of deep connection with the Valentino's.

"At first, she thought I might have sent it, since part of my logo was on the box?" I didn't mean for the words to come out like a question, but I couldn't help it.

Neil squeezed my shoulder. "I ordered all of Maggie's business paraphernalia from an online company. The logo was a freebie distributed for general use by the same site."

115

Special Agent Salazar flipped open a small leather-bound notebook. "The name of the site?"

Neil rattled it off.

"What's the name of your business, Mrs. Phillips?" Special Agent Feist pinned me down with his neon blue stare. If these two were doing a good cop/ bad cop routine, I couldn't pick out which was which.

"The Laundry Hag Cleaning Services."

"Laundry hag?" Salazar asked.

I shrugged. "It's hard to forget."

"Indeed," Special Agent Feist said. The two exchanged an unreadable look. Jeeze.

"Why did you go to the Valentino residence yesterday?" Special Agent Feist asked.

"Candie sounded so upset, I urged her to call the police about the dead bird, but I figured she wasn't thinking straight. I wanted to make sure she was okay."

"Why didn't you call the police, Mrs. Phillips?"

"My cell phone was out of juice and Neil left his at Dr. Bob's office."

"Dr. Bob?" Special Agent Salazar cocked his head to the side, studying me like an ameba under a microscope.

"Our marriage counselor," Neil supplied. Again with the silent communication. I wanted to elbow Neil in the gut. Did the entire world need to know we were in therapy?

"So that's why I didn't call Detective Capri." I finished lamely.

"What happened when you arrived at the Valentino residence?"

I retold the story, as much as I could recall anyhow. Neil kept quiet, probably so we didn't look like a couple of stooges working from a well-rehearsed routine, like our inquisitors.

"Detective Capri mentioned you have an ongoing relationship with the Hudson police force."

As succinctly as possible, I told them about the C.I. position and the events which had led up to it.

"So you took the note from the Valentino home without their knowledge." Special Agent Salazar crossed his arms over his chest and waited for conformation.

"No," I responded, but didn't elaborate.

"No?" Special Agent Feist didn't move, but something in his demeanor changed.

Neil poked me in the middle of my back, where they couldn't see. I sighed. "I made a photocopy to bring to Detective Capri."

"Are you aware, Mrs. Phillips, that Mr. Valentino had no knowledge of the first note?"

"I have no idea how he could have missed it. I left it on the tray of his fax machine." Unless Valentino had hidden it, like he'd attempted to hide the dead bird from the police. Why he'd lie about the note, after calling in the FBI, I couldn't begin to guess.

"Tell us about your whereabouts this morning, Mrs. Phillips."

His words didn't inform as to whether I was a suspect or not, but as I ran through my schedule, I realized it didn't matter. Because of my busy life, I had an alibi for almost the entire day.

117

Neil sucked in an audible breath when he discovered I had been back to Dr. Bob's, but didn't comment. The two special agents nodded as I gave them names and contact numbers for all of the people I'd spoken with. Part of me hoped they would run down Neil's day too, because even if my law-abiding husband fibbed to me, he'd play straight with the feds.

"So you didn't drive past the Valentino estate at any point today?" Special Agent Salazar had finished note-taking and looked at me. From his slightly melodic accent and dark features, I guessed he had some Arabic blood. He certainly didn't glow in the dark like I did during a New England winter.

"No, they're kind of out of the way. The closest I came was driving past the turnoff on my way to Walmart. I wasn't due to clean their house until Friday morning." Neil's grip on my shoulders tightened to near pain and I winced. "I was probably going to cancel anyhow."

"Why?" Special Agent Feist inquired.

I thought the answer was obvious, I wanted nothing to do with whatever oddness was happening with the Valentinos, but the men waited for a reply. "I'm looking into expanding my business, taking on more work."

Special Agent Salazar snorted. "In this economy? Good luck."

A perverse part of me was delighted to have gotten a human reaction from the stalwart FBI special agent. The larger part asked, "Any more questions, gentlemen?"

"I think we're done for now." Special Agent Salazar flipped his notebook closed. "We'll be in touch."

"Please let me know when you find her." Too concerned with the prospect that I was "a person of interest," my brain hadn't registered the nightmare Candie was enduring.

Special Agent Feist turned and looked at me. "We'll be in touch." He parroted. Neil followed them to the door.

"Shit," I muttered. "Shit, shit, SHIT!" God, the Phoenix wacko had taken Candie. Or maybe not. She might have been traumatized by the fricasseed Falcon and taken off on her own. Except, according to Capri, there had been another note left with ransom instructions. Thank the Lord I'd made a copy for Capri. For some reason, Valentino hadn't bothered to divulge that detail to the feds.

Neil returned and leaned on the counter so his face was a few inches from mine. "You went back to Dr. Bob's." He pointed out.

"So did you." I retorted. Neil blinked and I hid a smile, having taken him off guard.

"Just to get my phone." His eye contact was direct.

"I could have retrieved it for you." I said.

"Yeah, and I would have asked you to, except you didn't tell me you were going back there today." He pointed out.

What was it about some men that they could spin anything to make a woman doubt her own thoughts? In one statement, he revealed that he had no reason to hide his cell phone from me and made me feel guilty about

119

withholding the Dr. Bob visit. Damn his reasonable hide!

"So, I went back to Dr. Bob's today." I told him.

The corner of Neil's mouth hiked up and laugh lines crinkled around his eyes. "Really? I had no idea."

"I kind of hate him a little bit." I divulged.

"He seems like an okay guy to me." Neil extracted his now cold tuna casserole from the microwave and scraped the plate. "This stuff reeked *before* it sat for forty minutes. I'm not hungry anymore."

"So, wanna tell me about your day?" *Please, please, please, tell me all about your day,* I silently begged.

Neil rinsed the plate and set it in the dishwasher. "Right now, I just want to go to bed. Even if it is in a camper."

"Sorry," It wasn't hard to sound sincere, since I was sorry, for a multitude of reasons. Glancing at the clock, I realized it was practically Thursday. "Oh, no Leo," I groaned

"Is he sleeping over, too?" Neil didn't sound like he was joking.

"No, I promised him, I'd look for more work, so I could hire his friend."

"You have to stop taking in strays, Uncle Scrooge. I understand you want to save the world, but this is ridiculous."

"I told you I'd send Marty away if you wanted—"

"I don't want you to send him away." I looked at Neil and he shrugged. "He's your brother and Penny's his, well, I don't know

120

what, but sort of family I suppose." Neil took a breath and shook his head. "But this thing with Sylvia and Eric, Candie Valentino and now Leo's friend...?"

"Richard." I supplied.

"You don't have to be so involved with every person you meet. I mean, I love that you are, you have a generous heart, but really Maggie, you're...."

"What?" Dear God, was Dr. Bob right? Was I spreading myself too thin and neglecting Neil and the boys? "What do you want me to do?"

He rubbed his face with one hand, his stubble rasping against his palm. "Hell if I know. It might be nice to go a few days without a visit from the law though."

Ten

    True to his word, Neil was up before dawn. Despite my exhaustion, I had a lousy night's sleep, partly due to the lumpy mattress in Marty's built-in double bed. The space heater had kept the inside of the camper warm and while the small space had a worn quality to it, I was surprised by how tidy everything seemed. Towels were neatly folded in the cabinet by the bathroom; dishes were clean and stacked in a wire holder next to the mini fridge. The indoor/outdoor carpet still held tracks from a carpet sweeper. Either Marty had turned over a new leaf, or Penny was a pretty decent housekeeper.

Neil conked his head on the small doorway leading from the bedroom to the living/dining area. "Christ," he muttered, stuffing his arms into his jacket. I could see the appeal of these things, in spite of the numerous pitfalls. Looking decidedly rugged with a day's worth of stubble and severe bed head, I imagined touring the continental US with him, waking early to see the sunrise and then hitting the open road. I sat up, still fully clothed.

"Morning," I greeted him. He grunted and sat down on the loveseat to lace his boots so all I could see were his denim-clad calves. I guess he hadn't slept well either.

"Sorry, I didn't want to wake you."

In theory, I could have gone back to sleep, but what was the point? After flicking off the space heater, I pulled on my own coat. "Not a problem. I think I'll go jogging after I take the kids to school."

Neil nodded absently. ""How are they planning to keep a baby in here?"

I shrugged. "From what I can tell, Penny, like my brother, doesn't think very far in advance."

"When's our next meeting with Dr. Bob?" He asked and my esophagus tightened. I'd need to tell him about the 'homework' soon. Lord, help me.

"Next week," I answered.

"Just let me know when, so I can be sure to have the time set aside."

Deciding a little deep sea fishing expedition was in order, I cleared my throat. "Wow, I'm surprised you're picking up all this overtime. Someone I spoke to recently mentioned that Intel's cut way back on overtime."

I watched him closely for any reaction, a stiffening of the shoulders or a wary glance, but came up empty when he turned to the door. "I'm somewhat essential to a project the higher-ups are attempting to crank out post haste. I guess I'm exempt from the rules for the time being."

I hurried out into the pre-dawn gloom and skidded on the frozen bottom step. Neil steadied me and gripped my arm, so another spaz-attack wouldn't see me on my butt. I blew a lock of hair out of my eyes and dove back in. "So, you're doing the same job as always?"

"What I do isn't exactly like the daily grind, Uncle Scrooge. Sort of like, yesterday you were cleaning houses and today you're...?"

"Running the kids to school, Sylvia to her utility companies and then picking up your mother for a luncheon."

"Good one," Neil shook his head and clomped up the stairs. I scurried in his wake, since his large form broke the wind a bit.

"I'm serious. Someone in her circle is retiring and she wants me to pick her up for a luncheon." I lowered my voice as we entered our slumbering house. With no lights on, no smell of coffee, no running feet or cussing mouths, it didn't feel like home.

Neil shut and bolted the door behind us. "And you're going?" His tone was thick with disbelief.

"She sprung it on me and we've been a little harried...." My explanation rebounded off of Neil's back as he strode toward the

124

bathroom. I could follow him, but I was in desperate need of a caffeine fix. Plus, what was I supposed to say; his mother strong-armed me into attending and I'd been so worried my marriage was falling apart that I'd waited too long to decline?

I made a super high-octane pot of coffee and listened as the shower started. *Go on chicken, he wanted you in there yesterday.* That wasn't my mother's voice. I should listen anyway, since my imagination was spiraling out of control. Neil had a plausible explanation for his absences; Dr. Bob had been his suggestion, he didn't mind the thought of me checking his phone for odd numbers—

"Odd numbers," I murmured aloud. Neil's keys, wallet and cell phone sat waiting patiently in the dish on the entry table, next to my purse. Extracting my phone first, I keyed in latest entries. And yup, I was right, the number I'd found at Sloan's house was still saved in the memory bank. On impulse I hit send, assuming no one would pick up before the plumber's butt crack of dawn, but I might glean a little something from voicemail.

"You have reached Dr. Robert Ludlum, marriage facilitator—" I squeaked and hung up the phone. I knew that number looked familiar, but I hadn't envisioned Dr. Bob's involvement.

To be sure, I picked up Neil's phone and scrolled through the contact list. Sure enough, Dr. Bob was catalogued and the number matched the one I'd liberated from Sloan.

It seemed odd to me that Sloan had scribbled Dr. Bob's number on an envelope next to the phone in the house he moved into *after* his divorce. As a marriage facilitator—I struggled to wrap my head around that word choice— I'd expect Dr. Bob might have been called in before the lawyers. Sloan's current address in heartbreak city didn't bode well for my own marriage.

"Uncle Scrooge, have you seen my blue shirt?" Neil stood in the doorway, a towel wrapped around his hips. He raised an eyebrow when he noticed his phone in my palm.

Quickly, I set his phone down and plowed past him to the laundry room. "In here. I moved most of your work clothes onto the drying line last night. More efficient with Marty and Penny sleeping in our room, don't ya think?" I babbled while rummaging through the hangers then came up with the button-down in question and offered it to him. He didn't take it. One hand secured his towel and the other pointed his phone at me.

"What was that all about? You're being secretive and sneaky and I want to know why." His mouth was set in a grim line.

My lips parted, but only a breath of air came out. What to say?

"Please talk to me, I'm worried about you." Setting his phone down on the dryer he shut the door and we were plunged into darkness. I reached for a light switch, but he grasped my hand in his own.

"You are the most difficult person to have a discussion with, you know that?" His breath whispered along my left ear, sending chills down my spine. "Splitting an atom involves less effort than getting some info out of you."

"Better get out the water board slick, because I've got nothing for you."

"Is that so?" A faint fluttering sound and Neil's towel pooled at my feet. He kissed me and proved that I did in fact have something for him. Smart man and one helluva multitasker.

* * * *

"That was so wrong," I mumbled gazing at my poor, violated washing machine with a satisfied smile. Bet the manufacturer didn't have that in mind when they offered a five year extended warranty. Were outside vibrations covered under normal wear and tear?

"What's wrong is we're sneaking around like a couple of teenagers in our own house." Neil bent over to step into his pants and then hissed out a breath.

"Your shoulder?" I asked. Neil had made a mess of his rotator cuff— during a classified mission he couldn't tell me about— which was the reason he was no longer part of the SEAL teams.

Wincing, he straightened and reached around to massage the area. "The cold makes it worse."

That and hefting his not-so-dainty wife against a major appliance for a solid ten minutes. Guilt made my cheeks burn. No more excuses, I needed to get into shape, for Neil's sake.

I helped him ease his shoulder into the blue shirt and did the buttons.

"Crap, I'm going to be late." Neil opened the door to the laundry room and gazed at me

127

for a minute. "How about you meet me for dinner tonight? We might as well take advantage of the built-in babysitters. Wherever you want to go."

"What time?" I smiled, thinking it had been awhile since we had a date night.

He shoved his feet into steel-toed boots. "I'll give you a call later, after I see what my day is shaping up to be."

"Sounds great. Call my cell; I'll be all over the place today." Sighing, I watched him stride to the car. What a man.

"You look like a cat that tipped over a milk carton." Sylvia said from the living room, a note of sadness in her voice.

"How are you feeling?" I closed the door on Neil and turned to face my friend. The air mattress squeaked as Sylvia scooted forward in an effort to dismount.

"Like death on a cracker." Shifting her weight, she rolled off the inflate-a-bed. "What time is it?"

"Almost six. I'll drive you over to the electric company's office as soon as I drop the boys off."

Sylvia stood up and teetered a bit. Having no idea how much she'd imbibed the night before, I couldn't tell if she was hungover or just tired. "Thanks for the offer, but I can handle it. And thank you for putting me up last night."

"Anytime, Sylvie. Help yourself to anything in the kitchen. And I'll advise you to get a shower in before the rest of the house comes alive."

She nodded, and winced, as if the small movement pained her. I watched her shuffle off to the bathroom, sorrow curdling in my throat. Seeing her all discombobulated was almost worse than seeing her drunk. Typically, Sylvia was all grace and poise and I didn't know if Eric or her unemployment was to blame for her current state.

My mind still churning, I dressed in sweats and retrieved Josh's iPod, settling it in the little case that strapped onto my arm. I layered in a coat, gloves and earmuffs, which I discarded after realizing I wouldn't be able to use the ear buds while wearing them. The little case didn't fit over my goose-down jacket, so I abandoned the coat as well. Maybe I'd run faster in order to keep warm.

Scanning the playlist, I selected *Money for Nothing* as my warm-up song. As the drum beat blared in my ears, I stretched my calves, hamstrings and rolled my shoulders a bit like the way Neil always did before he hit the treadmill. Proud that I'd picked up a few things whilst ogling, I strode to the front door full of purpose.

Oh, holy Mary, mother of God, it was cold! I shot a longing glance at my coat, but between jogging and fiddling with the portable music player, I had enough coordination issues to deal with. I carefully made my way down the steps, avoiding icy patches. Thankfully the street was clear and the sand/salt combo spread by the town kept the ice at bay. I headed down the hill in the opposite direction from the last time, wanting to start fresh.

Without any conscious effort, my footfalls seemed to sync with the tempo of the song. The sun was still below the horizon but the sky grew lighter as I made my way around a bend. Breathing was a challenge and the sensation I was sucking down little daggers with each inhale had me gasping, even though my muscles were raring to go. In through the nose, which seemed to have frozen shut, and out through the mouth. Cripes, how long was this song?

Slowing to a walk, I unsheathed the iPod and thumbed the little wheel thingy, hoping to find something inspirational. Choosing Better Than Ezra's *A Lifetime*, I doggedly stumbled onward. My pace was slower, but the band was right, three and a half minutes really did feel like a lifetime.

I made it through most of the song before the wheezing grew too insistent to ignore. The song finished and I sought the player again, stopping at the bottom of the hill by the intersection leading out of the neighborhood. Moving off the road, in case a car drove by, I thumbed through the list again. What now? Robert Palmer maybe? Or no, that kick-ass Billy Squire song they used on the commercials for *Burn Notice*. What was it called again?

Shit, Josh had shown me how to search by artist, but I'd forgotten. I made a few requests from a menu button and spotted an artist menu. I was so busy fiddling that I didn't notice the car at first. After all, there were plenty of nine year old blue Ford Escorts in the area and some of them even had a *Support the*

130

Troops magnet on the left rear panel. But it was the other decal, with the Laundry Hag Cleaning Services and my cell phone number that nearly stopped my heart. No, this couldn't be right. Neil had left our house ten minutes ago. His car should be at least eight miles away by now. He'd said he was late, had hustled off without giving me a kiss goodbye because he was late, damn it. What would he be doing, not even a mile from our house...?

My vision clouded over and I bent at the waist, struggling with the urge to vomit. He'd just left me, after we'd had so much fun sullying the washing machine, and now he was parked in someone else's driveway? The double entendre made me gag.

"Move," I muttered under my breath. Standing and gawking wouldn't get me anywhere and the sweat I'd accumulated from my exertion was solidifying on my skin, the cool morning air chilling me to the core. Unfortunately my feet took the command in the wrong direction. Without intent, I made my way to a copse of evergreens in the adjacent lot and leaned against a pine for support. Without my electric blue parka, I blended in with the Spartan landscape and I hunkered in to watch for Neil.

In the back of my mind, I knew I couldn't stay here forever. Neil's typical shift started at nine, which roughly translated into ninety minutes from now. I'd be a hag-popsicle by then, plus kinda late getting Josh and Kenny off to school. The thoughts buzzed around like disgruntled bees, but I didn't budge from my bird's eye view of the front door.

The house was a fixer-upper cape cod with a tiny screened-in back porch tagged on as an afterthought. A small building, probably a garage, squatted perpendicular to the main house. Both sported aluminum siding in a Robin's egg blue and were trimmed in white. The gutters needed to be cleaned, as the house was surrounded by leafless elms and oaks, and there was a big sheet of plywood over one of the upstairs windows.

My hands were numb inside my dollar store knit gloves when the front door opened and Neil stepped out onto the porch. He smiled at someone who remained out of sight and spoke softly, too far away for me to hear. Frozen fingers gripped the tree as I leaned closer, hoping to catch a vibe from the scene, but it was over quickly and Neil trotted down the steps and backed his car out onto the road. Counting to fifty, I unglued my hands from the poor pine and scooted across the open area to the house. No way was I leaving until I knew who lived inside.

Eleven

"**D**oes this look all right?" Dressing for a society luncheon was not on my list of top ten favorite pastimes and neither Marty nor Penny had been any help, so I accosted Leo as he answered the door.

Standing in the foyer of my in-laws estate in Cambridge was like entering a new world. The floor was Italian marble, the statuary classic Roman design and the curtains were thick, allowing only the softest glimmer of light in to illuminate the interior. I'd only been to the estate a handful of times, but on every visit I couldn't help but hum that ditty from Sesame Street. *One of these things is not like the other....* My Gap pants and faux Prada purse certainly didn't belong.

Leo ushered me into one of the many sitting rooms and turned me around for a 360 degree inspection. "I like the pearl color of the blouse on you, very new money in combo with the black slacks, if you get my drift, but those shoes—"

I held up a hand to his lips. "I know they're awful but I didn't want my feet to freeze."

"How many times do I need to tell you, invest in a pair of classic black pumps and you won't go wrong." It wasn't a question.

"I've told you I can't walk in heels," I shuffled my gray winter boots, adjusting the pants so they hid more of my footwear. "Picture me in heels, walking across an icy parking lot. Now look me in the eye and tell me the vision doesn't include an ambulance."

"Darling, where you're going, you won't have to walk further than the valet drop off in front of the building."

I cringed. "Yikes. This doesn't sound good for me. Got any tips, oh czar of haute couture?"

Leo leaned in and wrapped an arm around my shoulder. "You look great and unfortunately it's too late to do much about the shoes, but your manner needs some work." He had the grace to shift his weight and glance away.

"Hit me," I sighed.

"Well, you need to remember not to exhibit fear. Show no weakness. They can smell the stink of apprehension like bears emerging from hibernation. So whatever you do, don't limp or you're done for."

I glared at him as he fiddled with my diamond necklace. "Way to pep me up before the big game there coach. Now that you've

134

filled my head with that lovely comparison, how do you suggest I cage the fear?"

He winked at me. "You could go with the classic 'picture them in their underwear'."

Gack. Not if I didn't want to gouge out my own eyeballs.

"Seriously Maggie, You're a hard working self-employed woman with a hotty of a hubby who comes from money. Do you really feel inferior to Laura's gaggle of persnickety geese?"

Yeah, I did, but I wasn't about to reveal that to Leo, who was a God, but his resume said otherwise and he might take offense. "Speaking of my self-employment, I made a few calls this morning and I have some leads for night cleaning gigs. Tell Richard to call me and we'll try to meet up for the interviews."

Leo kissed my forehead. "Bless you and your efficient attitude. I told him we could count on you."

"I meant what I said; you're pairing up with Marty whenever you're free."

"Why don't you just ask Neil to help? "

I swallowed around the tennis ball lodged in my esophagus. "Neil's been...busy. Lots to do, at work I mean." The loathsome quiver in my voice slipped out. After seeing the pretty mid-thirties mom preparing her two sons for school inside the run-down house, I didn't know what to make of Neil's stopover. Like any true Southern Belle, I'd decided not to think about what I'd seen, at least until tomorrow.

Leo spun me around, but I couldn't meet his gaze. "What's going on?" he whispered. I opened my mouth to answer, but Laura chose that moment to breeze in, full steam ahead. I imagined if a female praying mantis wore designer suits; she'd dress like my mother-in-law. Laura sported an expensive and masterfully cut black suit which accentuated her lean frame, the skirt stopping just above her knees. A celery green mandarin collar wrapped around her graceful throat and added to the image of predatory hunger. She was a beautiful, deadly force of nature. Just like her son.

I blinked repeatedly and Laura frowned at me. "What are you wearing? And why do you look like you're about to cry?"

"Go easy on her boss lady. Our Laundry Hag looks like she was ridden hard and put away wet."

Laura's nostrils flared and I swore I saw smoke. "Oh honestly, Leopold! Could you be any more vulgar?"

"It'd take some doing." Leo murmured and tossed me a wink before exiting the room. My smile was wan as I faced my doom.

"You look lovely, Laura, And I'm fine really, just my allergies acting up." I didn't let her comment about my wardrobe bother me; it wasn't even a blip on the radar at the moment.

Laura shot me stink-eye for a moment then presented her back and called out. "Leopold, we're leaving now. If anyone from the office telephones, forward the call to my mobile phone."

"Will do, Mrs. P," Leo hollered from the kitchen.

136

"You took a full day off?" I marveled as Laura slid her arms into her wool coat. She shooed me outside and shut the door. "And why shouldn't I? There is more to life than work, dear."

Missing a step, I caught myself on the iron hand rail and glanced around, nervously watched the sky for the four horsemen of the apocalypse. Good thing I wasn't in heels, I might have broken my neck.

Laura frowned at my display and then shook her head. "Really Margaret, you need to pay attention."

Nodding, I remoted my Mini open and bit my tongue. This was shaping up to be a long afternoon.

Laura gave me directions with the efficiency of a drill sergeant and soon we were idling in Boston lunchtime traffic. I wracked my brain for some benign topic, but Laura had her own agenda.

"Neil mentioned that the two of you were in therapy."

I gagged on my own saliva. "Well...um...that is—" Former SEAL or not, I was going to beat him to a quivering pulp.

"Really dear, you don't have to be so ashamed. Many a strong marriage require an intervention at some point."

"My marriage doesn't need an intervention—" I protested but Laura wasn't finished.

"After all, men and women think differently, experience the world differently, so it's perfectly acceptable to call in a trained professional for interpretation. I hope you

137

checked out the woman's credentials though. Lots of these so called "therapists" are nothing but hacks who've invested fifty dollars to print up an online degree. A classical education is best."

"He's a PH.D and Neil did the research, so—"

"Really Maggie, you rely on my son too much. While Neil is perfectly capable, you should take some pride and accomplish things for yourself. Set a positive example for Kenny and Josh; teach them to value strong, smart women so they will...."

As Laura droned on and on and on, I concentrated on the ancient rusted-out Volvo in front of us. The damn thing was practically held together by bumper stickers, both political and irreverent. My favorite was *fat people are harder to kidnap*. I laughed out loud, then started to cry, imagining poor Candie Valentino. Was she all right? I sobbed as my brain presented all sorts of grotesque possibilities.

"For heaven's sakes, what's the matter with you today? One might think you were—" Laura snapped her teeth together with an audible click.

I sniffled and reached for the pack of tissues in my cup holder. "What were you about to say?"

Laura shook her head, her champion poker face firmly in place. The drive progressed in silence.

* * * *

138

"And without further delay, I give you the woman of the hour." The speaker clapped as she stepped away from the podium. Having never been to a retirement luncheon before, I'd entered the posh hotel conference room clueless, but education was quick to slap me upside the head. We sat at a table near the dais, front and center with a clear view of the women on the stage. The gathering wasn't a ladies who do lunch affair, it was a feminist rally, each speaker driving home the point that a woman could and should do anything.

Except pee standing up. I thought to myself, but having no cronies with me, I contained my snark and tried to look engrossed in what the speaker said. The guest of honor was probably in her late sixties with diamond ice chips for eyes, and had an impressive resume. A self-made millionaire, who'd gone to college on a full academic scholarship—one of the first females to do so—and she'd amassed several rallies for equal rights during her tenure. In her spare moments, she'd studied political science and had been of critical importance to the Massachusetts state government. Unfortunately, all of her time moving in political circles had rubbed off and she droned on for what seemed like hours. While I admired her accomplishments, I wished I could admire them from a greater distance.

Surreptitiously, I glanced at Laura, who'd introduced me as "my daughter-in-law who runs her own business," to everyone we'd hobnobbed with. If anyone asked for further details, which few of them did, Laura made some vague reply and changed the subject. Her gaze was locked on the woman at the podium, and I puzzled over her. Obviously, Laura wanted to hide my cleaning lady status. She'd never approved of my desire to be home for the boys, but despite the progressive message of the afternoon, I knew most of the women in this room hired people just like me to take care of the nitty-gritty, be it answering phones, doing the laundry or scrubbing their porcelain thrones. So why had she forced me to come to this event? It didn't make sense, but I planned on hashing it out with her on the ride home.

The speaker took a breath and my cell phone went off. Laura glared at me as *I'm Too Sexy* resounded in the lull.

"'Scuse me," I smiled at the speaker and scooted for the exit. The phony expression fell away as soon as I was in the clear and I flipped the phone open. "Great timing Neil," I said, letting the sarcasm drip.

"Did I pull you away from something riveting?" I could hear the smile in his voice and my heart stuttered.

"How's your day going?" I asked, hoping he'd reveal what had gone on after he left.

"A cesspool of stupidity, and that's being kind. Sweet Jesus, I sound like my mother." Mock horror drifted through the phone.

I laughed, since I'd thought the same thing. "You still want to meet up for dinner tonight?"

"It'll have to be late, if that's okay. We have union engineers coming in and they have very specific hours, which us non-union plebes need to work around."

"How late is late?" I asked as my eyelids slid down. So damn tired.

"I was thinking eight. You decide where you wanna go?"

"How about that pub we went to after we moved here, you know with Sylvie and—" I swallowed, attempting not to choke on the memory.

If Neil picked up on my mood, he didn't say anything. "Okay, I'll meet you there at eight. Oh, I meant to ask, any word on Candie Valentino?"

"Detective Capri won't return my calls and I'd rather be filleted than traipse into the Hudson police station without a reason. Besides, it's not like I'm in the inner circle when it comes to the Valentinos. No matter how worried I am about Candie, it really isn't any of my business." Wow, I almost believed the words I'd spoken.

Neil didn't call me on my fib. "I gotta go now, Uncle Scrooge. I'll see ya at eight."

I closed the phone and opened my eyes. A woman was staring at me from the alcove by the restrooms. I wondered if I'd been talking loudly, having never quite mastered a proper indoor voice. Dressed in a form-fitting pinstriped business suit, I guessed she was another escapee from the luncheon; she appeared to belong with the women who move mountains society but we hadn't been introduced. Her ash blonde hair was coiled in an intricate rope at the nape of her neck and she appeared to have the grace to manage heels

141

and ice at the same time. I smiled at her, but she continued to stare.

I checked the time on my cell phone and wondered if I might just wait out here.

"Excuse me?" The business blonde approached me. This close, I could smell Shalimar perfume and a tinge of worried sweat. "Did you say something about Candie Valentino?"

"Do you know her?" I asked. Yup, definitely needed to work on my volume control.

"I'm Amelia Kettering. Candie was my roommate in college, but I haven't seen her in years." Amelia spoke with the same subtle drawl as Candie so I could believe they were both from Texas.

"Maggie Phillips," I extended a hand which Amelia shook firmly. "I was Mrs. Valentino's cleaning service," I answered, unsure of whether I'd be asked back and if I'd go after a kidnapping.

"Wait, Candie's living *here*?" her brown eyes seemed a little too big for her sockets.

I nodded. "They moved to Hudson a few months ago." I remembered how alone Candie seemed, flitting about the big house, always glad to see me. After witnessing the interaction with Markus, I gathered she was starved for company. Here she had a friend less than an hour away. "She never called you?"

Amelia shook her head, every hair lacquered severely in place. "No, I had no idea. I haven't seen her since before she was married." A far off look stole over her features.

I wanted to know why Amelia hadn't
been invited to the wedding, but didn't want to
appear rude. "Were the two of you close?"

"Very, until she met Markus anyway."
Bitterness tinged her words. "She didn't have
time for anyone but him, he saw to that."
Amelia shook her head. "How is she?"

The doors to the conference room
opened and a herd of women appeared,
stampeding for the restrooms. I glanced at
Amelia, wondering what protocol dictated in
this situation. Should I tell her Candie was
missing, presumed kidnapped? If Amelia was
anything like me, she might shriek or pass out.

"Um, maybe you want to call Markus." I
suggested, but Amelia shook her head.

"He made it plain that I was to have no
contact with either of them; he didn't want
word of our relationship to get out."

Laura pushed her way through the
crowd, searching for me, a black scowl firmly in
place. I estimated about seven seconds until
she bore down on us. "Relationship?" I
prodded.

Amelia met my gaze. "Candie and I
were lovers."

Twelve

"So, Ms. ..., Sampson is it?" Alan
Garner, department head of staffing and
personnel for Safari Power Solutions, looked
up from the clipboard he held between us like a
protective shield. His baby-fine blond hair was
neatly combed back against his skull and his
slight frame trembled as he reached for a set of
horn-rimmed glasses on his tiny desk. "Tell me
why I should hire you."

I smiled, doing my best to radiate
confidence. "Well, I'm prompt, thorough and
discreet and my team is handpicked and totally
flexible." My peripheral vision picked up on
Richard Head as he squirmed in his seat. Leo's
love interest was dressed in a crisp black shirt
and tan trousers with a perfect crease on each

pant leg. A bit much for a cleaning interview, but at least he didn't look like a slob.

"My rates are reasonable and I pride myself on a job well done." I continued, wondering why I was here. Job interviews were not my forte, and groveling to clean a bunch of corporate bathroom stalls seemed utterly pathetic. And what exactly had I been thinking when I'd used my maiden name? Sampson's Cleaning Services sounded decent, even if it was no Laundry Hag, and with Marty on board, it was even accurate. Possibly, I was afraid that Lucas Sloan—who still hadn't paid me—might be somehow involved in the hiring process. Or maybe I was hiding from Markus Valentino, CEO of this and several other companies because Laundry Hag would ring a bell with him. And no other business that I'd contacted was interested in hiring an unknown service. Promising Leo I'd find work for Richard was only part of it though, because I needed the extra income to foot the insurance plan Marty and I had settled on. Oh what a tangled web we weave.

Garner smiled at me, a polite expression with no teeth bared. "Do you know what it is we do here?"

"Something to do with batteries," I shrugged, as if it didn't matter to me. And it shouldn't, because as Laura had pointed out on the return trip from the luncheon, I was hardly more than the hired help. Unfortunately, I was too interested in what kind of operation Valentino ran, because I had no other way to investigate him.

145

Yeah, that's right. I wanted dirt on Markus Valentino, anything that might point to Candie's whereabouts. He'd hidden the first note about the phoenix from the FBI, I was sure of it. And after meeting Amelia, I'd settled on an image of Valentino as a school yard bully who wanted whatever someone else had.

I needed proof to bring to Capri and the FBI. And to find evidence, I needed access to one of Valentino's offices, preferably after hours when he would be elsewhere.

Richard cut his eyes to me. No doubt, he thought I was a moron, and I promised myself I'd rectify the situation as soon as possible, for Leo's sake.

Garner stared at me for a moment, probably wondering if I was as vapid as I seemed, but then he couldn't see my sensible shoes. I stayed silent, letting the chips fall where fate willed them. He fidgeted with his pocket protector and removed a pen to write something on his clipboard.

"Do you have any references?"

I dug through my tote, pulling out a sheet of paper with my phony references. Sylvia, Leo, and Detective Capri were all listed along with contact info. Garner's hand shook as he reached for the paper and I wondered if he might be ill. His skin was the color of wet concrete and the trembling was pronounced. Parkinson's maybe.

"When can you start?" He asked; his smile less glacial this time.

I turned my head and looked at Richard. He wasn't exactly leaping for joy. In fact, he appeared bored. "Tonight if you want,"

146

I answered, figuring Leo would cover if Richard had other plans.

Garner nodded, as if my reply suited him. "Be here at eight. I'll notify the security desk of your arrival. We'll issue badges for you and your crew by next week."

I stifled a wince. Crap, eight, when I was supposed to meet Neil for dinner. Sure, I could send Marty in my place, but that would leave Penny alone with the boys and me unable to snoop.

"How about a tour?" Garner rose from behind the tiny desk in his windowless office.

"Sounds like a plan." I said, following suit. Richard remained seated.

"Richard," I prompted. "Mr. Garner is taking us on a tour now. So we'll know our way around tonight?"

"Tonight?" Richard asked, blinking up at me.

"Yes, when we come back here. To clean." Had he been asleep through the entire interview?

"Oh, oh right. " Richard got to his feet and I prayed he would follow as I trailed Garner, who'd been conferring with someone outside and missed the entire exchange.

The level we were on was self-explanatory, with cubicles and a break room, as well as a couple of offices like Garner's. Here, we'd be responsible for vacuuming the indoor/outdoor carpeting, emptying waste baskets and scrubbing down the john. Yippee.

"Our primary function is sales and protection plans for companies who have purchased our battery back-ups. This is the

147

customer service floor. The clean room surrounds the perimeter of the area, which is why there aren't any windows in here. All high security." Garner explained as he shuffled past several empty offices. "You will not have access to the lab, as several experiments may be running at any given time and our engineers are very sensitive to any, ahem..., interruptions."

"Understood," I said, a little disappointed. The name, clean room just beckoned to my inner neat-freak and I wanted to see for myself if it lived up to the hype.

We loaded onto an elevator and Garner pushed the button for the third floor. The first floor was the lobby, where I'd met up with Richard. We'd just left the second and I crossed my fingers that pay dirt would be waiting on three.

The elevator slid open and I gaped as a huge mahogany desk was revealed. The woman behind the desk seemed completely dwarfed by the thing, which was clean of any of the normal desktop clutter. No coffee mugs holding pens, no piles of paper, no family photos or beanie babies. A sleek computer monitor, a phone with more buttons than NASA control and a leather-bound book were the only occupants.

"Sierra," Garner addressed the woman who personified my vision of the naughty librarian. Her glasses feathered out at the sides and her tight and fuzzy ice blue sweater enhanced her boobs, which were as big as mine, but much more perky. I wished I could ask her where she purchased her underwire bras. She glanced at Garner and held up a well-manicured finger while she finished her typing.

"How are you, Alan?" Her low, husky voice sounded too intimate for the professional setting. Sierra rose from her chair and glided around the desk. Her black pencil skirt cut off just above her knee but seemed indecent as it clung to her flesh. Garner swallowed audibly, but Richard still appeared bored. Definitely gay.

"I wanted to introduce Ms. Sampson and her associate, Mr. Head." Props to Garner for not choking on the name. He was obviously more mature than yours truly.

"They're part of the new cleaning service."

A light went on behind Sierra's eyes, making her all the more resplendent. "Excellent, I'll just go notify Mr. Valentino and we'll check his schedule...." She hustled behind the desk and Garner and I watched, each in our own stupor, him being lust-struck and me fighting panic. I did not want an encounter with Valentino when I was so close to my goal. His inner sanctum lay just beyond the frosted paned double doors and I scrambled for an out.

"No need to bother him, he's a busy man, I'm sure." I stammered. Not to mention a cold fish. Who goes into work after his wife has disappeared?

Sierra smiled at me like I'd just won brownie points. "Oh, Mr. V insists on meeting any new team member, even the cleaning staff. We're all like family here, you see."

Garner nodded as if his head was on a spring. "Family, that's right."

149

Frigging great, family wages.

Sierra spoke into a small device, which I presumed was an intercom. "When you have a moment Mr. Valentino—"

"Be right out," Came the clipped reply.

Surreptitiously, I shuffled back so I was partially obscured behind Richard and stared at the double doors.

"How's your daughter, Sierra?" Garner filled the quiet.

"Zoe's doing well, thank you Allan. She's been asking after you." Sierra focused on me. "Allan volunteers as the community soccer coach, he's wonderful with the kids."

Garner blushed and mumbled what I presumed to be a thank you and lapsed into silence again.

"Now who do we have here?" Valentino boomed from the now open doors.

"Margaret Sampson and her associate, Richard Head, our new cleaning service." Garner said, his tone implying that he'd escort us from the building at Valentino's command. Clearly, Valentino took great pains to approve anyone who had access to his building.

"Pleased to meet you," I mumbled, just as Richard sprang to life.

"Oh, Mr. Valentino, it's an honor, sir." He reached his hand forward and shook with fervor.

"Er...yes. A pleasure." Valentino dropped Richard's hand and glanced at me. Force of will alone let my gaze meet his. No hint of recognition lit in his eyes and he turned away almost immediately. "Well, I have something of a personal matter to attend to so if you'll excuse me...?"

He pivoted and said something low to Sierra and I silently prayed it wasn't a get this woman out of my building order. Striding back through the double doors, and pulling on a wool overcoat was the work of moments and my pulse throbbed in my eardrums while mutely watching.

"Be sure to dust the wires attached to the computers. The last service was sloppy about it."

I started breathing again as the elevator doors swallowed him.

* * * *

"Absolutely not," Richard stared at me like I had a dust rag nestled between my ears. "How can you even suggest that?"

"For the love of grief, Richard, what did you expect?" I snapped on my rubber scouring gloves and propped the bathroom door open with a full bucket of water. We'd been in the building for ten of the longest minutes of my life. Richard was a whiner and a complainer to the nth degree and it was all I could do not to club him with my mop. "Haven't you ever cleaned a bathroom before?" I asked, figuring it was a rhetorical question. My jaw hung open when he glanced away. "You haven't, have you?"

Richard puffed up like a blowfish under siege. "Mother takes care of the cleaning, she's very particular." The way he said mother reminded me of Norman Bates in *Psycho*. I shivered involuntarily.

151

Even insidious premonitions couldn't curb my tongue though. "So why on Earth would you want to tackle a cleaning job?"

He shrugged. "Leo asked me to come with you, said you needed help."

Leo was going to receive a serious beating when next we met. "Is that so?" Help didn't look to be on Richard's agenda this evening. He'd dawdled at the security desk, chatting up the night guard while I made three trips upstairs with my supplies. I'd vacuumed and dusted the outer area before he graced me with a cameo. And then the whining started.

"Richard, you have a choice here. Either pull on a pair of gloves and help me scour out this restroom or go home without pay." I may be a push-over, but even the laundry hag has limits.

"I'm allergic to latex," he informed me.

"I bet you say that to all your dates." I grumbled. He looked confused as my pithy remark flew over his head. I pushed past him to the cart and grabbed a bottle of ammonia. "Fine, go dust the offices."

"Dust is bad for my allergies."

I scrunched my eyes shut and sucked in a breath. Did I really cancel a date with Neil, who was not happy with me *again*, to work with Dick Head? "I mean it Richard; you're not getting paid to watch me bust my hump here. Find something to clean or scat."

He scowled at me for an indeterminate amount of time before I turned my back. Part of me hoped he'd disappear; it felt like a new kind of torture to pay someone to annoy me while I cleaned. I'd never bitch about Marty's

152

work-ethic again. Then too, I wouldn't have to sneak away from him to search Valentino's office.

Luckily, I'd noted that while the third floor was monitored on security's bank of screens, Valentino's office wasn't. I could just prop the door open, go about my business and the night watchman would be none the wiser.

Scouring the bathroom only took a few minutes, since it was in decent shape to begin with, and I signed the little chart when I finished and placed one of the *Caution: Wet Floor* signs in front of the door. Hefting my bucket of scummy water, I noticed Richard was halfheartedly arranging a tray of snacks in the break room. He so did not deserve Leo and I planned on telling my friend so at the first opportunity.

"I'm hitting the third floor now. Leave the exhaust fan on in the john so the floor dries before we leave." My tone was matter-of-fact, but my heart rate jumped as I thought about the task ahead.

"Oh, I'm coming!" Richard sprang to life like he'd just shot up adrenaline. "I want to see what's in Valentino's office."

"We're not going up there to snoop." I fibbed while gripping the bucket in a shaking hand. Crap, I should have seen this coming after the way he'd greeted Valentino earlier, but I'd been so busy fading into the wood paneling that Richard's reaction hadn't sunk into my skull.

"Come on, I bet his office looks like Spacely's Sprockets. You know, I read an article about him once in *Wired*. Apparently, he's a

153

real control freak, wants to approve every nuance of every sale. He's also a real hustler when it comes to bidding on big projects."

"So you're a tech-guy?" I resisted using the word geek since I wanted him to keep talking.

"I dabble," Richard replied with false modesty as he pushed the cart onto the elevator. "Valentino's interesting, kinda like Bill Gates. He's completely self-made, just a few lucky brakes and stellar timing equals a multimillionaire. From what I read, he's developing the next generation power supply, based on solar technology. Tons of backers and he's invested a huge chunk of his own fortune into the project. His corporate stock has gone through the roof with just the whispers of what this new battery can do." The elevator opened with a ding and we unloaded onto the third floor.

I nodded, deciding I'd pay Richard in full, if for nothing more than information. "What exactly can it do?" I asked, while taking out some furniture polish to treat Sierra's desk.

Richard leaned in close, like he was passing on top secret intelligence. "Until now, solar power has been a daytime only source of energy, because the sun goes down at night. Well, last summer MIT developed this new catalyst made of all non-toxic materials. Valentino's working on a storage unit that will house fuel cells so the solar panels collect the sunlight during the day to split water into hydrogen and oxygen for storage, Then at night, the cell will recombine the elements and poof, 24/7 energy."

154

I cocked my head to the side. "What good is that?"

Richard gave me a *are you totally stupid* look. "Just end global warming and provide cheap, unlimited energy to the entire planet is all."

"But aren't solar panels like crazy expensive? And kind of fragile?"

Richard's indignation was palpable. "With the technology we have available, manufacturers are working on super thin collectors. The holdup is storing the energy."

"And that's where Valentino comes in." I nodded. "What's it called?"

"Falcon. Like the bird of prey." He was obviously tickled by the name. I was simply unnerved. Again with the birds, this couldn't be pure coincidence.

"Are falcons anything like hawks?" I asked, trying to sound disinterested.

Richard rolled his eyes. "Duh. They are in the same order of birds, *falconiformes*."

Well excuse me, Dr. Do Little.

The wall clock chimed ten and I took a deep breath. "I'm going to vacuum in here. Can you do me a favor, Richard? I left my invoices in my car. Do you think you could grab them for me?" I tossed him my keys.

Richard sighed, but I switched on the vacuum before he could come up with an excuse. He punched the down arrow on the elevator while I concentrated on dragging the carpet to make tidy patterns on the knap. As soon as he was gone, I shut off the vacuum and bolted to Valentino's office. The doors were locked.

I had maybe fifteen minutes before Richard realized there weren't any invoices in my car, other than gas station receipts, and came back, so I scuttled to Sierra's desk. Leisurely, I rubbed across the surface, ignoring the camera mounted in the corner. "Key, key, key..." I chanted under my breath, aware that precious seconds were slipping away. The longer I fondled the desk, the more likely the guard would be to come check on me. Still rubbing in useless circles with my left hand, I slid my right down to open drawers. Her top drawer revealed only the leather-bound book, a tidy row of pens and a stapler. I reached under the desk and felt a button, probably a security alert, and I was careful not to trigger an alarm.

The bottom drawer held a bevy of manila file folders. I pretended to drop my rag and ducked behind the desk to reach inside the drawer, checking for a key secured inside. Nothing. The files were mostly marked with a name, client ID number and date, except for one halfway back, which was blank. Shaking hands tugged it loose and I opened it while holding my breath. Several envelopes, like you would get from a bank teller were lodged inside. I opened one and thought Eureka! As a shiny brass key fell into my sweaty palm.

"Let's get cracking," I muttered, pretending to bash my head against the desk and rub for the camera's benefit. Wheeling my cleaning cart in front of the secured office I stowed the rag and made a show of emptying the trash. If anyone had been watching me, they must be bored senseless by now. Keeping my mental fingers crossed, I scurried for the office. I inserted the key with a whispered prayer and exhaled loudly when it clicked the lock open. After parting the doors, I flicked on the lights and scanned the room. An antique cherry desk, much like the one at his house, held a computer and matching bookshelves lined the walls. Most of the shelves had been drafted for storage purposes, but a few technical manuals interspersed the clutter. The mauve carpeting looked odd with all of the dark, masculine furniture, but I wasn't here to critique the décor.

I strode to the desk, having no clue what I sought, but the need to find something gave me a natural high. The first thing I noticed was the lack of pictures, just like Sierra's. Valentino practiced what he preached, but my heart broke for Candie. Every wife should know her picture was proudly displayed in her husband's workspace.

"There I go again with the shoulds," I chastised myself and opened a few drawers. Paperclips, legal pads, post-its still in the wrapping. No clues here then.

"Stop right where you are." A harsh voice commanded my attention.

Busted. And not by Richard. But I knew the man, even if I'd never seen him in person before.

Come on, you worthless seven pounds of gray matter, churn out some brilliant excuse. Nothing surfaced and Lucas Sloan was closing in.

"Well, well, if it isn't the laundry hag," he smirked.

157

Thirteen

"This office is strictly off-limits. What are you doing in here?" Sloan withdrew a walkie-talkie from his guard uniform.

"Um, cleaning?" I gestured to the mountain of supplies just beyond the door.

"Valentino asked you to clean his office?" His gravelly voice was laced with skepticism. I nodded eagerly, praying I could talk my way out of whatever Sloan had in store.

"So why did I see you scrounging through the desk out there on my monitors? And how come you're in here, with all of your cleaning stuff out there?" He raised one eyebrow and I swallowed. Crap, there must have been a second camera monitoring behind

Sierra's desk. What, Valentino didn't trust his employees?

"Sierra promised to leave the key with security, but I guess she forgot. So I took a shot that it was still in her desk. And I was just figuring out what I need in here. Mr. V was in a hurry this afternoon and I didn't get a chance to scope out his set up." Queen of B.S. working her magic.

"I'll have to verify that with Tom." Sloan obviously didn't buy my excuse. "Step outside, hands where I can see 'em." It wasn't a request.

Circling the desk, I moved purposefully out into the reception area and headed to my cart. "I hope this won't take too long, I promised my partner we'd be done in a half hour." My nerves prickled like a startled hedgehog.

Sloan spoke into his hand unit. "Yeah, Tom, did Sierra or Mr. Valentino leave instructions for the cleaning service to take care of Mr. Valentino's office?" I held my breath and accepted a time of reckoning was at hand. Static crackled over the walkie-talkie and the reply came, too low for me to hear.

"You do that then. We'll just wait here." Sloan stared at me, a self-assured smirk on his face. "Tom's calling Mr. Valentino at home, just to be sure."

Not wanting him to see my panic, I bent over and stared at a bottle of Windex.

"Hands where I can see them!" Sloan ordered and I whirled to face the barrel of a gun leveled at my head. I raised my arms above my head, too fearful to feel ridiculous.

159

"Away from the cart, now." His eyes cut to Sierra's desk and I took the hint, stepping out of reach of my stuff.

"This is just a simple misunderstanding. Do I look like a corporate spy to you?" I wiped my sweaty palms on my bleach-stained jeans.

"Don't play games with me, little girl. I know you lied about your identity to get this job. I ran your social security number myself and out popped the Laundry Hag Cleaning Services, much to my surprise. What I don't know is why you lied, when you could have used me as a reference. I intended to find out."

The radio squawked and Sloan reached for it with one hand while training the gun on me with the other.

His dark eyes narrowed. "He did. Huh. No, no that's it for now." Sloan replaced the unit on his belt and holstered his weapon while I concentrated on not keeling over in relief. Valentino had vouched for me? He must have recognized me then, but the question remained, why?

"I want some answers." Sloan crossed his arms and stood with feet planted. The man was huge, bulkier than Neil and maybe an inch shorter, he towered over my five four stature. The thought of my husband gave me an epiphany. Maybe I could still spin this in my favor.

"My husband and I are having some troubles," I told him. "Our marriage counselor, Dr. Robert Ludlum, suggested we take a break, to reevaluate our priorities."

Something flickered on Sloan's face at the mention of Dr. Bob. "That sounds like the quack all right. Next thing you know, you'll be sitting in divorce court, wondering why you listened to the bastard to begin with."

Nodding I caught his gaze, hoping to fabricate a little solidarity between Dr. Bob's hapless victims. "I guess I needed a clean break, you know? Using my maiden name was just a knee-jerk reaction."

"Still doesn't explain why you didn't list me as a reference."

I shrugged, striving for an unsure posture. "You hadn't paid me yet and I didn't receive any feedback, so how was I to know if you were happy with the results. I couldn't take the chance; I *need* this job, especially if I'm headed for divorce court."

Sloan scrubbed a hand over his face. "I know what you mean. Between lawyers, court fees and supporting two households, I'm seeing red wherever I turn."

I shot him a confident smile. "So, can I get back to work now? I wanna be out of here before midnight."

"Sure, sure. Tom will be leaving as soon as I finish my rounds. If you need anything hit star three for the security desk." My new buddy tipped his ball cap at me and sauntered to the elevator. I made a show of pulling out a roll of paper towels, the Windex that almost got me killed and spritzing the open doors to Valentino's office.

The elevator dinged and Richard stomped past Sloan. "There are no invoices in that God forsaken vehicle!" He snapped.

"Really? I could have sworn I put them there earlier. Sorry about that, I guess I'll call

161

Mr. Garner tomorrow. Would you mind vacuuming in the office?" All this acting was giving me a migraine.

Richard grumbled, but I could tell his protests were halfhearted as he unplugged the vacuum and jauntily pushed it toward the open doors. I wanted to sag as the tail end of adrenalin departed from my system, but I was still on camera.

All that effort and I hadn't unearthed anything noteworthy. The idea that Valentino had recognized me but played dumb this afternoon and then supported my phony claim turned my knees to jelly. What was his deal? He'd called the FBI about his wife's possible abduction, but didn't care enough to console her when she was shaken by the dead bird or display her picture in his office. I thought back to my brief conversation with Amelia. He wanted what someone else possessed and now someone else had his wife. But where the hell did I fit in?

Realizing I was standing around staring at nothing, I dropped the window supplies back into the cart and extracted my Swiffer duster to do the blinds and windowsills. The drone of the vacuum emanated from the open office, but it didn't sound like Richard was moving it at all. I couldn't muster the will to care, for once not at all concerned about my reputation. No way would I come back here, as I planned to tell Garner tomorrow. I refused to be a pawn in whatever twisted crap was going on with Valentino.

Strangely detached, I watched the duster slide gracefully over the blinds, trapping grit and allergens in its fluffy grip. I held it up to my face, thinking it looked like a bird after a mud bath. *Falcon, Hawk, Phoenix,* ran through my head again and again. Falcon was Valentino's potentially Earth changing solar storage unit, the hawk had been charred and left for Candie and the Phoenix had kicked it all off in that first note. The note Valentino hadn't wanted the FBI to see, but my paranoia had daunted him.

Shaking my head, I discarded the skanky duster in the trash and removed the garbage bag and placed it on my cart. Was I coming between Valentino and something he wanted? Truly, I didn't believe the man was dangerous, but did I really know of what he might be capable when pushed. Perhaps my reprieve tonight was his way of setting me up for something more sinister.

Inhaling, I coughed and almost doubled over from the choking smell of a too full vacuum bag. "Hey, Richard, finish up, we're heading out."

No force on the planet would make me come back here.

* * * *

Neil was sprawled on the air mattress by the time I walked through the door. The chiming clock on the mantel tolled twelve as I dropped my coat on the hall tree and stumbled toward the bathroom.

A quick shower and I supposed the worst of the astringent smell was off, but I shampooed twice to be sure. Not having the energy to properly dry myself off, I swathed my

163

dripping carcass in a terry robe and blotted my hair with a towel. I combed through the tangles, ripping a few strands out, not caring all that much. The pain kept me from tumbling face first into the mirror.

I shut off the light before opening the door. A quick check on the boys revealed everyone in bed and asleep. My feet dragged on our thin carpet as I headed for the air mattress. Given my exhaustion, I flopped onto the makeshift bed with enough force to wake the dead, but Neil didn't stir. I listened to his even breaths until sleep claimed me.

Although physically spent, my mind agitated like an unbalanced load of wash and I wasn't surprised to find myself in a basement, having no memory of how I'd gotten there. Little light permeated the crusty arrow slit window several feet above my head and the smell of mildew overpowered my nose. I turned, squinting into the darkness in hopes that I'd spot an exit. A clinking noise, like metal on metal caught my notice and I headed in the direction of the sound, feeling my way along the damp walls to orient myself better.

"Hello? Is someone there?" I called out, stumbling over a crate I hadn't noticed in time. The clinking grew louder and blood roared in my ears as my pulse rate kicked up beyond jogging levels. I walked for what seemed like forever, the basement bigger than I had first realized. My hand hit a pipe and my eyes abruptly adjusted to the dim light. I'd reached what looked to be a large cylindrical tank with several pipes leading out like a mechanical spider with crooked legs. Deciding to back away and go around the tank, I stumbled and screamed as my ass met the concrete.

My teeth snapped together with such force that I saw stars. I groaned and pulled my feet underneath me, ready to start out again when I caught sight of what I'd tripped over. A woman was handcuffed to one of the pipes, a gag tied around the back of her head. Scrambling forward, I reached behind her to untie the fabric. The light was too dim to make out her features.

"Maggie, you've got to get out of here!" Her eyes were wild as she glanced from me to the far corner of the room. "He'll kill you!"

My fingers followed the handcuffs that wrapped around the pipe, seeking a spot of rust or some other weakness that I could use to free her. "Who did this? Who brought you here?"

She yanked away from me, sliding down the pipe as far as she could go. "Leave me! Just get yourself out of here, now!"

I grabbed both of her secure wrists and tugged against the resistance of the pipe. A pop sounded, followed by a slow hiss and my vision was again obscured. Steam billowed from the tank and choking smog filled the air. I cringed away while keeping a hand on her.

"Who's doing this?" I asked again, tugging on her arms. She cried out unintelligibly, and kicked me away with her foot. Some distant voice told me I was doing more harm than good, but I ignored it while I scrambled toward her. "I won't leave you! Help me get you free!"

165

A high keening sound pierced the air and my gaze shot to the tank a second before the pressure reached critical....

I jolted up in bed, breathing hard, shaken to the core. Damn my overactive imagination right to the depths of Dante's Inferno.

"You okay?" Neil's deep bass rumbled in my ear and he put his arms around my heaving chest. I nodded and rested my head against his shoulder and focused on taking even breaths. "Just a dream." I mumbled inanely.

He stroked my back. "Candie Valentino?" He asked.

"You know me too well." I mumbled. "There's no mystery left in our relationship."

"Is that a bad thing?" Neil kissed my neck and I sighed and shook my head.

He really was too patient with me and I felt compelled to apologize again for ditching him last night. "I'm sorry about dinner."

He pulled back and searched my eyes for a moment. "Yeah, me too. I feel so cheap and used after yesterday morning...."

I chuckled. "You do not so quit trying to guilt me. Besides, I promised you a rain check and my agenda is clear for the next forty-eight hours. How about tonight?"

"Sounds like a plan." Neil agreed, then groaned when the alarm on his phone sounded. "God, I hate this!" He reached over and silenced the noise.

"By this you mean...?"

"This damn schedule. I don't mind the twelve hour shifts normally, but I'm starting to believe I should just sleep at work until this damn project is resolved."

I didn't like that idea at all. "How much longer do you think—?"

"No frigging clue. It's like all the engineers have us running around chasing our tails while they dither about minutiae that gets us nowhere. The back-up power supply, the electrician, the frigging color of the processor for chrissakes. Borrowing trouble and squandering time if you ask me." He rose gracefully from the air mattress but for once I wasn't fixated on his backside.

"Power supply?" I asked my voice faint and hollow in my own ears. "Which company are they using?"

Neil pulled a T-shirt over his head and stepped into a faded pair of blue jeans. "Changes from minute to minute. The bid went to Safari, but there have been a few glitches with the latest model for upgrades and the higher-ups are nervous; don't want to take the risk. But they've already shelled out a tanker's worth of capitol to buy a contract and no one wants to eat that kind of loss."

"I didn't think Intel would outsource like that." Intel was the lifeblood of our community. If you didn't work there, someone you knew did. Intel employees donated time and money and equipment to help upgrade the schools, library and even the Hudson P.D. Heck the new theatre at the high school had been named after the company. I couldn't fathom a situation where they looked outside their own walls when they had many of the best technical minds in the country at their disposal.

"Budgets are tight everywhere and it doesn't make sense to devote someone from manufacturing or design to come up with a solution when we could purchase one with a lot less cost and effort."

His explanation made sense. A great deal of sense, but I couldn't get past Valentino's involvement. "The man's dirty Neil, I can feel it." I pounded on my chest for emphasis.

"His wife was kidnapped and someone's been sending him gruesome warnings. That doesn't make him Snidely Whiplash."

I almost told him about my cleaning job at Safari the night before, but I didn't want to fight with him when he was on his way to work and already in a pissy mood. The more I thought on it, I was sure Valentino had only played ignorant when we'd been introduced yesterday. Not that I was particularly memorable, but coupled with the fact that he'd granted me a boon and not had my hide arrested for snooping, something was off.

And with my day free, I was determined to find out what.

Fourteen

I *might be able to get into this exercise thing.* I told myself as I stumbled back up the hill. Not that I was enjoying the physical exertion, but it gave me a good reason to check out the house where Neil had stopped yesterday. His car wasn't in the drive this morning and I'd waited in my skulking spot for ten minutes, until my toes went numb. Eventually, I would break down and ask him why he'd stopped there, who owned the place and why he hadn't told me about his detour, but for now, I'd go the Nancy Drew route.

My song—Blue Oyster Cult *Burning for you*—finished halfway up the hill and the only sound came from my sneakers hitting the pavement and a less pronounced wheezing.

169

Tempted to stop and switch songs, I pushed harder, my thighs going from a slow burn to a fiery inferno. Almost there, a few more steps and the torture would be behind me. I promised my aching body I would reward it and walk the final half mile.

An engine purred from behind me and without looking I moved to the shoulder of the road. I had no idea what side I was supposed to be on, it wasn't like driving a car, so I was jogging with the flow of traffic and would continue to do so until told otherwise.

"Mrs. Phillips?" I jumped at the sound of my name, glad the music was off. I wasn't coordinated enough to jog and look over at the same time, so I slowed my pace to a walk.

"What...can I... do for... you?" I huffed. The silver car was a BMW and very new, judging from the look of it. The man who'd addressed me was unfamiliar, dressed in a gray suit with an exceptionally hideous red tie. Large sunglasses hid his eyes, but a friendly smile lit his face. The car and the suit was a little too over the top for my neighborhood and if he hadn't called to me by name I would have assumed he was lost.

"My employer would like a moment of your time." The man said with an apologetic smile. "If you would be so kind to get in the car, I'd be happy to give you a ride."

"Who's your employer?" I asked.

"Mr. Valentino."

I stopped cold and the car, which had been keeping pace with me, did as well. "Are you kidding?" Had I passed out from lack of oxygen or stumbled into a mafia movie? Who the hell made an offer like that? Markus fricking Valentino, apparently.

The driver answered as if I'd asked a genuine question. "No Ma'am. If you would just get into the vehicle please...."
"Not gonna happen, buster." I told him while searching for a shortcut he couldn't follow.

Before I could decide on a course of action, the window in the rear of the car rolled down and a new voice commanded my attention. "Either get in the car, Mrs. Phillips or I'll be forced to alert the authorities to your trespassing on my property."

The man himself. Valentino's eyes were hidden behind designer sunglasses, but I could feel the intensity focused on me. I really didn't want to fend off the Hudson P.D. or—shudder— the feds. He had me over a barrel and he knew it, the smug bastard.

I drew up as tall as my five-foot four-inch frame allowed and reached for the handle. Valentino slid over, probably wanting some distance between his Armani suit and my sweaty stench. The leather interior cradled my sore backside and I took a moment to feel for my cell phone, ready to call in the cavalry, or Marty, if the situation went south.

Valentino waited for the car to start moving before he turned to face me. "I applaud your tenacity, Mrs. Phillips. I understand you aren't the type of woman to give up but you're in way over your head and mucking up my affairs. I cannot allow that to continue."

I swallowed at the perceived threat, calling myself all kinds of stupid. No one knew

I was with him and if he wanted me to disappear, I'm sure he'd be able to arrange it.

"Why didn't you stop Garner from hiring me?" I asked, fear making me bold. "And why did you cover for me last night. Wouldn't it have been easier to have Sloan call the cops and keep me under police supervision?"

Valentino rubbed the bridge of his nose. "My father taught me to keep my friends close and my enemies closer. I'm not sure which category you fall under, but you present a problem in either case."

"I only want to help Candie." I told him honestly.

"That makes two of us, but you are in no position to help her. I am able, but not with your constant interference."

I pondered his words. He said he could help Candie, not that he would. "Tell me about Amelia Kettering." I ordered.

Valentino removed his sunglasses, his eyes wide. "Who told you about her?"

He didn't have to sound so incredulous. "She did. From our conversation, I gather she doesn't hold you in high esteem."

"Jealous harpy," Valentino muttered, then sighed. "Candie went through an experimental phase in college, not so uncommon. Amelia built it up to be more than it was. Started threatening to tell Candies' parents about their relationship, hoping they'd sequester her away from the world. A classic, if I can't have her, no one can. Candie ended their affair and asked Amelia not to contact her again."

"Your suggestion, I suppose?"

172

Valentino didn't respond, but I had my answer. No matter what he said, I knew this man didn't put up with threats in any form.

He smiled, just a wry quirk of his lips. "I can tell you've painted me as the villain here, but I assure you I've always made her well-being a top priority."

I pondered that for a moment. "Do you know where she is?"

"I'm sure Candie is safe. It's no secret that she was unhappy here and it's easy to believe she's taken off for a bit. She always did have a love for drama, but I'm involved with several projects which require my attention and I can't run after her like some moon-struck adolescent."

Unbelievable. He was claiming she ran off in a fit of pique. And he hadn't denied knowledge of her whereabouts. I gazed out of the car window sightlessly for a minute. If what he said was true, then why had he bothered to call the FBI? And what about the notes and the dead bird? I was dying to ask him about Falcon, but afraid to push too hard.

"What did the other note say? The one you found after Candie disappeared." I asked him, not believing for a second he would tell me.

"Telling you that defeats the purpose of asking you to back off from your investigation, does it not?" He reached into a pocket of his overcoat and extracted a business envelope. "For your trouble."

I starred at the offering. "Buying my silence, Mr. Valentino?"

173

"Think of it more as a peace offering. As well as compensation for all your hard work. I asked Sierra to include a letter of recommendation, so you won't be forced to make up references in the future."

I blushed to the roots of my hair. Was it my fault that all of my clients left the area, or died, after utilizing my services?

"And here we are." The car stopped and I recognized the ugly camper out the front windshield. The dutiful chauffer had merely been circling our development until Valentino spoke his piece.

"Take a vacation, Mrs. Phillips. You've earned it." He pressed the thick envelope into my hand and before I knew what was happening, I stood on the sidewalk, watching his taillights disappear.

I opened the envelope and blinked. Cripes, that was a wad all right. The aforementioned letter was in there as well, a glowing reference from one of the area's top businesses. Between the two, I could set up a slew of gigs to keep Marty employed full-time and branch out into other offices. There would be a nest egg for my little niece or nephew and plenty left over to narrow the financial gap for our family's needs. Neil wouldn't have to work so much overtime. The thought of having him home more was the greatest temptation.

The dream of Candie chained to the boiler haunted me as I trudged up the steps and pondered my next move.

* * * *

"Wait, wait, back up a minute. You got in the car with him?" Neil was seated across

174

from me in a booth at our favorite pub. Despite having worked a fourteen hour day, he'd arrived as if fresh from the shower. I, who actually was fresh from the shower, had already dripped some nacho cheese onto my dark blue cable-knit sweater. Damn tricksy appetizers.

I took a pull off my light beer and grimaced. Since I hadn't finished my exercise regime, I denied myself a full calorie beverage. That alone should teach me not to get into the car with strange men, Marty aside. "I know it was stupid, but—"

"No excuses, Uncle Scrooge!" Neil raised his voice, but the place was busy with the Saturday night crowd and no one glanced our way. "You tell me you know your actions were thoughtless and then try to reason through it! Like any justification is enough of a reason for putting yourself in harm's way!"

"Simmer down, Neil. I promise; it won't happen again." I reached for his hand across the table and twined my fingers with his. This was not the scenario I'd imagined while scouring the bathroom floor earlier today. And I had no one to blame except for my big, fat, mouth. Couldn't I have waited til desert to tell him about the encounter with Valentino?

He scrubbed his free hand across his face and sighed audibly. "Maggie, I'll admit you were right about the fax. Valentino's got something going on and I seriously doubt he's been completely upfront with the feds. I understand you are worried about Candie, but please accept that you can't do anything here. You need to stop painting a target on your ass. I'm begging you, stay out of the investigation."

"What about the money?" I whispered, feeling dirty just considering holding on to it.

Neil shrugged and leaned back in his seat. "I believe you've earned it. What you do with it is your call."

Our entrees arrived then, a chicken Caesar salad for me and a ½ lb. burger with the works for Neil. I snitched a fry and chewed, while mulling over Neil's position. Undoubtedly, my actions would give him an ulcer, but I needed to see Valentino one more time, if only to return the money. Despite what my husband said, I couldn't justify keeping the windfall, no matter how tempting. My mother would have applauded my ethics, even if I felt like the biggest idiot on the planet for refusing a hefty boon.

"Tell me about the luncheon. Did you ever find out why my mother dragged you there?" He bit into his burger with relish and I tried not to envy his choice. Or snatch it out of his hands.

"How's work going?" I changed the subject while dousing my salad with the pitiful side cup of dressing. Man alive, they were stingy with the condiments.

Neil swallowed and set his food down. "Spill, Uncle Scrooge."

I rolled my eyes. "You know how she is, always trying to hold a mirror up to my face and pointing out the flaws. The luncheon was a visual aide, to illuminate all of my deficiencies." Speaking of which.... "Why the hell did you tell her we're seeing a counselor? She blindsided me with that little nugget and I almost crashed the car on purpose, just to get her to back off."

"There's no shame in therapy, Uncle Scrooge. I had to deal with a shrink every time I came back from a hairy mission, sometimes for months. It's not fun, but it can help, if you let your guard down. And you're not deficient. My mother views life differently and she's convinced her way is the only one."

My knee bounced frantically under the table. "I still don't like the world thinking there is something wrong in our marriage."

I'd hoped Neil would assure me there wasn't anything wrong between us, that we were hunky-dory. He didn't say a word as he tucked in to his burger. I studied him for a moment, wondering what was brewing in that super-sized brain, when he gestured to my salad.

"You're not eating. Is it all right?"

Crap, nothing was all right, at least anything I'd touched. I was the Anti-King Midas, turning everything I contacted into a steaming pile of cow dung. Though I couldn't claim credit for Candie's abduction, Eric's affair, Leo's piss-poor taste in men, guilt assaulted me on a chromosomal level.

And I knew Neil's crazy hours had something to do with me, even if only remotely. "Let's see if we can get into Dr. Bob tomorrow." I said before the thought had registered.

Neil wiped his empty hands on the checked napkin confusion marring his perfect face. "Nice segue. Tomorrow is Sunday; he probably doesn't have office hours."

Damn, I hadn't thought of that. Normal people were off on weekends.

My expression must have reflected my disappointment because he smiled reassuringly at me. "I'll give him a call; see if he might make an exception for us. If not, we'll do something else, okay?"

"Sounds like a plan," I forced a smile and picked at my salad. We didn't talk much after that; Neil was content to finish his fries and order another drink and I didn't want to resume fighting stance. I shifted in my seat, seeking to ease my discomfort, but the source was internal. Being with my husband used to ease my frazzled mind, help chill me out, but that reassurance was noticeably absent. I found myself incapable of reading him anymore, like he'd shifted walkie-talkie frequencies and I'd missed the changeover. Too many doubts filled my head. Was Neil having an affair? His odd work schedule, the random stop down the road the other morning and something in his manner of speech, like he chose his words with great care, all pointed to some duplicity. Or was I simply neurotic?

"Earth to Uncle Scrooge," Neil snapped his fingers two inches from the end of my nose.

"What?" My temper showed through furrowed eyebrows.

"Well, I was going to suggest a game of darts, but since you're off in la la land..."

My spirits lifted. "May I go first?"

"Do I look stupid to you?"

I just grinned. "Age before beauty then."

There aren't many things in life I excel at, but playing darts is one of them. I'd actually bilked half a SEAL team out of several hundred dollars back before I'd married Neil.

178

"You're a woman full of contradictions." Neil scowled at my fifth bull's-eye. "You're so uncoordinated; you couldn't hit water if you fell off an aircraft carrier—"

"Flatterer," I threw another dart and the scoreboard lit up like a Christmas tree.

"But you cream me and every other person you've ever gone up against in darts. How is that possible?"

"Dunno," My eye trained on the small target, I tossed my final dart, ending the game. "I have good aim, when I concentrate. Most of the time, my head is buzzing with superfluous crap and I don't pay attention, just stumble into spaz-ville."

"With a little more focus, you could have been a great marksman."

"Guns freak me out." I shuddered. "You ready to go?"

Neil waved to our server and she hustled off to prepare our bill. Since we'd met at the restaurant, we had to drive home separately. For my purposes, the arrangement would be best, as much as I longed to cuddle up next to him in the truck he'd rented while the escort was being serviced, there was something I needed to take care of first.

"I'm just gonna stop at the store, get something for breakfast and an extra gallon of milk, for Penny." I fibbed as he dug out his credit card. Neil smiled.

"See you at home, then."

My heart ached as I donned my coat and headed toward the exit.

179

Fifteen

I first noticed the headlights in my rearview mirror after I made the turn into the Valentino's neighborhood. The vehicle, probably a truck or an SUV from the position of the headlights, was several hundred yards behind me, so I dismissed the nervousness as best I could. Yet after three turns, with the houses situated fewer and farther in between, the lights still pursued me. My cell phone trilled, but I ignored it as I maneuvered my Mini around dark patches of what I assumed to be ice. I needed one of those hands free devices, but even if I'd had one, I would have let the call go to voicemail. My agenda was set; chuck the envelope back at Valentino, stop at the store so I wouldn't arrive home empty-handed and avoid another confrontation with Neil. Nothing to discuss with anyone else.

Having never been to the Valentino's at night, I drove slowly, not wanting to miss the turn. Those damn headlights were gaining and I considered pulling over to let the vehicle pass. Some buried instinct kept my foot on the accelerator. I scolded my imagination for working overtime as I pulled up in front of Valentino's mansion.

The headlights followed me and an involuntary shudder ripped through my body. I grabbed my tote and climbed from the car. What were the chances that Valentino would receive another visitor at this exact moment, so late at night? Maybe it was the man himself, yet I couldn't picture Valentino driving anything that big. Eyeing the distance to the front porch, I was set to run when a door slammed behind me. A stream of obscenities caught on the wind along with my name spat like a bitter pill and I spun to face my doom.

"Just going to the store? For chrissakes, Maggie!" Neil thundered as he closed in on me. My mouth opened and closed a few times, but I couldn't force a sound out. I didn't realize I was backing up until my butt hit the side of the car. Large evergreens obscured the moonlight and a predator stalked through the shadows. Though Neil would never hurt me physically, I knew I'd pushed him too far.

His hands clamped down on my arms and I winced, even though it didn't hurt. His eyes blazed with fury as his grip tightened.

"Do you have a goddamned death wish? Why the hell can't you leave it alone?"

181

"I have to give him the money back," I whimpered, but my excuse only enraged him further.

"Mail it to him, then! Fed Ex, UPS, hire a fuckin' courier for all I care! You have plenty of reasonable options, yet you choose this!"

With a muttered expletive he dragged me into his arms. His embrace held more anger than relief, his body trembling at the contact. I remained stiff, waiting for the next wave of rage to knock me on my ass. It didn't come, and he pulled back, then dragged me toward the open truck door. He'd left the engine on, ready for a swift getaway.

"Wait, my car!" I squealed, but he didn't slow his forward progress.

"Screw the damn car. It's a clown car anyway."

"Hey!" I lashed out with my foot. Nobody insulted my Mini—even if he was rightfully beyond furious— and got away with it. The toe of my boot connected with the back of his shin and he grunted, but continued on, undeterred. There was a high probability that once Neil had me in the truck, he'd lock me up for the foreseeable future. I glanced at my car, and at Valentino's front door, wishing for an out. I squinted at the house; sure my eyes were playing tricks on me.

"Neil, wait—"

"Stow it Maggie, I don't want to hear it." His words held a warning which I stoutly ignored.

"But Neil, I see—"

"Get in the truck Maggie, or I swear I'll hogtie you in the bed for the ride home." He was

182

serious, and unaware of what was happening right behind us.

"Listen to me, damn it! I think Valentino's house is on fire." I blurted before he could toss me headfirst into the cab of the truck.

He blinked twice, his jaw making an awful cracking sound as he ground his molars together and I pointed frantically to the smoke billowing out of the open front door.

"Christ Almighty!" He shoved me into the truck anyway and hollered, "Stay in there and call 911!" before slamming the door with enough force to rock the vehicle and sprinting toward the house.

"No!" I shouted, even as I fished out my cell phone. Punching in the number, I watched my husband mount the steps and push the door open. Smoke billowed out around him before he disappeared. God, what was he thinking? We didn't even know if someone was *inside* the house!

"911, what's the nature of your emergency?" A dulcet voice queried.

"The Valentino's house might be on fire and my idiot husband is inside playing hero!" I screeched.

"Might be on fire?" The operator asked.

"There's smoke coming from the front door."

"Ma'am, are you within the residence?" She asked the question with a bit more urgency.

"No, I'm outside but my husband just went in."

"Okay Ma'am I need you to stay away from the structure in question."

"Of course I'm going to stay outside. Contrary to popular opinion, I don't have a death wish."

"Ma'am I need you to calm down and give me an address."

I rattled it off, my gaze locked on the front door, willing Neil to reappear. Damn his hero complex!

"The fire department is en route. Ma'am, please remain on the line and brief me of any changes. Can you see your husband?"

There was a loud boom as flames shot out of a side window and I yelped. Though my sense of direction sucked, I was sure the blast had originated in the kitchen. The operator asked for an update and I stuttered out some sort of reply.

"Has your husband returned?" She asked again.

"No," I whimpered. "Please, tell them to hurry." God, it wouldn't end like this, would it? Neil furious and suicidally altruistic while I bore impotent witness. Swamped with anxiety, I squeezed the phone tighter.

It seemed an eternity passed before the sounds of sirens pierced the still night. The western side of the house was mottled in flames and Neil still hadn't emerged. I opened the truck door and flung myself to the ground, going down on one knee in my haste to intercept the firemen. They needed to know Neil was still inside and make finding him a priority. I must have announced my intent to the operator because she nattered on about the need for me to stay out of the way. Snapping the phone closed, I stuffed it in my coat pocket.

"He's in there; my husband went inside the house!" I shouted as firemen swarmed off the huge engine like angry bees from a disturbed hive.

One tall man nodded in acknowledgment and ushered me to the side of the driveway. "Is anyone else in the building?"

"I don't know. Please, find him."

"We'll do our best, Ma'am. Stay here." Again I was left without a purpose and I hugged myself, for once able to ignore the cold.

My vantage of the front door wasn't nearly as good as from the truck, but for once I felt no desire to obstruct. A prayer left my lips as I observed the activity, the firemen staking out positions around the foundation, some disappearing into the house.

The noise was unbelievable. I'd never thought about what fire sounded like and tears streamed down my face as I thought of Neil and possibly Mr. Valentino deafened and disoriented within the inferno. The lights from the truck parked on the grass reflected off the undamaged portions of siding, casting moving shadows everywhere.

"Come back to me Neil," I whispered. At that moment, I resolved that no matter what was going on, whatever Neil's secret might be I'd deal with it as long as he came out alive.

Then, in the flickering light, a figure emerged, and I squinted, endeavoring to adjust my eyesight. The figure appeared oddly misshapen, no wait! He was carrying something. Despite the warning to stay back, I

185

dashed forward, but stopped in my tracks. It wasn't a fireman carrying Neil as I'd suspected but Neil hauling Valentino over his shoulder. He stumbled a bit and two firemen emerged behind him, taking the unconscious man off his shoulders.

"You stupid fucking hero!" I bellowed and rushed forward.

* * * *

"How come you get to take ridiculous chances with your life and I'm read the riot act for putting a toe out of line?" I huffed at Neil. My husband reeked of smoke and sweat and a streak of soot decorated his jaw, but he was otherwise undamaged. We sat in the cab of his truck, which we'd moved onto the street, along with my Mini, and watched the firemen work. Mr. Valentino had been carted off in an ambulance, still unconscious and probably suffering from smoke inhalation. Neil had taken a few hits from an oxygen mask, but refused any other medical aide. Stupid, stubborn man.

In spite of the smell, I was curled up into his chest, holding on to reassure myself he wasn't hurt. His hand stroked my hair absently as he stared at the activity before us. The fire, (I'd been right, it had started in the kitchen,) was mostly out and a few firemen coiled up the long hoses.

"Trained SEAL here, remember? And I don't take chances without a reason." His voice was rougher than usual and I brushed away a fresh onslaught of misery.

186

"Do you want to go home?" I asked, turning my head so I could read his expression. "You probably want to take a shower."

He met my gaze and his lips twitched. "Smell that bad, do I?"

I burrowed deeper. "Not at all." He smelled alive, so it wasn't a lie.

"If it's all right with you, I wanted to wait until the Fire Marshal determines the cause." He coughed on the last word and I sat back, worried that my added weight hindered his ability to breathe. He scowled then pulled me closer and I resettled with ease.

"What do you suspect happened?" I asked, recalling that the front door had been left cracked open.

Neil grunted and we watched another police car roll in to join the melee on the lawn. Neil inhaled and I listened contentedly to the steady thumping of his heart. "I'm sure whoever did this made it look like an accident, a grease fire or faulty wiring, but Valentino was already unconscious when I found him." He coughed again and cleared his gravelly throat. "My own damn fault it took so long. I headed upstairs first, since that's where the lights were on. I would have been out several minutes sooner if I'd started in the kitchen."

"Don't do that to me ever again." I whispered, fighting the tears that threatened to spill over.

His index finger tilted my chin so I met his gaze. At point blank range, Neil's hazel eyes possessed the power to hypnotize and he unleashed it now. "I'm sorry I scared you." He had too much class to point out that it was my

187

fault he was anywhere near the blaze to begin with.

All those times he'd been deployed on missions, where people shot at him, tried to blow him up or take him captive, I'd worried, not knowing where he was, if he was safe. I thought I knew real terror. But those wild conjectures of my imagination were nothing next to actually seeing him in danger, knowing it was my fault....

I gave up the fight and allowed myself to cry. Neil didn't say anything; he just let me sob and held me close. His understanding made it worse because I was such a hypocrite. I'd worried him, by involving myself in dangerous plots, and the fact that I hadn't sought out trouble didn't matter. I silently vowed to exercise more caution, and remember this fear before courting trouble again.

Minutes passed by the time I'd regained my composure, the scene out the window had changed. The lights from the fire truck and other emergency vehicles had been extinguished and there was considerably less activity from the few remaining civil servants.

"You got yourself together?" Neil asked. I sniffled and nodded. "Good, because I think we're about to have company." A knock on the window made me jump and I used the sleeve of my sweater to scrub my face. Between the nacho cheese stain and the smears of soot, it was probably a lost cause anyhow.

Neil rolled down the window and as my vision adjusted I started at the compact silhouette. "Cripes, what are you doing here?"

Neil smirked and shook his head while Detective Capri scowled at me.

"You took the words right out of my mouth, Mrs. Phillips. I received a call from dispatch, informing me that, quote; "my go-to girl had stepped in it again." End quote." She made little twitchy bunny ears with both hands to underscore her point.

I opened my mouth, but shut it for lack of a good retort. Coming off of a useless adrenaline rush, and basically mired in guilt, I wasn't up to my usual verbal sparring at the moment. But I wasn't about to apologize for my piss-poor luck, either, so she could go stuff herself.

Neil, as always, sized up the edgy atmosphere and said the right thing. "Maggie, explain to detective Capri about the envelope you were trying to return." He squeezed my arm, applying gentle pressure, attempting to send me a nonverbal message. Too tired to read between the lines, I did as he suggested, leaving nothing out, except for my fib about the store and our heated exchange before we'd noticed the fire.

Capri could have been a master poker player, since her expression rarely changed from stone-cold sober. She did wince when I admitted I'd climbed in the car with Valentino, but didn't interrupt the telling. My voice petered out, but I'd gone over the essentials.

"So Valentino gave you money to keep you out of his business," She mused, then glanced toward the house. "I wonder where the feds are, I'm pretty sure that's a detail they'd be interested in."

189

I grimaced, imaging the two stalwart
FBI special agents in my homey little kitchen,
but didn't protest. I needed to help Candie in
any way I could, especially now that Valentino
would be in no position to do the job.

"Do you know how the fire started?"
Neil asked in a mild tone. My gaze cut to him,
but I schooled my features almost immediately.
So that's what he'd meant. Give Capri the low-
down and then ferret out a few details of our
own. Basic *I'll scratch your back and you
scratch mine* technique. The man was a master
manipulator, just like his mother.

Capri appeared lost in thought,
probably mulling over my deluge of
information, seeking the common thread to tie
this dung heap up. "An overload in the kitchen.
The circuit breaker didn't trip like it should
have." She mumbled the words as if on
automatic pilot.

"What about Markus?" I asked,
remembering how Neil said he was already
unconscious. "Has he come to yet?"

While Neil's probing question made it
through her lowered defenses, mine must have
triggered red alert. Her gaze snapped to mine
and her lips compressed in a grim line. "He'll
be all right. I wouldn't recommend visiting him
in the hospital though, I'm sure the feds will
post a guard. You two should go home." Crap, I
guess goodwill chat time was over.

Neil nodded in a succinct message
received motion and turned the key to the
truck's ignition. "Detective, would you have
someone drive Maggie's car home? I think
she's a little too shaken up to drive right now.

Whenever you get the chance will be fine, we'll be home all day tomorrow."

What a rat-fink! In one blow, he'd ingratiated himself to Capri by subtly promising to keep me off her radar for a while and managed to limit my means of transportation for the foreseeable future. The high handedness made my stomach twitch, but I couldn't muster the will to fight his sense. Tomorrow was another day.

Capri nodded and smiled at my self-appointed handler. "Not a problem. Keys are in it?"

"Yes," I ground out, unwilling to thank her for aiding Neil in imprisoning me. Since I had no plans, no cleaning jobs, or social commitments, it wasn't really such a bad thing and I was a little shaky, though I refused to admit it. But the *principle* of the matter..., grrrrr.

Neil, the bloody Boy Scout, thanked her again and shifted into reverse.

"Happy?" I asked him as we turned out of the development.

He didn't answer but his satisfied smile practically blinded me as we passed under a streetlight.

191

Sixteen

I had no desire to get out of bed Sunday morning. Sleep came in fits and starts since we'd hit the sheets around three A.M. So I listened as Penny trundled down the hall from my bedroom and took her early morning soak in the tub. Water gurgled through our ancient pipes as she emptied the bathwater and I closed my eyes when she fired up my hairdryer. The next time I regained consciousness, the spot on the air mattress next to me was empty and someone had started coffee. Judging from the industrial strength fumes, Marty had heavy-handed the Folgers into a dinky paper filter. My brother should have been the cop, the way he ruined coffee, yet drank it by the gallon.

"What time did ya'll come in last night?" Penny's drawl drifted along with the smell of browning sausages.

"Sometime after midnight." Neil responded and I heard Marty's raspy chuckle.

"Must have been one helluva date. The way you two go at it, I'm surprised you don't have half a dozen kids by now."

I covered my head with a pillow and groaned. As much as I loved my brother, I wished someone would staple his lips together. Lord, the last thing this dysfunctional household needed was another baby on final approach.

My ever tactful husband refrained from recommending birth control to my brother, the jackass. With the pillow over my face, I didn't catch his response, but then, if I wanted to be part of the conversation, I'd get my rear in gear and join them.

Staying where I was seemed simpler, even if I couldn't stop the mental slideshow of the last few days. Sadistic marriage counselors, cheating husbands, secret lesbian lovers, oh my! Never mind the fine concoction of bribery and arson I'd choked down yesterday.

"Come on, Uncle Scrooge, up and at 'em!" Neil yanked the pillow off my face and knelt on the floor next to me. He'd showered when we'd arrived home and still smelled of Irish Spring soap.

"What's on the schedule for the day, warden?" I asked, struggling to sit upright. He handed over a steaming mug, light and sweet, just the way I liked my morning brew. I took a sip and the bitchiness abated somewhat.

"Serious R&R. I promised to take the boys skiing. My mom still has my old equipment and Leo should be by soon to drop it off."

Oh the horror. My face must have reflected my opinion because Neil chuckled. "You can rent whatever you need." He shook his head at what must have been a terrified look. "Or spend the day in the lodge in front of the fire if you prefer. Bring a book and take it easy."

Hmmm. Slide down a mountain on my ass in the freezing cold or curl up with a novel and a cup of hot chocolate. Was there really a choice here? "What about my car?" I pushed my hair back from my face and took another hit of caffeine.

"The good detective already had someone bring it by." Neil snatched my coffee mug and took a sip. I watched him for a beat and a light bulb went off over my head.

"Ah so that explains the sudden urge to go skiing."

"What?" He lowered the mug and blinked at me innocently. Too innocently.

"Can't keep Maggie in the house, so you'll take her out of town?"

He scowled. "Can't a guy just want to spend a day doing something with his family?" If I didn't know better, I might have thought he was sincere.

"I'm sure that's part of it, but ..."

He blew out a breath, the veins on his neck bulging visibly. "Fine, I want to get you away from this craziness for a bit, sue me."

194

"Not likely, I do your books, remember pal?" And those books backed up his story about the overtime. Since Neil's paycheck was deposited electronically, I didn't have an actual hardcopy of the hours he'd logged, but from my estimate the day before, the money was all there. Maybe Neil hadn't been lying to me; maybe I was just paranoid because of Sylvie and Eric's situation and Dr. Bob's innuendos. Wouldn't be the first time my imagination backfired on me.

He kissed my nose. "I'm going to get the boys up. Can you be ready to go in an hour?"

"Not a problem." I said, fully relaxing for the first time in days. We'd do our family day and tomorrow, I'd confess my shamefully suspicious thoughts in front of Neil and Dr. Bob as penance. Finishing my coffee, I literally rolled out of bed and trundled down the hall to the miraculously unoccupied bathroom. Several fists pounded on the door while I worked shampoo into my hair, but I ignored them.

Humming, I toweled off and flipped on the vent fan to abate the steam. Brushing my teeth, drying my hair and braiding it so it wouldn't get in my way if I did attempt to ski, only took a few minutes and I swathed myself in a super thick bathrobe before vacating the room.

The pounder turned out to be Marty. "Jeeze, hag, take all day why don't you?" He griped as he pushed me into the hallway, slamming the bathroom door in my face.

I dressed in a turtleneck that I seldom wore because it made my head look gigantic

195

and a bulky cable knit sweater layered on top. Fleece jeans and heavy knee-high socks completed the ensemble. I might par boil in the outfit, but I refused to spend another second underdressed in the bone-cracking cold.

Leo had appeared and helped himself to coffee. He sat, dishing with Penny who was wolfing down about half a loaf's worth of French toast. Josh and Kenny were physically present, but their eyes held the distant look of preteens who hadn't gotten the requisite fourteen hours of sleep.

"Hungry?" Neil asked as he flipped sausage patties onto a plate.

"You're cooking?" I stared dubiously at the spread. I thought for sure it'd been Penny's doing. "What's the occasion?"

Neil shrugged good-naturedly and turned back to the electric griddle. I caught Leo's stare, but said nothing as I took the sausage to the table.

"So the Dragon Lady is on her way to torture the city of New York. She'll be gone for a couple of days." Leo informed me as he slid a steaming mug of—bless him—fresh, nontoxic coffee in front of me.

"Hmm," I said, reaching to fork up a slice of French toast, but Kenny snatched it first. "Work or pleasure?"

Leo rolled his eyes. "You know Laura takes no pleasure in anything unless it involves breaking someone's spirit. But I think this would fall under the category of relaxation. She went with a friend. Ralph is ecstatic; he gave me the day off. I'm sure he's going to use the

196

empty house as an excuse to order all sorts of fatty take-out and watch CNN all day."

"So, do you have any plans?" I asked as Neil set down a fresh batch of French toast. He cast me an indecipherable glance but turned away before I could question him.

"I'm keeping the day open for Richard. Unfortunately, he's a night owl and I'm a Lark so I probably won't hear from him until about noon."

"Hey, do you want to come skiing with us? You can keep me company in the lodge while the guys are busy being physical." I asked, enjoying the image.

There was a loud clatter, followed by a curse from the kitchen and I turned to see Neil, his hand shoved under the running faucet. "Oh, sweetie, did you burn yourself?" I jumped up scurrying to his side. "Here, let me look."

I reached for his hand, but he drew back, scowling. "It's fine."

"Let me just run and get the burn ointment. Kenny is the first aid kit in your room?" I was halfway down the hall when Neil caught my arm.

"I said I'm fine. Just forget about it."

"What's the matter with you?" I asked. He opened his mouth to reply, but his words were cut off by the ringing doorbell.

"Let me see who that is, then we'll finish this." I marched to the front door, pulling it open.

"What are you doing here?" I asked Detective Capri. "Someone's already returned my car."

Capri proffered her gloved hand and a thrice folded sheet of white paper. Her face gave away nothing. "Mrs. Phillips, we have a warrant to search your house."

* * * *

My family, plus Leo, clustered in the living room while one of the uniformed officers under Capri's command kept an eye on us. Kenny bounced on the air mattress, excited because his house was being searched and sacked. "I can't wait to tell the guys at school about this!" he kept saying. Josh sprawled on the floor and commanded his brother to shut it every thirty seconds like clockwork.

Penny, her feet up on Marty's lap, allowed Leo to hold an ice pack on her forehead. The three of them took up the couch. Neil prowled the room, the copy of the search warrant in his hands. I'd tried to talk with him a few times, but he brushed me aside, so I stood in the corner, arms wrapped around myself. Sounds of drawers being emptied, papers fluttering to the floor and the soft murmur of animated discussion drifted from the hallway.

"Maybe one of us should watch them, make sure they aren't planting evidence." Marty said for the fifth time.
Neil growled unintelligibly from the corner. I slid him a look, but he turned away, his shoulders unnaturally stiff. I strode over to Marty and lowered my voice.

"They're looking for Candie Valentino, Sprout and I'm pretty sure they didn't smuggle her in under their department issued coats."

198

"Ten frigging minutes," Neil muttered and shook his head. I understood what he meant. Ten minutes more and in all likelihood, we would have been on our way out of town, blissfully unaware that our house was being ransacked. I was sorry his Sunday plans had been spoiled, but really, wasn't it better to be here for the search?

"I still don't understand," I said to the officer. "Markus Valentino claimed I was blackmailing him?"

"That's right." The answer came from Detective Capri, who'd appeared in the foyer. "He said you came to him demanding a certain amount of money for proof of life on Candie. That, when he delivered the aforementioned monies, you refused and laughed at him. He also implicated you in the arson at his estate."

"I saved his worthless ass." Neil seethed. "How dare he—?"

"Detective, I think I've got something here."

Capri turned and the officer handed an envelope over to her. Still wearing latex gloves, she slid its contents out, scanned them briefly before meeting my gaze. "A check from Markus Valentino."

"I worked for him, you know that!" I shouted at her.

"This is quite a hefty sum for a cleaning service. Bag it." She ordered her aide.

"Let me explain—"

"You'll have plenty of time to explain down at the station. "Margaret Phillips, you are under arrest for extortion. You have the right to remain silent...." Capri droned on, a flash of

199

pity in her eyes while one of the officers handcuffed me.

I blinked back tears and Neil was at my side, ready to surge into battle if need be. "I'm sorry I ruined your plans for today," I told him, my voice wobbling.

He ignored my apology, focusing on what mattered. "Don't worry Maggie, we'll fix this. I'll call my Dad and we'll get you a lawyer. Don't say anything without a lawyer present, got it?"

I nodded as my police escort ushered me out the door. "I won't, I promise."

Neil already had his cell phone to his ear as he watched me escorted to and loaded in the back of a black and white cruiser.

"Maggie!" The slamming car door didn't cut off her strangled cry as Sylvia skidded on her icy driveway, running for all she was worth. I watched sadly as one of the police officers shooed her away.

Josh and Kenny stood at the window, their faces heart-wrenchingly desolate. Sure, I'd been arrested before, but never in front of my family, never for something so serious.

Capri turned to say something else to Neil before she stomped over the crusty snow.

"How could you do this?" I asked her, keeping my voice quiet.

She didn't turn to face me. "It's my job."

"You know I didn't have anything to do with Candie's disappearance. You know that!"

She ignored me as the vehicle backed out of my driveway. I slunk down in the seat, not wanting any of my neighbors to catch sight of me in total disgrace.

My brain was still absorbing how Valentino's phony claim had justified the warrant when the cruiser stopped. Capri helped me from the backseat. "Take her straight through booking then stick her in the tank until her counsel arrives." She walked off, leaving me burning holes in the back of her retreating skull.

Booking involved a great deal more paperwork then I'd ever imagined. Not that I'd imagined it often. I almost felt sorry for the paper pushers who dealt with this every workday. There was also fingerprinting, both digital and hard copy on paper, and the infamous mug shot photos. I was offered a phone call, which I refused for the time being. Then I had to cool my heels until my counsel showed up.

Thank God Laura wasn't around. The fur was really gonna fly when she caught wind of this kafuffle.

I sat on the concrete floor, doubly glad I put on insulated jeans that morning, and watched people come and go. Mostly police officers, who were easy to spot, not just from their uniforms, but their purposeful stride. Business was slow, but then, this was Hudson on a Sunday, so there really wasn't a huge, nasty element for these law enforcement officials to contend with. I watched Special Agents Salazar and Feist come in, striding past my cage with a self-important air the local cops lacked. No doubt, they had been to see Valentino first thing that morning and were gearing up to interrogate me.

Taking Neil's advice, I remained quiet, pulling facts together in my head. Confident that Neil and Ralph would find me the best lawyer money could buy, I wanted to be ready to give him everything I knew. Sadly, it really wasn't much.

Seventeen

"**I** told you, I don't understand why he gave me so much money, other than to bribe me to back off from investigating him." Frustration oozed from my pores and I glanced at Darryl Brentwood, the lawyer Neil's father had recommended as "a real son-of-a-bitch." Coming from the original, it was high praise indeed.

Brentwood shrugged his massive shoulders, indicating I should suck it up for now.

Special Agent Feist rested his steepled fingers on the table in front of him and quirked an eyebrow. "Civilians don't investigate, Mrs.

Phillips. They both observe and assist the police. Or they stalk."

I didn't like his implication and the second-grade name calling chaffed my already itchy skin. No need to wonder who was playing bad cop. I blew out in exasperation. "I didn't find anything to report to Detective...er...to you."

"Why didn't you simply inform us about Valentino's payoff when he gave it to you?" Salazar's reasonable tone didn't fool me for a second. There were no good cops in this room.

"Honestly, I was too stunned at first, then since I planned to return it to him—"

Feist cut me off. "You wait until well after dark on a Saturday night and then proceed to the man's place of residence to return so-called free money? I'm having a hard time swallowing your story, Mrs. Phillips."

Part of me wanted to tell him to choke on it, but common sense reigned. "Look, I know it was weird timing, but I know myself and I wouldn't have been able to sleep if I let it go until morning."

Brentwood patted one of his gigantic mitts on my tightly clenched fist. I jumped, having forgotten he was there. "Other than Mr. Valentino's claim that Mrs. Phillips was extorting money for information, do you have any proof that she was involved with Mrs. Valentino's disappearance?"

Special Agent Feist dodged the question. "Mr. Valentino was attacked in his home last night. A physical examination of his person revealed someone had hit him over the head with a blunt object, rendering him unconscious before the fire started. It is our belief the attacker then set the house on fire, with the intention of murdering Mr. Valentino and having it appear to be an accident."

"My husband went in the house; he saved Valentino's life. And I'm the person who called 911. Do you think we would have done those things if we wanted Valentino out of the picture?"

Salazar studied my face. "It's not unheard of for a first time offender to panic, have an attack of conscience and retrench at the eleventh hour."

Darryl stood and waved dismissively. "Gentlemen, you have nothing on my client but circumstantial evidence and the word of one man who deliberately withheld evidence early in the investigation. The record shows that Mrs. Phillips worked with Detective Capri, even before the kidnapping. You are wasting her time and your resources holding her here. In addition, you have tarnished her good name and I plan on advising my client to sue for defamation of character. Considering her business will potentially suffer, I'm sure we will have a strong case against both the Hudson police and the FBI."

I sat back, very impressed with the real son-of–a-bitch. Special Agent Feist opened his mouth but no sound emerged. Salazar's lips made a thin white slash under his grim stare.

"Now, if you'll excuse me gentlemen, this interview is over. I will need a moment to confer with my client before I take this before a judge."

Effectively dismissed, the FBI drones rose simultaneously and exited the interview room. I glanced at my lawyer, his pearly white grin shocking next to the ebony of his skin. "Thank you, Mr. Brentwood. That turned out better than I had hoped."

"Don't thank me until after you get my bill, Mrs. Phillips. And I meant what I said; you have a very strong case for defamation of character."

"Not interested. They really are just doing their jobs."

Daryl grunted. "As your counsel, I'll advise you to stay away from Valentino and the remainder of the federal investigation. Coincidental or not, you don't want your name to constantly pop up on the Fed's radar. I'll also advise you to abandon your ties with Detective Capri and the confidential informant position. Being a rat never pays."

On that ominous note, he lumbered out. I brooded while a uniform escorted me back to the holding area. The sounds and smell of the police station hovered around me, the moans of drunken citizens who had partied too much on Saturday night drying out in the cell next door, burnt coffee and nervous sweat lodged in my nostrils, ringing phones and the constant murmur of voices too far away to distinguish.

Breathing through my mouth, I waited to be released. Brentwood had been right; Hudson was a small community and I might lose clients because of my arrest. I rubbed my hands over my eyes. This couldn't have happened at a worse time

"Margaret Phillips," A young female officer, almost pixie-like in appearance, called and I stood back from the door as she unlatched it. Brentwood towered over her, flashing me another of his quick, confident grins. "The charges have been dropped." He reassured me.

Brentwood, took my arm and guided me to what I assumed was the check-out desk. I saw Neil first, pacing like a caged panther and my father-in-law, Ralph Phillips scowling at his son's back. I swallowed hard. This wasn't going to be fun.

"Maggie!" Neil was at my side, relief and fury battling for control of his expression. "Are you all right?"

The short answer was no, but I nodded because I didn't want to be responsible for another second of his distress. "I will be once I get home."

Ralph stood by Neil's side, his face grim. "Say the word, sweetheart and we'll own this whole damn building."

"I'm fine, Ralph really. It was just a mistake." Although I knew his reaction stemmed from a thirst for blood more than genuine distress for my situation, I was sort of flattered.

"Maggie, can I speak with you?" Capri had approached and I turned to scowl at her plum-colored suit, sidearm strapped visibly under her unbuttoned jacket.

Neil bristled like an irate hedgehog, but I placed a hand on his arm, signaling that I could handle the confrontation. "Don't worry,

207

Capri, I'm not lawsuit happy. I have to live in this town, too."

Her gaze steady, she nodded once. "That's good to know, but it's not what I want to speak with you about."

"My wife isn't about to say anything without her attorney present. Come on Maggie." Neil pulled on my arm, but Capri blocked his path. Tension radiated off him in waves and I was afraid if Capri didn't move her bony ass, Neil would knock her down then be charged with assaulting an officer.

"Neil, it's all right. Let me talk with her and be finished with this mess." He didn't budge. "Please," I wasn't above begging.

Capri was smart enough not to smirk as I signaled Brentwood. "May I have another moment of your time?"

"I'll wait here." Neil said.

We followed Capri's brisk stride to her office and Brentwood shut the door.

I opened my mouth to tear a strip of flesh from her hide, but my lawyer spoke first. "I want it on record that my client is cooperating in full with this investigation."

"Noted. Maggie, tell me more about your encounter with Valentino. What was your impression of his attitude at the time?"

I thought back. "Confident, arrogant even. Pretty much the same as the other encounter I had with him."

"Did he seem at all upset? Angry?"

"Only when I mentioned Amelia Kettering. He seemed jealous of her former relationship with Candie. Perhaps he felt threatened."

"I've run a background check on Ms. Kettering. Everything seems simple enough. She's single, thirty-five years old, an advertising executive for a national firm. She moves around quite a bit, rents instead of owns. She's not flush with money, but she is comfortable financially. Do you believe she might have anything to do with Mrs. Valentino's disappearance?"

"Not unless she's a brilliant actress. She seemed genuinely surprised that Candie lived nearby, and shocked when I told her about the kidnapping. I don't think her reactions were feigned and she didn't strike me as the vengeful sort."

Capri glanced at Brentwood. "For the record, I want you to understand that I never believed you were capable of extortion and that I trust your judgment. However, the feds are in charge of this investigation. I'm required to follow their playbook. I hope this won't affect our future working relationship."

I rolled my shoulders back, stared her in the eye. "Detective, do you honestly believe everything is going to go back to the way it was? Finding a cleaning job in this town will be like searching for a specific tick in the forest. It's a small community, word will spread and my reputation will be in tatters. The last thing I'm worried about right now is feeding you more information."

"Noted," Capri said again and I turned to the door. "For the record, I only wanted to help Candie Valentino."

"Funny, me too. I suggest you look into Valentino's business dealings, specifically a project named falcon. My impression is he cares more about that than his wife."

I left without a backwards glance. The cops had the ball and they could stuff it for all I cared. Finding Candie cost too high a price for me to even consider paying.

"My office will bill you." Brentwood said as we parted ways in the lobby.

Case in point. I sighed and gestured to Neil. "I want to go home now."

"As you wish, milady."

* * * *

As the sun headed toward the western horizon, the calls began. My arrest in connection with Candie Valentino's disappearance wouldn't hit the newspapers until Monday morning, but word of mouth was almost as reliable. Every stinking job I'd lined up for the following week had been canceled. I was a pariah, not convicted by the courts, but by my community. No one wanted a possible extortionist/ arsonist mopping their floors.

After the fifth cancellation, I shut my cell phone off. Penny, eyes wide, squeezed Marty's hand as they watched me prepare dinner. The greens were washed and chopped and I kept busy sautéing pine nuts in extra virgin olive oil for a salad topper. A mountain of chicken cutlets sat warming in the oven and the rice pilaf stood ready, awaiting distribution.

Neil was propped up against the refrigerator. Flanked by his offspring, three sets of hazel eyes bore witness to my every move. I loved them, but the staring was driving me nuts. The relief at my quick return home had evaporated as reality of what was next for

210

our family to endure settled over us. The Laundry Hag was officially *persona non grata*.

"We don't need the money; we were getting by just fine before you started cleaning houses." He said for the fifth time.

"You're absolutely right." I agreed, scooping the nuts onto a paper towel to cool.

"Maybe we should head out." Marty offered.

Normally, I would fight him on it, but arguing required more fire than I possessed at the moment. "Do you have somewhere to go?"

Marty's lack of reply was answer enough. "Boys, wash your hands and set the table please. Neil, would you call Sylvia, see if she would like to join us for dinner?" The salad alone could feed fifty after all and I didn't want to think about her sitting all alone, abandoned.

"Sure thing, Uncle Scrooge." Neil picked up the phone, but put it down just as fast. "Maybe I'll walk over there instead, I could use some air." He headed out of the room to get his jacket.

"What would you like to drink, Penny?" I opened the fridge, surveying the beverage selection.

"I'll get it myself. " Penny drawled but I cast a black scowl over my shoulder. This was not a night I would tolerate someone taking over. I needed to stay busy and hold onto the illusion of control.

"What... Do... You... Want.... To... Drink." I bit out.

Penny and Marty exchanged silent communication. "Milk, please." She squeaked.

I poured an enormous glass of milk, then turned to Marty. "And you?"

"How about a beer?"

I didn't bother to look. "We're out. How about milk?"

"Sounds like a plan." My brother grumbled.

"Milks all around," I announced and emptied the gallon into various cups.

"Let me carry those for you, sis." Marty reached for the glasses, but I jerked them back. Milk sloshed over the rim, slopping onto my sweater and landing with a splat on the floor.

"Jesus, Marty," I began as the liquid seeped into the fabric.

My brother hung his head. "Sorry, I'm so sorry, Maggie."

I knew he was referring to more than the milk. Harnessing my temper, I headed for the laundry room and a mop.

Wisely, Penny and Marty shuffled into the dining room to assist Kenny and Josh with table duty. I'd just emptied the bucket into the kitchen sink when the doorbell rang. Grumbling, I slouched down the hall. "Neil, did you forget your key...?" I trailed off when I saw Leo on the other side of the door. He looked pale and shivery, understandable since he stood in the cold, coatless, but the stricken look on his face told me more than the weather was to blame for his haggard appearance.

"Come in here before you freeze." I hauled him inside. "Where's your coat? Lord above, it must be in the single digits out there."

"Maggie, I'm so sorry."

"Not your fault I'm nosy and got in over my head, Leo." I snatched a blanket off the air mattress and wrapped him up. "Let's go in the kitchen, the oven is on and you'll warm up faster."

Obediently, Leo shuffled after me. "I have to talk to you, in private." He cut his gaze toward the dining room where Marty had dropped some silverware.

"Can it wait until after dinner? We're just about to sit down and Neil should be back with Sylvia any time now. You're welcome to stay and—"

"Now, Maggie." Though his tone was forceful, I worried he might start to cry if I refused.

"Let's go in my bedroom." I led the way; calling out to the assembled family members that I would be back shortly.

"What's going on?" I asked as soon as he shut the door. "I can't remember ever seeing you this upset."

"It's Richard."

Concerned, I rubbed his arm. "Is he all right? Was he in an accident?"

"No, he's fine, just a real dickhead." Leo snorted. "Dick Head, the dickhead, why didn't I see it?"

Ignoring the unmade bed, I pulled Leo over and sat down. "Wanna tell me what happened?"

Leo nodded, misery incarnate. "He stole files from Valentino's office."

"Excuse me?" I was sure I hadn't processed his words correctly.

213

"When he went cleaning with you. I didn't know, until I went to his house this afternoon. His mother let me in, you see. She's so sweet, if a bit demanding and Richard didn't know I was there. He was in the shower and I decided to wait for him in his bedroom. The computer was on and I must have nudged the keyboard or something because this file opened up. It had Valentino's corporate logo on the header, so I knew it wasn't his. From what I could tell it was quarterly stock reports for Safari and a list of shareholders. So I started, you know, scrolling through the files. And I found this status report for something called falcon, as well as a bunch of bank statements. I knew it couldn't be a coincidence."

I closed my eyes. "Damn it all to hell and back."

"There's more. I searched through his room and found this."

Where he pulled the manila file folder from, I had no idea, but my curiosity subsided as I leafed through its contents. Pictures, all of Valentino and Candie, some cut from magazine or newspaper articles, others paparazzi-style candid shots of one or both subjects walking, talking to someone. Dozens of clippings pertaining to Falcon, Safari Power Solutions, and Candie's disappearance.

"This is bad, Leo."

Leo lost the battle and his face crumpled. "I'm so sorry. Maggie. I confronted him about it. He claimed he had a source who fed him the information online, that he was just monitoring the project, the company. I knew he was B.S.-ing me though. I mean,

214

where does he get the money for the rent, if he's not working? His mother's a retired kindergarten teacher for God's sake. He has to be some sort of corporate spy." A tear slid down his cheek.

My brain was on a tilt-a-whirl. "Leo, listen to me. This is not your fault, you hear me? You had no way of knowing what Dick Head was up to. I didn't know and I was right there with him. But now that you are aware of what he's been doing, you need to tell the police. He might be involved in the kidnapping." If so, he was probably half way to Zimbabwe by now. I looked back to the file, my heart like a hunk of granite in my chest. I really didn't want to have another run-in with the law today.

Leo nodded. "I'll go right now. I should have gone there first, but I wasn't thinking." I offered him the file; sorry my fingerprints were on it, but in his distress he fumbled and papers fluttered to the carpet.

"Sorry, Maggie, I'm so sorry...." Leo droned on but I tuned him out while I restacked the clippings.

"No freaking way," I said as one headline caught my eye.

"What is it?" Leo stoppered his verbal diarrhea of apology and leaned over my shoulder.

"Maybe nothing. Go now, ask for Detective Capri. I'll have Marty drive you."

Too upset to even make a joke, Leo jumped up. He opened the door to Neil, fist aloft, poised for knocking.

215

"Neil, go get Marty. He's going to go to the police station with Leo."

Neil cocked his head, studied me. "You don't want me to ride with him?"

"Not this time, slick. We need to have a chat."

Eighteen

"**S**on of a bitch." Neil said as he accessed Safari's corporate website. "Here it is in black and white. Why didn't I pick up on this sooner?"

I leaned over his shoulder, kissed his cheek. "You've been busy. Why would you notice?" I couldn't suppress my grin. It wasn't often I figured something out before Neil.

Candie Valentino, not Markus, was the owner of Safari Power Solutions. True, Markus was the business tycoon, the man behind cutting-edge advances, but fifty-one percent of the company's stock was held by his wife. She came from money, a true Dallas socialite and sole heir to her father's oil fortune.

217

"Okay, let's assume the feds know all this. Chances are, Candie's WASP parents, not Markus Valentino, called in the FBI. Valentino's under the gun because he's late bringing his new project, falcon, to fruition. He's made big promises and backed them up with smoke. Meanwhile, his existing customers are all sorts of pissed off, because he's not paying as much attention to them. The market is shaky right now and he can't afford his stocks to tank when he's invested so much in falcon. What better way to gain a little sympathy than a stalking threat, followed by his wife's disappearance? The question is, was it a voluntary disappearance?"

Neil looked stunned, then a slow grin broke across his face. "You think she's just hiding, faking the kidnapping for her husband's sake?"

"I'm not sure. I'd like to believe Candie is incapable of this sort of duplicity, but there is a possibility she's part of it. But like I said, the feds probably know all this. And Valentino's under a microscope. What better way to divert attention from him, than to set me up as blackmailer?"

Neil's fists clenched on the arms of the desk chair. "If this is true, you were arrested as a red herring, so Valentino would feel confident enough to make his next move. Then, the feds would close in. You really should sue, Uncle Scrooge. Or at least let me beat the snot out of them all."

Not the most romantic offer, but it filled in the cold pit in my stomach with light and warmth. "Never mind that now. There are still

218

pieces missing. First, we don't know if Candie is involved or not. If not, then Markus has an accomplice. While he may have sent those faxes and the dead bird, he didn't bash himself over the back of the head, then set fire to his own house. My money is on Dick Head. It's too coincidental that he hooks up with Leo right after I started cleaning for the Valentinos. Look at the facts. He uses Leo to get to me and the guise of the cleaning gig to nose around Valentino's private office. He has a stalker-esqe file on them, for Pete's sake."

Neil mulled that over, absently stroking my arm. "Then again, he could be just some whacked-out groupie. Valentino might've hired some random thug. You can buy anything on Craigslist."

"Or it could be the guy who was driving us around. Or possibly Sierra. As his personal assistant, she could cover for him at any point when he was out doing something unscrupulous. Then too, there's Lucas Sloan. Lord knows that guy has so much financial trouble, he'd get in bed with the devil for a few coins to rub together." I looked Neil in the eye. "Whoever it is, they've decided to take Valentino out. Chances are high the police have a guard posted at his hospital room door in case the perp has another go at him."

The corner of Neil's mouth kicked up. "Perp? You're really getting into this."

"Not like I had much of a choice." But he was right, I realized. While running my own business had been kind of cool, it didn't occupy my mind the way the CI position did. I turned to my husband. "With cleaning, there was

219

always going to be a need to do it again and the effort is often overlooked. Helping out Capri made me feel as if I was making a real difference, not just a temporary one."

Neil reached out, pulled me onto his lap. "You make me absolutely crazy, you know that?" He said as his hand stroked lazily through my hair. "All I want in this world is to protect you and the boys and to see that you're all happy. Figures that the only way for you to be happy is pasting a giant bull's eye on your forehead."

"That's not true, I'm happy doing stuff with you and the boys."

His hand stilled and dropped to the arm of the chair once more. "Are you? Is that why you went out of your way to invite Leo to come skiing with us?"

My mouth dropped open. "Was that why you were in such a snit this morning? Neil, Leo gets like two days off every six months, otherwise your mother keeps him chained to a radiator. I thought he'd like a change of pace. Besides, you know darn well that I wasn't going to ski and I know you needed a little physical action."

"Speaking of which..." Neil mumbled, before claiming my lips.

Someone knocked on the door.

"Go away," We shouted in tandem.

"Maggie, I need to talk to you." Sylvia's meek plea seemed even more pathetic filtered through the door.

I rested my forehead against Neil's. "Cripes, I should hang up a shingle next to Dr. Bob's."

"Come on in, Sylvia," Neil called out as I scrambled off his lap.

"Hey, you guys. Sorry to interrupt."

"We're used to it." Neil said easily. "I'm going to see what's left from dinner."

"Save me something," I pleaded as he shut the door. On a sigh, I turned to face my friend.

"What's up, Sylvie?" My heart broke as I watched her wring her hands. Sylvia had changed so much in the last week. Her usual confidence in tatters, she looked like a little girl who'd been abandoned in a foreign city.

"Well, first, I wanted you to know how grateful I am that you've been here for me. I know I'm weird and out there and you don't get all my new age hocus pocus, but you're still here for me." Her hands gestured wildly. "And I wanted to tell you, I've decided to sell the house."

I dropped back into the padded chair. Crap. "When?"

"As soon as possible. Eric promised I could have the house, since he's the one who still has a job, but of course I can't pay for it on my own."

"Where are you going to live?" *Please don't move away.* I kept the selfish plea to myself. Being on the outs with Hudson society, I needed the one true friend I had here.

"I haven't thought that far ahead. I'll stay in the house until it sells, then I guess we'll leave it up to fate."

Fuck fate. "Have you thought about looking for a job in Boston? You could find a small apartment."

221

"I really don't want to live by myself in the city,"

"Then you could commute. Whatever you have to do, I'll be here to help."

Her smile was small, but genuine. "I know you will Maggie. And look, I'm sorry about your cleaning business."

"All good things must come to an end." The sage words sounded hollow in my ears.

"No, no, I mean, pushing you into it in the first place. I can't help but feel that if it wasn't for me, all these awful things wouldn't have happened."

"It wasn't all bad. I met some interesting people and I have excellent stories to tell at social functions."

"Yeah, but—"

"Really Sylvia, you didn't dupe me into this and I guess being self-employed wasn't in the cards. Come on, let's go have some dinner."

* * * *

Neil was snoring on the air mattress next to me when Marty returned. I eased to the floor and signaled to him to meet me in the kitchen. "How did it go? Where's Leo?"

Marty ignored my questions and poked his head in the refrigerator. "Any food left?"

"Marty, I'm dying here."

"Mind fixing me something to eat before you expire?"

Grumbling, I shoved him aside and withdrew the plate I'd saved for him. Popping it in the microwave, I fetched a beer out of Neil's hidden stash in the garage. "If you want this, you'd better dish." I waved the bottle under his nose.

"You're a shrewd negotiator, Laundry Hag." He snatched the bottle and twisted off the cap. "Leo's fine, a little shaken, but he'll be all right. I offered to drive him back to your in-laws, but he insisted on driving himself."

"Are the police going to question Richard?"

"How the hell would I know? I'm just your lousy errand boy."

"Oh quit that poor, poor, pitiful me act. Wait until your kid is born. Being a dad will redefine you understanding of put-upon."

Marty shuffled his feet, his gaze focused over my shoulder. "The baby's not mine, Maggie."

I blinked stupidly. "Pardon?"

"I met Penny at a restaurant outside of Charleston. I was working on a road crew and me and the guys would stop in every day for lunch. Penny was real nice to all of us, bringing us free fries or slices of pie. Anyway, I stopped in late one night, and saw her walking through the parking lot. She was with this guy and I could see through the window they were yelling. So when I saw the guy hit her, I got in the middle of it. I mean, I couldn't just let some asshole pound a pregnant girl, ya know?"

"Wait, wait, slow down. What guy?"

"Penny's high school boyfriend; the father of her baby."

Behind me, the microwave dinged. We both ignored it, lost in the gaping chasm of words unsaid. I wanted to yell at him, but seeing the bags under his eyes and the hangdog

223

lines around his face, I didn't have the heart for a verbal flogging.

"How did she end up with you?"

My words jolted Marty out of whatever he'd been brooding over. "She was living with the guy and after I beat the piss out of him, I convinced her to press charges. But his Dad was the local sheriff and she was convinced he'd be out in no time and come after both of us. So, I sold my car and bought the RV."

I needed to sit down. "Jesus, Marty. Does he know your name?"

My brother shook his head. "We've never been properly introduced, other than my fist to his face."

"You're damn lucky you weren't slapped with an assault charge." His gaze skittered away and I groaned. "Oh, shit, don't tell me..."

"I don't guess I need to."

Cripes, what a frigging disaster. "He'll be looking for her, Marty. She's carrying his child. You need to go to the police, get a lawyer."

"I can't do that, Maggie! Penny's so stressed out, I'm afraid she'll lose the baby. This house isn't exactly the sea of tranquility, you know?"

I slapped my hands on the counter. "How can you dump this on me, Marty? How can you be so selfish as to drag my family into your problems this way? Again! Just what exactly is wrong with you, that you screw up every frigging thing you touch?"

"That's enough, Uncle Scrooge." Neil said from the doorway.

224

"Oh, we're not even in the same dimension as enough! I'm just warming up here and—"

"Marty, go to bed. We'll talk to you tomorrow." Neil's tone was hard and unyielding. "Maggie, come outside with me a second."

I took one last look at my brother's devastated face, before closing my eyes. "I'm sorry Marty, I didn't mean—"

"Save it, Laundry Hag." Marty nodded to Neil, then stormed down the hall. At least he had enough sense not to slam the door. I launched myself from the barstool and flung the microwave door open.

"God, can you believe him?" I asked as I scraped the food into the trash. "Running from a damn assault charge with a pregnant stranger riding shotgun. Un-frigging-believable"

"Maggie, come outside." Neil repeated the command.

"I don't want to go outside, it's too cold. Hey!" I shouted as the fleece comforter from our makeshift bed was tossed over my head. Neil spun me until I was swaddled like a mummy and lifted me off the ground in a fireman's carry.

"What the hell are you doing, you'll hurt your shoulder." My words must have been muffled by the blanket because he patted my backside once and didn't respond.

A lock clicked and I hissed as the freezing air stung my bare feet. Neil must have put on boots because I heard the distinct crunching of snow as I jounced along like a tuna in a net.

225

"Seriously Neil, how much did you like dinner, 'cause we might experience it again if you keep bouncing me around."

"Quit your bellyaching, we're almost there." Another light slap on the butt. He was having way too much fun with this.

"Almost where?" I asked at the same time a door squeaked open. The world came back into view as Neil set me down and the comforter fell away from my head. My feet were planted on the steps to the RV.

"Are you out of your ever-loving mind? The heater isn't on, we'll freeze to death."

Pushing past me, Neil kicked off his boots and flicked the space heater on. "See, no popsicles in here. Besides, you needed to cool off. Come in and shut the door before you let the heat out."

"Wiseass," I grumbled, hopping over the small puddles of snow his boots had left behind. Tempted though I was to hog the blanket, I sat down next to him, so close that our thighs touched, and flung one corner over his shoulder.

His arm wrapped around my waist and he sighed. "Let it all out, Uncle Scrooge."

I blew out a sigh. "My brother's an idiot."

"That's not exactly a news flash."

I rolled my eyes at him. "You know what I mean. Part of me wants to box his ears for not thinking this through, for dragging us into the muck with him."

Neil made a sound of commiseration. "And the other part?"

226

I looked him in the eyes, a small smile turning up the corners of my mouth. "I'm very proud of him, for standing up for someone weaker than himself."

Neil smiled back "Me too. He's not just a selfish kid anymore."

"Oh, he's still a selfish kid," I said. "And he got in way over his head this time, but the reason he did, the fact that he wanted to help someone other than himself...."

"It changes things," he finished for me.

I sniffed, my nose dripping unattractively, whether from the cold or emotion I couldn't tell. "So, what do we do now?"

"Well, tomorrow, we contact that lawyer, explain the situation and see what he advises and take it from there."

I groaned. "I'm going to have to sell a kidney to pay for this."

"Worry about that later." He leaned in, kissed my neck followed by a quick hit to the corner of my mouth. "Since we're out here, all alone in the cold, you wanna share body heat?"

"That," I told him "is the best offer I've had all night."

Nineteen

"**H**ave the two of you worked on that
homework assignment I gave you?" Dr. Bob
asked. He sat in a rolling desk chair, his little
notebook perched on his lap. He'd chosen a
green sweater-vest to wear over a pinstripe
dress shirt. His glasses now sported tape at the
bridge and a safety pin over one ear. The effect
was almost painful with his graying comb-over
and pleated khaki pants.

Neil's eyebrows met dead center above
his nose. "What's this?"

"We made a sizeable dent in it last
night," I chirped. I'd been willing to forgo
another round with Dr. Bob, but Neil had
insisted. Marty and Penny had gone to Boston,
to consult with the attorney and the boys were

in school. Since the Laundry Hag's services weren't required, I had nothing better to do.

Dr. Bob clucked at the mystified expression on Neil's face. "Maggie, we all need to start off on the same page here. Your husband obviously didn't know about the assignment, did you Neil?"

"This is the first I've heard about any homework."

"Well, next time, I'll be sure to relay all after-session work to *both* of you. For now, would you like to tell me about some of the difficulties the two of you have been encountering lately?"

Neil and I looked at each other. "Not particularly," we said in unison.

"Come, come, you two are obviously in marital counseling for a reason. Tell me what brought you here."

I figured he wasn't referring to Neil's Ford Escort. I cleared my throat, wondering what to say. Neil took the ball and ran.

"Well, I guess we're here because we need to communicate better."

Give the man a gold star.

Dr. Bob crossed one leg over the other, and I saw one shiny penny glinting in its loafer prison. I'd bet my left arm it was a 2009 vintage coin and the other was an exact match. Heads up, of course.

"In what area, Neil?"

Yeah, in what area, Neil?

Watching my husband flounder was a new experience for me. He waved his hands in little circles and shot me a helpless look. I commiserated with a mental, *yeah, this sucks doesn't it, slick?*

I'd rather have another round with the FBI.

"Well, Maggie, um... she's great and all, it just that..." Neil gestured helplessly as he ran down. Oh, how the mighty have fallen.

"Just, what?" Dr. Bob prompted, leaning in, clearly scenting a weakness. "Well, she uh, hides stuff." He smiled in triumph.

"Me!" I exploded out of my seat. "I hide stuff? What about you Mr. *I'm working overtime*? Where have you been sneaking off to?"

Dr. Bob patted the air in a classic settle down motion. "You'll get your turn, Maggie. Remember, we're attempting to create a safe, nurturing environment here. Outbursts will only undermine our work."

Yeah, it'd be a real shame to lose this gem. I gazed heavenward, but sat.

Neil frowned at me. "What do you mean sneaking?"

"It's not my turn," I seethed from between clenched teeth.

"I'll give you my turn. Just answer the damn question."

"You can't give me your turn, you have to finish. Besides, I'd like to know what you meant about me hiding stuff. I assume you're not talking about your car keys."

"Answer my question and I'll answer yours."

"Oh *that's* mature, Neil. What are you, five?" We were both on our feet, noses less than an inch apart, me on my tiptoes so not to be loomed over.

"Folks, folks. You are communicating a bit too loudly. If we could all just reclaim our seats...?"

Smoke practically billowed out of my nostrils. By God, I was the one in the right here. We sat in unison and I had to fight not to cross my arms over my chest.

"Perhaps we ought to follow this path a little further. Now Maggie, what you said about the overtime—"

"Hey! It's his turn, you said so."

Neil rolled his eyes. "Now who's being mature?"

I growled at him.

"Maggie, it's your turn now. Please say what's on your mind."

I was pretty sure he didn't really mean that. "Neil has been going into work a lot more often than usual. Earlier days, longer nights. He claims it's because he's logging overtime on this project which he can't tell me about, but when I called his desk last week...," Was I really going to say it?

"Do go on, Maggie." Dr. Bob said. The man was practically drooling. I ignored him and turned to face my husband.

"You weren't there. The man who answered told me Intel had shelved all overtime, due to the economy. Then I saw you, at that house down the road." Tears stung, demanding release, but I curled my fingers into my palms, digging my nails into flesh. I was not going to cry.

"Shit," Neil said. He scrubbed one hand over his face. "Shit."

My heart stopped mid thump and died in my chest cavity. Only sheer force of will kept me from curling into the fetal position by the loafers, to brace for the hit that was coming.

"God, Maggie, I'm sorry. I'm so, so sorry."

No, no, no, no. NO!

Detached from my feeling center, I watched his head shake. Back and forth, back and forth, back and forth.

"Just say it." I whispered.

His shoulders shook. "I didn't realize how it would look. No wonder you've been acting like a lunatic lately." He started to laugh. "No wonder you made me sleep in that god forsaken camper!" Tears streamed down his face.

"What's the joke here?" Dr. Bob's expression could only be called bewildered.

"Maggie thought I was screwing around on her," Neil giggled.

Not the reaction I would have picked.

"Are you?" Dr. Bob's tone was deceptively mild.

Neil's laughter dissolved like sugar in acid. "Of course not." He looked at me. "I love you and only you. I'm sorry you doubted me for even a second."

"So where have you been spending your time, Neil?" Dr. Bob asked.

Neil hadn't forgiven the accusation. "I'll answer, but only because I'm positive Maggie wants to know, too."

"I've been working. That much is true. Just, the overtime hasn't been with Intel. They have scaled back on overtime, that's also correct."

I swayed on the chair, having visions of Neil selling his body for profit before I got a hold on my runaway imagination.

"I've been doing odd jobs, roof and window repair, a little plumbing. The woman from our neighborhood? She's the room mother in Kenny's class. We got to talking one day when I picked the boys up and she mentioned a pipe burst and her husband was away on business. The plumbers repaired the damage, but she had a huge hole in her kitchen ceiling, so I did the dry walling for her. I was just checking in on her that morning, making sure she didn't have any other problems."

I blinked. "So you've been working as a handyman?"

"Pretty much." He rested a hand on my knee. The Laundry Hag and the Handy Man, go figure.

"Why didn't you tell me?" Now that the stupor had ebbed, the anger was back. "God Almighty Neil, why did you hide this?"

"Because I didn't want you fretting about the money. No, hear me out." He insisted and I snapped my mouth shut. "You always worry about money, but it's been worse since we moved here. I didn't tell you about the overtime because you'd only worry more when there's no need. I thought doing this would kill two birds with one stone."

"Who's the other lucky bird?" I asked.

233

Neil grimaced. "Marty. I can't stand the guy, but I was afraid if I went off on him again like I did in December, he'd leave and you'd be crushed. Again. Don't you see, Maggie? Everything I do, everything I even think about doing, I do for you."

"Time's up." Dr. Bob announced.

* * * *

The feds were waiting on our front porch when Neil drove me home.

"I should have anticipated this." I sighed as the Escort rolled to a stop. "I suppose I have to talk to them."

"Do you want me to stay?" Neil offered.

"Don't you have work?"

"Yes."

"Then you should go."

He lifted my knuckles to his lips and placed a soft kiss on them. "Try and stay out of jail, okay?"

"I always try," I muttered and climbed from the car. Miracle of miracles, the sun was out and shining, and there was considerably less snow on the ground. Between Neil's revelation and the turnaround in the weather, I felt calm and more myself than I had in weeks.

Neither of the FBI special agents shared my mood. "We've been attempting to contact you since last night, Mrs. Phillips." Fatigue was evident in Salazar's voice.

I shrugged, inserting my key in the deadbolt. "I shut my cell phone off." Confident that my action wasn't a federal crime, I gestured for the two men to enter.

"I've seriously contemplated arresting you for

234

interfering with a federal investigation." Feist stated as I shucked my coat.

"Wanting to tangle with my lawyer again already? And here I thought you were searching for Mrs. Valentino. Would you gentlemen care for some coffee?" I didn't bother waiting for a response as I bee-lined for the kitchen.

"We need to ask you some more questions about your relationship with one Richard Head."

"He was dating a friend of mine, Leopold Rothschild. Leo asked me to hire him as my assistant. I did, he didn't work out, end of story." I pushed the on button for the coffee pot and spun to face my audience.

"Mr. Rothschild told us that he stopped here last night before coming to the police station."

"He was upset, he needed a friend. I'm sure you would feel the same Special Agent Feist, if someone you were romantically involved with turned out to be a stalker and/or corporate spy."

"How would you characterize Mr. Rothschild's reaction to his find?"

I scowled at Salazar. "I'm not sure what you mean."

"Was he angry?"

The tingle started along the back of my neck. "More devastated than anything. Leo doesn't open his heart very often; he's been burned before."

They exchanged glances and the tingling increased.

"Where were you between nine and eleven PM yesterday, Mrs. Phillips."

"Here. Why?"

"Is there anyone who can substantiate your whereabouts?"

"Neil, Penny, the kids, my next door neighbor, Sylvia Wright. Why do you need to know?"

"We're the ones asking the questions." Feist snapped.

I pushed past him, reaching for the phone. "I'm calling my lawyer. I don't know what the two of you are up to, but I'm sick of feeling like there's a giant target on my back."

Another silent communication passed between them. Did the FBI train them in mental telepathy? Salazar nodded once and Feist grunted, "Richard Head's body was discovered in an alley several blocks from his home. Medical examiner estimated the time of death between 9:30 and 10:30 PM."

"Shit," I dropped my weight onto a reluctant barstool. It groaned in protest. "I'm guessing it wasn't an accident?"

"That's classified." Salazar said in a mild tone. "We've been in this business for a long time, Mrs. Phillips. It's never a coincidence that the same person's name resurfaces time and again through the investigation. You are tied to every single person involved in some way or another. If you were us, what would you think?"

I didn't answer.

"Contact your counsel, we'll be in touch." Feist nodded once and led the way out.

I sat, staring into space. They were
absolutely right about my name cropping up,
but the reason for it was obvious, if only to me.
I was being set up.

Why? And by who? Coffee forgotten, I
paced the length of the kitchen. Who would
have anything to gain by framing me?

Well, Richard Head's killer, obviously.
Followed closely by Candie's kidnapper and
whoever had torched the Valentino estate. *It
might be all one person.* The thought sent a
shiver down my spine.

The phone rang. "Hey," Neil said. "You
all right?"

"Not so much" I whispered. "Someone's
setting me up."

The line was quiet for a second. "Get
changed into some sweats. I'll be home in a
few."

"Are you sure you won't get into trouble
taking time off?"

"Don't worry about it. Go get ready."

Twenty

"This is stupid," I huffed as Neil lapped me again on the high school track. We'd been at it for twenty minutes and I'd completed three laps to Neil's eight. He pinched my behind on every pass, unimpeded by the thick sweats covering my lower half. Miracle of miracles, it wasn't snowing on us and the temperature resided somewhere in the mid-forties.

Neil pivoted to face me, continuing to jog backward, the showoff. "Aren't you having fun, Uncle Scrooge?"

"You're giving me an inferiority complex," I grumbled, picking up my pace.

"It's not a competition, Maggie."

238

I shot him a dirty look and stumbled over nothing for my efforts. Neil's laughter faded as he turned forward and sped away.

I smiled to myself, glad my husband was having fun, even if I was the butt of the joke. Out of the multitude of worries I dwelt on, Neil's happiness was high on the list. Ever since he'd left his SEAL team, I fretted about my own hum-drum existence boring him to death. While raising two boys kept me busy, it wasn't as if I was saving the world, fighting terrorists or rescuing hostages. Cleaning and daydreaming didn't get the old adrenaline pumping the way Neil preferred it.

We'd settled into a routine soon after moving to Hudson, albeit a somewhat strange one. But between canceling the gym membership and my utter failure as a small business owner, I'd destroyed the little stability we'd built and were now forced into starting all over again.

Neil would adapt; Navy SEAL's are trained to acclimate in any situation. But there's a big difference between surviving and truly enjoying life.

Candie Valentino, from what little I'd seen of her, had been surviving. Markus, I wasn't so sure about. Although the man wore a slick veneer of confidence, my radar hummed that it was a false front, designed to fool people. The question was, who had he been fleecing and for what purpose?

"Come on Uncle Scrooge, kick it up a notch." He goosed me again.

"Hey, Emeril, keep your hands to yourself."

"Who?"

I shook my head. "You are completely devoid in pop culture knowledge."

"I can live with that. Seriously though, I think you're ready for the Social Security 5K."

"Did you think Eric and Sylvia were happy together?"

"Jeeze," Neil slowed to a walk. "How the hell would I know? Men don't talk about that kind of shit."

"Just from an observation standpoint. You spent time with them. Give me your impressions." I persisted.

One of the great many things I loved about my husband, he always considered my questions, no matter how ridiculous they seemed. "They put up a front when they were together. But if I were to guess, I'd bet that no, they weren't happy."

"Why?"

Neil scratched his uber sexy chin stubble. "They never sought each other out, when they were in public. No little glances, subtle touches, things like that. They looked good together, but I doubt there were any genuine feelings between them."

"See, you are good at this." I smiled at him. "I was kind of thinking the same thing about Markus Valentino. Like he was all for show, and Candie was the handy-dandy trophy wife."

But he shook his head. "Trophy wives marry into money, but Candie came with her own, remember? No, I think their marriage is more of a business arrangement. She's got the funding, he's got the know-how."

240

"So what went wrong?"

Neil shrugged. Then stopped dead. "Hey, I have an idea."

He grasped my arm, towing me across the football field and back to the car. "Where are going?"

"To get a professional's opinion."

He unlocked the car and took the time to open my door. "You have your cell handy?"

I flipped up the center arm rest, retrieving my phone. "Who am I calling?"

"Dr. Bob. See if he could meet with us for a few minutes."

"Now?"

"Why not? But he's not really going to be counseling us; he'll be meeting the Valentinos."

"I don't understand." I dialed anyway and listened as the phone rang on the other end.

"Dr. Robert Ludlum, marriage facilitator."

"Hi, Dr. Bob. This is Maggie Phillips. Neil and I were wondering if we could stop by to see you."

"Is something wrong? You two seemed to have reached an understanding this morning."

"No, we need counseling all right." Especially Neil and that slightly mad gleam in his eye.

"It happens I had a last minute cancellation so my three o'clock slot is free."

"Thank you. We'll see you in a bit." I shut the phone and slammed into the door as Neil took a corner at the speed of sound.

"For the love of God, what is churning in your head?"

Neil grinned at me and explained his plan.

* * * *

"There's something different about you, Mrs. Phillips." Dr. Bob scanned me from head to toe.

I'm Candie Valentino, I'm Candie Valentino. I offered him a shy smile and concentrated on a spot on the carpet. "Why thank you, sir."

Neil glanced pointedly at his watch. "Can we get this show on the road; I have a great deal of work waiting for me."

Dr. Bob seemed somewhat taken aback by Neil's uncharacteristic abruptness, but recovered quickly.

"How have things been going?"

I opened my mouth to respond, but Neil got there first.

"Fine, everything is just fine." He crossed one ankle to his knee and jiggled his foot.

"You seem tense, Mr. Phillips. Is there something you wish to share?"

I stared at my husband, but hardly recognized him. His usual humor and easy-going air had evaporated like mist on a sunny morning. What was left was a hard-eyed stranger wearing an expression like someone had slipped cat turds into his morning Wheaties.

"I need to get back to work, but she insisted on being here." Neil spat the words, jerking his head toward me.

"Work is very important to you then, Mr. Phillips?" Dr. Bob watched Neil closely, studying his every twitch.

"Well, someone has to make money and since she sits on her ass all day—"

"Hey now!" My character slipped and Neil's gaze met mine. Dr. Bob patted the air in a classic calm down gesture.

"You'll get your turn, Mrs. Phillips. Neil, may I call you Neil?"

His foot jiggled faster. "Fine," he clipped out.

"I thought your wife ran her own business."

Neil rolled his eyes. "Like she could make that work. She's a social pariah, just ask my mother. She tries to involve Maggie in the world, but my wife can't see beyond the end of her nose. It's one crazy scheme after another, with never one thought to sense and what's best for our family. For me."

Dr. Bob's eyes were as big as duck eggs. "I see. Would you like to respond to your husband's statements, Maggie?"

It's not real; he's playing the role of Markus. Even as sense whispered it, I sat stunned at the bile that had spewed from Neil's mouth. This was like my worst nightmare, my husband underscoring all of my deficiencies and attacking me for them. I needed a moment and while Dr. Bob gestured me onward, Neil, the real Neil, picked up on my conundrum. He

243

shot me a quick wink and addressed his audience.

"Go ahead, cry on his shoulder like you do with everyone else. Poor, poor wittle trust fund baby, too much money, not enough sense." His voice went high-pitched and girly. "Oh, boo hoo, no one understands me, no one loves me. My life isn't perfect. Boo hoo hoo. Well, it's time you grew up, little girl. Happiness isn't handed to you on a silver platter. Some of us actually have to work for a living, work to get the things we want."

"Mr. Phillips, please, restrain yourself. Maggie, tell us how you feel right now."

Rip roaring pissed. But even if Candie was angry, she was also afraid. Who wouldn't be, when confronted by such a domineering tyrant? "I guess, I feel awful. Everything he said is true, and I hate that he sees me this way."

Dr. Bob leaned back in his chair. "What can we do, do you think to change this?"

I mulled it over. "Well, I guess I could—"

"Here's a thought; how about you quit whining and be grateful I put up with your shit."

"Mr. Phillips, that's enough!" Dr. Bob's face was mottled red from the part of his comb-over to the neckline on his sweater vest. "Can't you see your tactless words hurt your wife's feelings?"

Neil shrugged and my eyes narrowed. I loved him, but in that instant, I wanted to hurt him. No, to annihilate him.

As if he read my mind, Neil relaxed and lost the asshole coating. "I'm sorry, Uncle

244

Scrooge. You know I couldn't do what I do without you, right?"

I smiled. "I see you, even when you are being a total prick."

Dr. Bob was lost. It was comical the way his head whipped back and forth between the two of us, trying to put his finger on what he'd missed.

"It's been a rough week." I told Dr. Bob. "Neil and I really aren't feeling like ourselves."

"Are you mixing medications, Neil?" Dr. Bob stared at my husband.

"Stress is all. Maggie is currently under investigation by the FBI. One of her clients was kidnapped, then a former cleaning partner showed up dead."

"Don't forget the arson. Oh, and the bribery / extortion thing."

Dr. Bob swallowed. "I see. And, uh, how does this make you feel, Maggie."

They say there are no stupid questions but that one came pretty damn far into moron territory. "Shitty, thanks for asking."

"Ah," Dr. Bob glanced at his wall clock. "I seem to have forgotten about another engagement, if you both will excuse me....?" His eyes begged the crazy people to vamoose and never return.

"Thank you for seeing us, I really feel like we've made a breakthrough here." Neil extended his hand. Dr. Bob backed into the door, fumbling for the knob.

"Really, no trouble at all." He managed to open the door and we wasted no time departing. I contained my hysteria until we reached the car.

"Now that was fun with a capital FU."

"You know he's watching us through the office window."

I turned and caught the blinds snapping closed on the second story. "You think he's phoning the police? Or a psych ward?"

"No, but I doubt he'll ever return our calls again."

Mock sniffling, I flicked a pretend tear away from my eye. "Hold me, Neil; I don't think I have the strength to go on."

Neil chuckled and opened the car door, ushering me to sit. "So what did we learn, class?"

Waiting until he'd buckled his seat belt I ran over everything in my head. "Markus is a domineering ass. Not that I'm surprised but having that kind of condescension bearing down on me was truly awful. Humiliating even."

Neil squeezed my hand in silent apology. "So, if you were really Candie...?"

"I'd kill the creep. Well, maybe not, but I'd do my damndest to ruin him. And I'm pretty sure she'd do the same."

"That's a big assumption. What do you have backing it up?"

"Amelia Kettering, first of all. What are the chances I get dragged to a luncheon and happen to run into Candie's former lover, and not only the meeting but coping to the relationship?"

"Pretty slim," Neil nodded. "Go on."

"That encounter always bugged me. I mean, Markus is a control freak, but no way could he keep Candie from contacting Amelia if

246

she really wanted. And don't forget, she's holding all the money, doling it out to his company as she sees fit. No, Candie is no shrinking violet, no matter what I thought at first. Money equals power, right?"

"In most cases," Neil confirmed.

"So maybe the bird was a test. Like one last chance for Markus to come through for her, to ride to her rescue. She sets it up so I'm involved by using my logo, just to ensure she'll have a witness there. Then, when he brushes her off in front of us, she feels justified to do whatever she pleases."

"Hell hath no fury like a woman scorned. But what about the fax?"

"She wasn't in the house with me when it came through. Supposedly, she'd gone to a spinning class, but how hard would it have been to fax it from the nearest Kinkos?"

"So you think she set up the entire stalker thing, the phoenix, the dead bird, her own kidnapping, all to teach Markus a lesson?"

"At first perhaps. She knew he was stressed, late with the deadline for his new project. Remember, Leo said Richard claimed that someone was slipping him the Safari information online? I bet you anything it was Candie. So, when it comes to light that Richard had all this insider information, Markus is top suspect. It's his wife that's missing, his company the deceased was monitoring. Who else could it be?" I dusted my hands off.

"She didn't count on you, on Markus setting you up for extortion. Maybe she found out about that and that's why she set the fire."

"Which means she has help. Someone who's monitoring Valentino for her. And not Amelia Kettering. Markus wouldn't let her within fifty yards of anything he owns."

"Someone who could be bought."

Our gazes locked and Neil banged a U-turn at the next light.

A rusty red Ford pick-up was parked in Lucas Sloan's driveway. Neil parked my Mini on the street and we both stared at the house.

"Call Detective Capri, we have no authority here." Neil said as my feet hit the ground.

"We're not going to make a citizen's arrest or anything. I only want to talk to him. Besides, he owes me for cleaning this heap." I chucked a thumb at the decrepit ranch.

"It's still nicer than our first place together, look at the bump-out bay window. You've got to admit, it holds potential."

I raised one eyebrow at him. "Someone's been watching *Trading Spaces* again."

Neil started up the path toward the side door. "I refuse to either confirm or deny, seeing as how it will incriminate me."

I crunched after him. "Shheeesh," I muttered, "What's with all the kitty litter?"

"It absorbs the water, from the melted ice." Neil waited to escort me up the stone steps. "Sand and Salt work for melting the initial ice, but water tends to migrate downhill and another sharp drop in temperature will cause refreeze. The Kitty litter absorbs the water. I guess it's better than a yard full of tampons."

"Well thank you, Mr. Wizard. And I do know about black ice. I meant, what's with the dump truck's worth of kitty litter?" I gestured to the heaping mounds of it, more even as we approached the side door.

Neil jerked to a stop. His good shoulder nudged me off to the side. "What does that look like to you?" He pointed to the front door.

"A pile of slush."

"Slush is gray or maybe dirt brown, not reddish brown." He caught my gaze. "Go call 911."

I latched onto his coat sleeve. "Nuh, uh. Not unless you're coming with me. No way in the seventh circle of hell will I let you charge into another potential crime scene alone."

A muscle jumped in Neil's jaw. "I'm not the suspect at this point. Someone could be hurt in there; I might be able to help."

"You're not a medic, Neil. And while we stand here, arguing, times a wastin'. You jump, I jump, Jack."

"Christ Almighty, save me from *Titanic* references." He led the way back to the car though, pulling a satisfied laundry hag in his wake.

Twenty One

Lucas Sloan was dead.

I knew the second the team of patrol officers, who'd responded to our 911 call, rushed out the front door and simultaneously vomited in the rhododendron bushes.

I hugged Neil's arm as the sound of retching drifted toward us. "I'm really glad we didn't go in there."

"She got to him first," Neil grumbled, watching another city vehicle roll to a stop.

"No way, it couldn't have been Candie." I did my best not to think about Sloan's now fatherless children.

Neil turned and stared down at me. "I thought we were on the same page with this,

Uncle Scrooge. Candie Valentino equals bad guy."

"True, but think about it Neil. Candie couldn't just be waltzing around town in the middle of the day; every cop and his Uncle Fred are looking for her."

Neil nodded slowly. "You're right. So if not Candie...Amelia Kettering?"

I shook my head and pointed at the officer wiping his trembling mouth on his sleeve. "Not a woman. Women are sneaky, preferring to use poison over a gun. Whatever's in there is grotesque enough to warrant the kitty litter to sop up blood, and is making the cops puke at the experience."

Neil narrowed his eyes on me, then smiled. "Very good points all, but we'll have to put the sleuthing on hold for today. School's out in ten minutes."

"One of us should stay here and talk to the homicide investigator." I bounced up and down on my toes. "You go on and pick up the boys; don't forget they have karate tonight."

"Maggie, we should both go," Neil bent over so he could speak directly into my ear. "Please, Uncle Scrooge, let's go about our business. If the feds show up and find you here...."

He didn't need to finish that statement. "Let me just make sure they don't need to question us first."

Walking over to the young officer unrolling yellow crime scene tape, I smiled, before realizing how ridiculous the gesture appeared under the circumstances. "Um, hi,

251

my husband and I need to go pick up our kids from school. Is that all right?"

"Ummm," the sweat on his upper lip and shifting gaze clearly marked him as a newbie. Many of the law enforcement officers at the Hudson P.D. were transfers from the much larger Boston police force, typically guys with families and had decided to get out of the trenches of the larger city. Apparently this poor shmoe had never worked a crime scene before, didn't know the procedure.

I used his ignorance to my advantage. "Here's my card with my cell phone number, if anyone needs to ask any questions."

He took the card, glanced at it, then back to me "Well, umm—"

"Thanks!" And I was off, bee-lining for the open passenger's side door of the Mini.

"Let's roll," I said to Neil.

"That poor guy is going to be reamed a new one for letting us go." Neil said, glancing in the rearview mirror.

"I don't think he realized we made the call. There were plenty of neighbors goggling at the scene and quite a bit of traffic on the thru street. I left him my card, but I'll call Capri as soon as we get home."

"So, she can chew you out?"

"No smartass. Because we know whodunit. We solved the puzzle, let her wrap the case."

"The feds won't be happy."

I shrugged, not giving two flying figs about what made Salazar and Feist happy, as long as the body count stopped.

Josh and Kenny were waiting at the curb in front of the middle school. I had to climb out so they and their bulging backpacks could squeeze into the backseat.

"How'd it go today guys?" I pivoted on the seat so I could see them.

"Okay." Josh said, immediately turning on his cell phone. The school prohibited text messaging and he was undoubtedly setting up a chat session with his pseudo girlfriend.

"Mom, can we get a dog?" Kenny asked all big-eyed pleading.

Neil shot me a look. This was a common question which usually sprang up every few months. Neil was pro canine and I straddled the fence. Before we'd moved to Hudson, I'd been able to deflect, claiming it wouldn't be fair to adopt a pet right before a major transition. Now, though....

"I don't know sport, we've got a lot going on right now and a pet is a big responsibility."

"Please, Mom, you won't have to do anything, I'll take care of him, I promise."

Yeah, right. We'd never had a pet before, but I was sure I wasn't the first mother in history to receive this sincere promise. No doubt, two weeks in the dog would be old hat and I'd be stuck walking and feeding and cleaning up after it.

"A dog might be good company for you during the day, Uncle Scrooge." Neil pointed out. "And you'll get more exercise because you'll have to walk it several times a day."

And scoop its poop. And spot treat the rug and chase it off the furniture, not to mention the additional vacuuming and dust mopping... Ugh. When had my eye begun twitching?

"A dog will just lie around all day, eating and sleeping and making a mess. I don't need any more of that kind of company; I have Marty."

Neil ignored my grumping. "What do you think, Josh? You want a dog?"

He didn't look up from his phone. "Whatever. Not like it'll happen, Mom always comes up with an excuse."

His tone sounded borderline fresh to me. "You might want to rephrase that statement, Joshua."

Green eyes rolled around in the kind of exaggeration only a pre-teen could manage. "'Scuse me, what I meant was, Mom's too busy being nosy and getting locked up to bother with an animal."

"Hey! Now just wait a minute—" My protest was cut off as Neil slammed down on the brakes half a mile from our driveway. We all lurched forward and were held in the vehicle by seatbelts and God's will.

"Maggie, drive Kenny home. Josh. Out. Now. We're walking the rest of the way." His cold tone brooked no argument.

"Neil, I can handle this." I muttered as I circled the car.

"I know you can, and would, but Josh and I need to talk. We'll see you at home." Neil shut the door behind me and tugged Josh to the side of the road.

"Josh is gonna get it." Kenny predicted from the back seat.

254

I was amazed at the changes in Josh, from even a few months ago. He'd gone from the little boy whose battles I'd readily fought, to a hormonal, snot-nosed pubescent young man in the blink of an eye. And I couldn't help thinking that my preoccupation with both crime and cleaning was partially to blame for his attitude realignment.

* * * *

Marty and Penny were parked on the living room sofa when I arrived home. Kenny tossed his backpack inside of the front door. "Hey Uncle Marty, do you wanna go lift weights in the garage with me?"

"Sure thing, tough guy." Mary handed the remote to Penny and stood, stretching his back. "I could use a little action."

"Keep it to half an hour; you have homework to do before dinner." I said to Kenny. He raced down the hall to change out of his school clothes.

I turned to face my brother. "How did it go?"

"Well enough, I suppose. The lawyer said he'd get back to me in a few days." Marty leaned down and pecked Penny on the cheek. "No worries, right?"

Penny offered him a wan smile and nodded. Seemingly satisfied, Marty left.

I searched out the front window for any sign of Neil and Josh. Fabric rustled as Penny shifted on the couch, cleared her throat.

"You could have told me, you know." I said, not bothering to face Penny. "I'm sorry you felt like you had to keep the truth from me."

"I'll leave, if you want." Penny's voice was small, reluctant. "I never meant to cause so much trouble."

I glanced at her over my shoulder. "Don't be stupid. You're more than welcome to stay here."

"But the baby's not Marty's. She's not kin to you."

I whirled on her. "Do you want my brother to be a father to your child?"

Shoulders slumped, she nodded.

"Then you and your child are kin to me. I have no idea what the two of you are planning, but you have family here, all right?"

"I'm so afraid Marty's going to get into real trouble. He's such a good guy and I couldn't bear it if he...." She stared off into space.

I knelt down next to her. "Listen to me. Marty's been in trouble before, and he's always wormed his way out of it." No need to point out that the team of Maggie and Neil usually had a hand in the extraction. "Everything will work out."

I could read the disbelief in her eyes. I sighed and settled on the floor more comfortably. "Did Marty tell you that Josh and Kenny aren't my biological children?"

Since I was watching for it, I saw surprise flitter across her face. "It's true. Neil was in the middle of an extremely hostile divorce from his first wife. I was hired on as their nanny."

256

"How old were they?" Penny questioned so softly, I barely heard it over the erectile dysfunction commercial blaring from the television. I clicked the set off.

"Josh was two years, nine months and Kenny not even a year old. Their mother was....well, let's say she was a piece of work and leave it at that. My mother raised me better than to speak ill of the dead."

Penny sucked in a breath, clearly at a loss for words.

"Yeah, so there I am, never having been around babies before, not a clue in the world as to what I should do. Neil was a wreck; she'd really messed with his head, you know? And as a Navy SEAL the amount of time he was around the kids was already limited, never mind custody arrangements and restraining orders. So I literally had no clue, no help, nowhere to turn."

She swallowed. "So, what did you do?"

I shrugged. "The only thing I could do, I dealt. " I smiled, remembering. "Neil didn't like me at first. In fact, he hated me."

Penny's jaw dropped. "You're kidding. You guys are, like, made for each other."

"Thank you. But neither one of us realized it at the time."

"So, what happened?"

The front door opened and a sullen Josh tramped through, followed by his equally perturbed father.

"That's a story for another time." I told Penny, rising to my feet.

Neil nudged his son into the room. Josh cast him a black look, then focused on his tattered shoelaces. "I'm sorry, Mom."

"A man looks a person in the eye," Neil informed him.

Josh looked up and I almost took a step back from the righteous indignation etched on his face. "I apologize for what I said earlier."

Typically, my first instinct was to shout, but every so often cool reasoning triumphed. "You hurt my feelings."

The cold look melted away and he shifted his weight.

"I think I'll go get dinner started." Penny stood with facile grace and made for shelter. I made a get outta here motion with my head to Neil and he nodded once before exiting silently.

"Talk to me, Josh. Did something happen at school?"

He didn't respond, so I pulled him over to the couch. "I can't defend myself if I don't know what happened to set you off."

His lip trembled and the words spilled out like a tsunami. "Sammy calls you Mother Mayhem. He said nothing bad ever happened until we moved here. Now, there's all this stuff about people being killed or kidnapped and houses burning down and you're always involved. I kept telling him it wasn't your fault; that you just happened to be wherever and know whoever. And then you get arrested!" Betrayal glinted at me from his green eyes.

"Aw, crap." I groaned and sat back. "Let me guess, Sammy's dad is a police officer."

258

Josh swiped at a few escaped tears. "His mom, too. So Sammy knows what he's talking about."

"Bull," I told Josh. "He might have heard that I was involved with a few incidents but I'm absolutely positive stuff happened here before I made the scene. And I was working with the police, remember? I've been trying to help fight crime, just like your dad did."

Inspiration struck. "Hey, pal, you know how Dad was always being sent to poverty riddled countries, places with terrorists and war all sorts of bad stuff? Did the whole country get together and say, "Hey, Neil Phillips is coming, let's tear this place up!"

Josh giggled and sniffed. "That's stupid."

"Exactly. You can't go blaming one person for the world's problems. Well, I guess you *could*, but that means you're delusional."

This time the eye-roll was playfully exasperated. "Mo-om,"

"What I'm trying to explain here is that I've ticked off some people around here, Sammy's folks among them. But is it right that they're spending their time griping about me when there are real criminals out there?"

"No, it isn't." Josh scowled. "I'll tell him that next time he opens his stupid mouth."

"Nuh-uh. You'll smile and walk away. Some people are just mean and petty and you can't win with them. So don't play his game, okay? You're better than that." I kissed his forehead. "And don't say stupid."

The doorbell chimed. "Why don't you go get changed and start on your homework?"

259

Josh nodded and I pulled my coat on, pretty sure my house didn't need another police interruption today.

"I was just on my way out." I told Detective Capri as I pushed past her, securing the door so she wouldn't be seen by anyone in the kitchen.

"What in the hell were you doing at Lucas Sloan's house today?" Capri flicked the business card and I winced in sympathy for the young officer who was probably donning a crossing guard uniform at this moment.

"He owes me money, for cleaning his house. Normally, I'd let it slide a while, but since my contacts have dried up thanks to my rap sheet, I didn't have much choice."

"Don't try to make me feel guilty. You're the nutcase who insisted on meddling where a civilian shouldn't like some goddamn vigilante."

"Well excuse the hell out of me! I thought you wanted me to nose around and find dirt for you! Isn't that what the CI position was all about?"

"You're not supposed to solve the flipping case single handedly!"

"Well, that's just what I did. Do you want to hear it or not?"

"Fine." Capri folded her arms across her chest.

So I told her about my ruminating with Neil, the role-playing session at Dr. Bob's, and Sloan's possible involvement.

"So, you see, Candie's behind the whole thing. It makes sense for her to off Lucas Sloan after his usefulness has run its course."

"You've got it all figured out, haven't you." Capri shook her head. "I see one big problem with your theory."

My hands slammed onto my hips. "And what, pray tell, is that?"

"We didn't find Lucas Sloan's corpse. It was Candie Valentino inside the house."

Twenty Two

Sleeping was out of the question. Knees curled under my butt, I perched on the couch in the dark, staring out the window as snow drifted by. The dying embers from the fire Neil started several hours earlier glowed eerily in the grate.

Logically, I knew I hadn't caused Candie's death. I didn't hack her into five pieces or toss kitty litter over the floor and the back path in an effort to hide the crime and make it look like Lucas Sloan had done the deed before rushing out to work. Fortunately for Lucas, he'd been in court, awaiting a new custody hearing with his lawyer at the estimated time of death, which the medical examiner placed between nine and eleven a.m.

After witnessing my distress, Capri had eased her own attack. "You did what you could for her, to find her. More than most people would bother doing for an acquaintance. The FBI accepted that you had nothing to do with this, even if your husband made the 911 call. Sloan verified you'd cleaned his house; that he owed you money. Between Dr. Bob and the FBI, you're solidly alibi-ed for this."

"Is that supposed to make me feel better?" I now whispered into the dark. That finally, the feds couldn't harass me about a horrible crime, just because my alibi would hold in court? A man and a woman were dead, two people who I'd met, who I'd believed the worst about, even for a short moment in time. Obviously, Candie hadn't staged her own dismemberment. I shuddered at the mental picture.

"Come to bed, Uncle Scrooge." Neil fumbled across the cushions a minute, before locating my foot, rubbing gently. "There's nothing else you can do for her."

"I don't understand this." Snow swirled and the house groaned as wind battered from the north. "None of it makes any sense. It's not about money, or technological accolades or revenge. So what's the point?"

"You're forgetting that whoever kidnapped Candie and set up first you, then Sloan, isn't a rational person. You're talking about a madman, someone who likes to cause suffering and chaos wherever he goes. There's no logic in that."

263

His sage words washed over me. "It's got to be about Markus Valentino. The Phoenix; the first letter. There was a reason Valentino didn't report the fax or the dead bird. He's hiding something. Someone wants him to suffer."

Neil groaned and sat up, the comforter falling into his lap. "So the feds, or detective Capri or whoever has to extract the whole story from him. What more can you do?"

"Nothing," I said. "You're right."

"Oh, music to my ears." Neil changed his hold on my ankle and pulled me to the air mattress. "Say it again."

"Not in this lifetime, pal."

He cupped my face in his hands. The kiss was soft, almost delicate, the merest brushing of his lips over mine. "You've done enough worrying in the past few weeks to last a lifetime. Give yourself a break."

Ready to take his advice I leaned up to kiss him when the phone rang.

Neil rolled off of me and flung a hand over his eyes. "Christ Almighty, it never ends." I scurried to the kitchen and forgoing the light, fumbled to answer the cordless.

"Hey Maggie, you're up." Sylvia's voice, more chipper than I'd heard in weeks greeted me.

"Is everything all right?" I asked her, wondering what demon spirit possessed her to call after midnight. "You haven't been drinking again, right?"

"No, but I was lying in bed and I had this epiphany. Can I come over?"

"Sure Sylvie. Come on over."

I hung up the phone and returned to the living room. "Sylvia's coming over. She had an epiphany."

"Cripes, she couldn't have had it during normal business hours?"

I flicked on a table lamp then went to the door, opening it for my friend. "Be nice or go sleep in the camper."

Neil grunted. "Is there a third option?"

Sylvia lighted onto the porch and shook the snow from her head. "Isn't it pretty?" She gestured toward the snow.

"Fabulous," Neil said and I shot him a withering look.

"What's going on, Sylvie?" I took her coat, hung it on the hall tree.

"Well, I couldn't sleep, thinking about poor Candie Valentino and Lucas Sloan too. First his marriage ends and now his house is the scene of a brutal murder. That's a lot of bad juju."

"Agreed." I gestured toward the kitchen. "Do you want some tea?"

"Not right now," She practically bounced down the hall. "So anyway, I thought about all the bad karma in that house and it hit me. A spiritual cleansing."

"A spiritual cleansing." I intoned, waiting for the punch line.

"Yes. So many people suffer from lack of positive energy. They get bogged down by the daily grind, become jaded, and lose hope. Like I did. You come in and cleanse their homes of dirt and grime, but the negative energy festers. What if, you offered a spiritual cleansing along with a physical one? I could teach people how

265

to set up their homes to encourage a positive energy flow, help focus their lives in a more productive direction."

"So, you wanna scrub the death cooties out of Sloan's house?" I set the kettle on the back burner, ignoring her refusal of tea.

She actually considered my words. "That's one way to view it. Think for a second, Maggie. Your business is suffering; this will open new doors for you and for me as well. We have an opportunity to help ourselves here."

I plunked two lemon zinger teabags into mugs. What was it Josh's classmate had dubbed me? Mother Mayhem. . "I don't know Sylvie; it's probably not wise for you to link your name with mine right now."

"We'd have to expand on your territory, maybe into Boston or Cambridge. I could offer spiritual counseling, maybe hold an internet workshop."

The kettle let out a shrill whistle and I removed it from the burner. "Sylvia, did you hear me? I think your idea is fantastic and I'm sure you'd have some takers, but you'd be shooting yourself in the foot by associating with me professionally."

"No, Maggie, don't you see? What better way to advertise that I can solve any metaphysical mess than by pairing up with the notorious Laundry Hag?"

I plunked the mug down more forcefully than intended. "Metaphysical mess, am I?"

Sylvia grinned and brought the mug to her lips. "Undoubtedly, but you're my metaphysical mess."

"Okay, so what would I have to do to be cleansed spiritually?" A vision of me sacrificing a live chicken under the full moon airing on You-tube flitted across my mind.

"Well, first we'd need to set up a website, maybe take out an ad in the paper. One of my former yoga students would probably take us on, especially if we offered her a trial discount." Despite her staunch belief in all things woo-woo, Sylvia's mind was sharp and tuned to practical matters.

"What are you two plotting in here?" Neil leaned against the doorjamb, squinting due to the harsh overhead light.

"My career comeback," I told him. "The Laundry Hag meets...?"

Sylvia cocked her head. "The balance guru?"

Neil made a face. "How about Sylvia's Shui-way?"

"Sounds like a sandwich shop."

"Well, since you're the mastermind behind the laundry hag you think of something."

I yawned. "Tomorrow will be soon enough."

* * * *

For once, the snow from the night before didn't hinder the morning schedule. Neil dropped Josh and Kenny at school on his way to another handyman gig. Sylvia returned at first light and we sat down to map out our business plan. Penny and Marty were still in bed and the house was blessedly quiet.

267

"I can't wait for spring." I told Sylvia over my second cup of coffee. "I want to walk outside and not be bundled up like a pig in a blanket."

"That's only natural." Sylvia didn't look up from her blackberry. She'd already filled half a page on her memo pad with names of her friends and clients who might hire our service to rid their homes of dirt and chaos. "Spring symbolizes rebirth and brings a lighter kind of energy along with the new possibilities."

"Yeah, I could deal with a few of those." I stirred my coffee and watched her work. Having always admired Sylvia's glass-is-half-full attitude, I kept my misgivings about the new business to myself. Personally, I wouldn't hire us, a Hag with a rap sheet and a Barbie Zen master, but hey, what did I know?

My cell phone pealed the standard ring for an unfamiliar number. I dug through my bag, wishing the technology gurus would stop making such dinky devises. My compact was bigger than my phone for heaven's sake and I tended to fat-finger the numbers on this munchkin model.

"I've got you now," I said as I flipped the top open. "Laundry Hag cleaning services, Maggie speaking."

"Is this Maggie Phillips?" The unfamiliar female voice sounded watery, even over the tinny connection.

"Yes, who's speaking please?" The call had come up private name and number. Not at all unusual in the age of rampant phone solicitation.

268

"This is Sierra, Mr. Valentino's executive assistant. I don't know if you remember me...?"

"Of course, what can I do for you?" I pictured the outrageously well-groomed bombshell that'd guarded Valentino's inner sanctum.

"I, um, I found something. Something of Mr. Valentino's. I think he might have killed his wife."

"Not possible," I said, even though her words peeked my interest. "Valentino's still in the hospital and he's being monitored by the FBI. No way could he have caused Candie's death."

"Yes, but I found this file locked in his desk. He hired a private investigator to follow her. In the report, the PI claims she was cheating on him, with another woman. I've worked for Mr. Valentino for a long time; he would never stand for that."

No he wouldn't. "But the timing...?" I mused aloud. Sylvia was watching me, her eyebrows furrowed as she listened to my end of the conversation.

"I think he might have hired someone. You know, before the fire? I don't know what to do."

"Contact the police, ask for Detective Capri. She'll put you in touch with the FBI."

"I know it's horrible of me to ask, but do you think you could come over and stay with me while they're here? I read about you in the newspaper and I know you know how to handle this sort of situation."

269

The wince escaped despite my best efforts. Holding up under police interrogation was not something I wanted people to remember about me. She made a decent point though. Valentino had set me up, cast suspicion on my good name and made my life hell. Didn't I have a vested interest in seeing the evidence of his perfidy?

"Where are you? Where's the file?"

"I'm at the office and I left the file on his desk. I didn't know what else to do."

She sounded so distressed, I made up my mind. "I'll be there shortly. Call the police now; they'll probably be right behind me."

"Thank you," Sierra sniffed.

"What's up?" Sylvia stood, stretching her back.

"I'll update you on the way." I snatched up my bag, unhooked my car keys from the ring, donned my jacket.

The drive to Safari took less than ten minutes and I filled Sylvia in on what Sierra had unearthed.

"So now you think Candie was innocent of staging the abduction? Valentino was behind it all?"

I made a left into the parking garage. "No, I think he played her, just like he did me. She stepped out, went back to her girls behaving badly phase, tried to undermine him by sneaking crucial information to Richard Head. He retaliated by hiring some thug to kidnap her, to show her who was in charge."

"What about the fire? I doubt that was part of his plan."

"Right, I think whoever took Candie got pissed off with Valentino, tried to teach him a lesson. Candie's death was part of it."

"But who?" Despite the heat pumping from the vent, Sylvia shivered. "Who killed her? And Richard?"

"That, I don't know which is why I agreed to come here. Maybe if I get a chance to look through the files, I can piece it all together.

"Do you want me to come up with you?" Sylvia asked, looking as though she might vomit if I said yes.

I shook my head. "No, the police will be here any minute." As if to punctuate my words, sirens blared in the distance. "Do me a favor though, call Neil and tell him what's happening. Marty too."

Sylvia squeezed my hand. "Be careful. And don't get arrested."

"I'll do my best."

Parking garages always creeped me out. Even though they were monitored via video camera, something about the absence of light, the absolute quiet unnerved me. I power-walked over to the elevator, assuming I needed to check in at the security desk before going up to see Sierra.

I pushed the down button and the doors opened immediately. Pools of filthy water, probably tracked in from various boots were visible on the floor of the car. I tip toed around them, and pushed floor number one. The car lurched, and I yipped in fright, but the ride progressed smoothly. Fishing in my bag so my

271

ID would be handy, I didn't pay attention to the lit numbers tracking the car's progress.

A soft ding sounded before the doors slid open. Where the heck was my driver's license? Security might give me a hard time if Sierra hadn't already notified the desk of my impending arrival.

Distracted, I stepped off the elevator, glancing up when my boot heels clicked against concrete instead of the anticipated carpet. The elevator hadn't delivered me to the brightly lit lobby. Instead I found myself in some sort of basement.

"Oh, what the hell?" Annoyed, I turned to face the elevator when I felt the prick of something sharp penetrate my jacket right below my left shoulder blade. Then a jolt of energy and unexpected pain ripped through my system and the world slid away.

Twenty Three

The smell of mildew invaded my
nostrils, forcing consciousness back.
Something gurgled, water I thought, rushing
through pipes. Face pressed against cold, damp
concrete, I had no idea if my eyes were open or
closed. I tried blinking, but nothing came into
focus. My body, sluggish and weak as a
newborn, didn't respond as I willed my arm
forward to check my eyelids.

My hands were tied behind my back.

What the hell happened? Remembering
the elevator, the basement, the sting as
something sharp bit through the layers of
clothing, I pieced together that' I'd been

zapped, most likely by a Taser or stun gun. Who'd done it though? And why?

"Hello?" My voice was as weak as my body, my tongue thick and heavy in my mouth. "Who's there?"

I listened, but no one replied. "Sierra?" She was the only person who knew I was coming. "What's going on?"

Footsteps sounded distantly and I struggled to sit upright, no easy feat with my hands tethered. Florescent light sputtered to life, blinding me as effectively as the darkness. Scrunching my eyes closed, I called out again. "Sierra?"

"Oh, she's not available right now. I have her stashed elsewhere." The man's voice and cadence sounded familiar and foreign all at once. I slitted one eye open but still couldn't see worth shit.

"Who are you?" I asked as I felt more than heard him move closer.

A high pitched giggle, almost effeminate was my only answer. Retrenching, I asked, "Why did you tie me up?"

"You've proven yourself to be resourceful and I can't have anyone mucking with my plans."

Dread, slimy and cold settled in my gut. "What plans?"

"The destruction of Safari and all of Valentino's minions, of course. The time has come, and out of the ashes of his wicked empire, the phoenix will rise and live for a thousand years."

Hell, my unconscious mind had set me up in a crappy B movie. This couldn't be real. "Tell me who you are, why you're doing this."

A flashlight with enough juice to power the greater Boston Area, clicked on directly in my eyes. I yelped and slammed my eyelids down before my retinas sizzled up like fatty bacon. The man laughed again, and perspiration popped out on my forehead as I picked up on the hysterical note.

"Every villain must have a foil and I am Markus Valentino's. My father was the lead engineer on Valentino's power solutions team in Austin. Unfortunately, he made the mistake of signing an intellectual property rights agreement that allowed Valentino to have first dibs on his every innovation. Years, I spent, watching him profit from my father's work, reaping all the benefits of someone else's labor. I watched as my father withered while that bastard flourished, married a rich debutante and soared to even greater heights. Too weak to fight the evil, I was with him when my father breathed his last. And then, Maggie, the most amazing thing happened. My father's essence filled me.

Sick. I retched in my mouth, swallowing the tangy bile back down since the damn flashlight was still trained on my face. This guy was disturbed on a level I'd never fathomed. Some survival instinct warned he wouldn't appreciate my take and I kept my lips compressed together.

"His final gift to me, my father gave me the means to bring Valentino down forever. I am my father reborn, the phoenix."

275

The man liked to talk and I decided to use it to my advantage. As long as he blathered his heart out, nothing bad could happen. Sylvia would come in eventually and the police were nearby. "That must have been hard for you, living your father's life instead of your own."

"Greatness demands sacrifice, but the rewards will soon abound. I thought Valentino's wife would be my first reward. She came to me, just as my father's spirit had predicted, offering to help on my quest. And for a time, I thought I could slip into his life, keep his woman for my own. But she was impure, sullying herself with her own sex. Sickening."

"Candie wanted you to bring Valentino to justice. She didn't see your vision." I prompted, trying not to wet myself in fear. God knew I didn't have the faintest idea what I was messing with and this guy was bat shit crazy.

Apparently, I'd said the right thing. The flashlight lowered and satisfaction emanated from him in waves. "You understand. I knew you would. Smart girl, devoted to her cause, just like me. It's not your fault you entered the game too late and on the wrong side. If you were beautiful, I might consider keeping you for my own. Alas, you are too ordinary."

"Hey!" Why the hell was I annoyed? Oh gee, Mr. Lunatic phoenix hack-em-up doesn't think I'm beautiful. BFD. Unfortunately, my logical brain was sitting backseat to adrenaline. "So, how did you find out that Candie was just using you and your vision to her own ends?"

"It was you, actually," I winced, not willing to take on responsibility for Candie's evisceration. "You mentioned it during your meeting with Valentino. His chauffer has proven to be a reliable asset, willing to record Valentino's conversations and sell them to the highest bidder."

I swallowed around the lump in my throat. "And Richard was another bidder."

My captor snorted. My vision had improved and I could make out a shadowy shape, small to average for a man. "What a waste of flesh. And his obsession with Valentino and his fortune was as disgusting as it was unnatural. Of course, I would have let him be, but Candie had brought him in, promising him all sorts of ridiculous rewards. I couldn't have an outsider privy to what happened in my company, could I? Putting out his light was pure pleasure."

So what we have here is a homophobic daddy's boy on a mission to kill, maim and incinerate anything in his path. Skippy. Unfortunately, I still didn't know who I was dealing with, and the deficiency put me at a serious disadvantage.

"So, what's next?" I asked, curious despite my better judgment.

The light bobbed as the man moved. "Well, Valentino's lost his wife, his reputation is in tatters and his home reduced to a pile of cinders. The only thing he has left is this building. But not for long." This statement seemed to amuse him and that chilling laugh reverberated off my concrete prison.

"You're going to kill me, aren't you?" Despite my question, I knew he wouldn't have explained all this if he intended to let me go.

277

The giggles cut off abruptly, and I winced as he crouched down beside me. A cold hand brushed my cheek and I flinched at his clammy touch.

"All good things must come to an end. I'll be sure to send your husband my regrets. He doesn't need to know you were running around using your maiden name, it will only add to his pain."

It clicked into place. "Oh my God, Alan Garner."

* * * *

Garner, the sick bastard, appeared delighted by my reaction. "Never suspected me, did you? Neither does anyone else. Sierra knows now, since I chloroformed her after encouraging her to call you. She and the others in this building will be sacrificed for the greater good. Fifteen minutes from now, they will be nothing but corpses buried under mountains of rubble."

"Why kill everyone? Valentino's your target; no one else has to die."

"Oh, but I want them to die. I want to feel their mortal lives ending, to acquire a piece of their souls and make it my own. Just like my father's. It's my destiny."

"I thought your destiny was to take Valentino's place." Nothing worse than a psycho who couldn't keep his story straight.

Garner shrugged. "I've learned to multitask, I can be both." With that, he stepped back into the darkness, directed the light in my face, interrogation style. "The end is upon you

Margaret Sampson Phillips. If you choose to repent, I will hear your sins."

"Freaking drama queen!" I shouted into the darkness. "You're nothing but a sneaky snake in the grass. You're pathetic."

In all the books I'd ever read, this kind of goading would see some volatile reaction from the antagonist. Garner laughed his creepy, girly laugh again.

"Oh, Maggie, still fighting the good fight. I admire your weak attempts to unhinge me, but they are all in vain. I have a plan you see, a flawless plan."

"From what I understand, every tech geek and his brother are racing to find a way to make solar technology a living reality. What makes you think you'll get there first?"

"I've been siphoning off money from under Valentino's nose for several years now. I've sent the little file Sierra phoned you about to the police. When he goes to jail for murdering his wife, I'll be ready to run things in his absence. And I'll be sure to visit him, to let him know who was behind it all. For a man as arrogant as Valentino, no torture could be worse than realizing he was had by one of his drones."

He chuckled, the flashlight bouncing maniacally as his body shook with raptures.

"They're going to investigate. Someone will discover you set the explosion."

Garner, still laughing softly, moved off and I panicked, trying to get my feet under me. Whatever he'd jolted me with still had my muscles twitching to the point my body felt like unset Jell-O.

"Since I told Markus that the maintenance staff was an unnecessary expense, he fired the lot when rough economic times struck. The hot water heater is going to overload, just another tragedy which could have been avoided with proper maintenance. Believe me; no one will bother looking further than Markus Valentino."

"You're wrong. Detective Capri won't be satisfied with a tidily wrapped case and coincidence. She'll find you." So would Neil, but I didn't want to make him a target.

"Ah, Maggie, I've enjoyed our chat. Try and take comfort in the fact that your essence will live on, through me." The light clicked off and I heard his footsteps fading away. A high-pitched whistling disrupted the gloomy quiet; bringing a distinct change in air pressure.

Panic snaked through my brain, muddying my thoughts. If this lunatic had his way, I'd never see my family again. They needed me to act, just as the innocent people in this building needed me to get off my keister and stop Garner. I didn't have a plan but one thing was clear, no way would I let him waltz out of here. Rocking to my feet, I stumbled toward the mechanical whine. Footfalls sounded to my left and I dogged him, hoping to take him by surprise.

Still unable to see, I focused on my other senses. The humidity had increased, similar to the feeling in the air right before a major rainstorm. Sweat trickled down my neck, chaffed the fabric around my bound wrists. The blood pounding in my ears roared, commanding too much of my attention. I stopped, focused on breathing through my nose and listened. The footsteps were gone.

Clink, clink, clink. The noise, too random to be mechanical was coming from my left. Was Garner there? I had no weapons and my hands were bound, sorry odds against a nut job and his Taser. The rubber soles of my sneakers made no discernible noise so I might have surprise on my side, as well as a rabid desire to live. The metal on metal sound grew louder and this weird déjà vu sensation tickled my brain.

"Hello?" I called out. "Is someone there?"

"You fool," My mother's voice hissed in reprimand, "He's *there!*" I ignored her and called out again.

The clanging increased to a frantic level and I staggered towards the sound. The basement was huge and my sense of direction severely compromised my barely stifled fear. My feet tangled in something and I went down hard, face first. Something light fluttered down wrapping me up like a gag gift.

"Crap," I moaned, sure my nose was broken. Blood, hot and tangy gushed down my chin. I rolled and bucked until the sheet which had ensnared me gave up. Good news was it had been covering a small window, and darkness turned to dimness. I wiped my face on the sheet and used my stomach muscles to pull me upright.

The elevator was nowhere in sight, but I made out the cylindrical shape which vibrated alarmingly on its concrete platform. More than five times the size of my own hot water heater, the prospect of that thing exploding was beyond terrifying. My ears popped as I swallowed blood, but I managed to lurch forward.

What I understood about hot water heaters couldn't fill a Dixie cup, but I did recall an episode of *Mythbusters* when the guys had intentionally detonated one by steadily increasing the pounds per square inch. The tank hadn't technically exploded, more of launched itself through the building which housed it, but considering the total destruction, I doubt anyone would argue semantics with the rubble.

It seemed to me the big thing was just an overgrown pressure cooker, and I did know how to work one of those. There had to be some sort of release valve, to ease the pressure and keep the thing from taking off like a rocket. If I were the guy to design this, where would I put it?

"Within easy reach," was the logical answer. Easy, that is when one wasn't disabled by bound hands. I was so focused on the tank; I almost missed the small shape tethered to one of the pipes. The clinks had originated from the metal cuffs imprisoning her.

I squinted and rushed forward. "Sierra?" Holy God, this was just like that dream, except, my mind had superimposed Candy Valentino as my fellow prisoner. Pushing the thought away, I turned around and groped with my numbing fingers, feeling my way to the flimsy gag. "Just hang in there, I've almost got this."

I yanked, and the final knot slipped free and Sierra bubbled over. "Oh, Maggie, I'm so sorry! It's Alan; he's lost his mind and I—"

I interrupted her with a sharp noise and spun around, assessing the situation. Not enough time to work her free first. "Sierra, do you know where the pressure release valve is for the hot water tank? We need to vent the steam before it goes critical."

"I don't, I'm sorry." She started to cry. "My kids, oh God, I don't want to die!"

"Listen to me; we are going to get out of this, you have to trust me. Sierra, listen to me." I squatted down with my back to her, my bound hands in line with hers. "Can you untie me?"

Her fingers fumbled, nails scraping my abused wrists. "I don't know, it's so tight and I can't see."

"You're doing fine." I coaxed, praying my latest harebrained scheme wouldn't be the last. Sierra worked the knot, each tug had me wincing. After an eternity she loosened the knot and I managed to work one wrist free of the rope.

"Maggie, please go. Save yourself."

Ignoring her plea, I turned my attention to the tank. Carefully, I stepped onto the concrete platform. Balanced on the balls of my feet, my forehead only reached halfway up the tank. Numerous warning stickers decorated the thing. Up above my head was a sticker and an upwards facing arrow labeled Pressure Relief Valve. Heat emanated from the cylinder and I could only imagine what sort of temperature was going on inside the tank. Standing on my tiptoes, I could see the release valve had been melted down to an unrecognizable lump of metal.

Shit, it had been a shot in the dark anyway. Of course Garner would have anticipated that I'd get free. In all likelihood, he got off on the image of my futile efforts. I stepped down, carefully avoiding Sierra. If I couldn't release the pressure by traditional means....

My gaze landed on a fire ax, enshrined in glass next to a doorway. My mind couldn't even imagine the possible outcomes, but I was operating under the idea that doing something was indeed better than nothing. The little metal hammer hung from a string next to the case and I raised it, looking away as the glass shattered. The ax was much heavier than I'd anticipated, but I had adrenalin driven panic on my side.

"Sierra, I'm going to get you free. As soon as I do, I want you to run for that door as fast as you can, all right?"

Even in the gloom, I saw the whites of her eyes as she focused on the ax. "What about you?"

"I'll be right behind you. Move your wrists as far apart as you can."

She did and shut her eyes. *Aim and concentration. It's just like darts.* I focused on the metal links on her handcuffs, holding the ax in a firm grip and swung. Unlike in the movies, the ax didn't cut clean through the chain, but it did manage to break a few links and not lop either hand off. Setting the ax down, I worked it, pulling her away from the pipe until the weakened metal gave way.

"Go!" I commanded. Sierra stumbled once, but jackrabbit-ed to the door. I gauged the distance between the tank and the door as maybe fifty feet. Time to see if my running skills were up to par. I stood ten feet back, ax poised over my head, waiting until she was safe. The door banged against the wall, my cue. *You could have been a great marksman.* Neil's praise funneled my concentration to the point I intended to hit. *Just a really big dart.*

"Here goes everything." I flung the ax at the tank.

Twenty Four

Not waiting to see if the ax hit its mark, I bolted toward the door. Great clouds of steam erupted with an angry whistle, scalding my bare hands and face, but I pushed on.

It was the longest sprint of my life, but I made it through the door, slamming it closed in my wake. Giant blisters bubbled up on my hands and the bright florescent lights blinded me after the gloom of the basement. Someone had sounded a fire alarm, and as I took the stairs two at a time. Breathing through my broken nose was out of the question, as I tasted blood with every swallow. Gasping for breath, I reached the landing for the lobby and flung the door open, revealing the security desk.

"Get everyone out of the building, now!" I shouted at the stunned guard and, having preformed enough heroics for one day, bolted for the glass doors.

"Hey, wait a minute, what the hell's going on? Did you set the fire alarm off? That's illegal, you know." The guard moved like a striking snake and grabbed my jacket. I slipped my arms out of it and kept going, not willing to play twenty questions right now.

"Maggie!" Neil, along with Detective Capri and the feds were on the sidewalk, heading into the building. "Good God almighty, what happened to you?"

I shoved at him, attempting to move us both to a safer distance. "Garner," I wheezed. "Alan Garner, did it all, he's going to blow up the building."

My words were like a brand to a herd of oxen. Capri got on the radio, screaming out orders and the feds circled me like vultures, their questions pecking at what was left of my damaged carcass.

"Where is it? What kind of explosive?"

"Basement, hot water tank. I threw an ax at it, but it might still go off."

"Get her to the car." Salazar ordered Feist. "Take her to the hospital, and have those burns treated."

"I'm going too." Neil looked more panicked than I'd ever seen him, almost like his skin was holding all of his vibrating energy together. He scooped me up, careful to avoid touching my skin.

"No hospital," I begged but was soundly ignored. Feist ushered us into the back of an unmarked black car and shut the door. I closed my eyes, my muscles still twitching. "Sylvia?" I asked Neil.

"She's fine. She took your car back home."

I took a deep breath, the first it seemed I'd taken in eons and doubled over from the pain. "Christ, what's happening?"

"Get us the fuck out of here!" Neil's hands hovered over me, his energy touching where skin could not. "You've been badly burned, Uncle Scrooge. We're getting you to the hospital."

"He wanted to kill everyone, everyone in the building, just because they worked for Valentino. He killed Candie, cut her up." Something drove me to get it all out, in case I didn't make it.

"We know. We found his DNA in Sloan's house. Valentino had all of his staffs on file. Being the paranoid sort, he did it without their knowledge."

"Isn't that illegal?" I really didn't care, but anything was better than focusing on the gut-churning pain.

Feist smiled. "Yes, it is."

"'You're gonna get burned,'" I murmured, sick at the irony. "Garner got his wish, Valentino's going down." That damn note had been an omen, and my sorry self had insisted on getting involved. What had I been thinking? The worry in Neil's voice, the frantic edge on his very presence iced my pain with grief

"I couldn't let him win. Couldn't leave the kids, leave you." My vision clouded, and tunneled. "So sorry," I whispered and lost consciousness.

* * * *

When I came to, I groaned, not from pain, but from the smells of the hospital. Gauze pads swathed my hands and head in a light, but continuous mummification. Someone was talking in the low, sepulchral tones used in rooms like this.

"Appears to be second degree burns. We've started her on a course of intravenous antibiotics to

288

prevent any infection, as well as low dose morphine for pain management."

My gaze cut to the I.V. stand that dripped clear fluid down into a tube connected to the needle in my arm. "Well, this sucks," I croaked.

Neil was at my side in an instant. "Hey there, hot stuff. How's it going?"

"It's going."

"Let's check those bandages," The woman I assumed to be the doctor smiled reassuringly as she unwrapped one arm. "Looking good."

I glanced at the puffy red skin covered with angry blisters and winced. "On what planet?"

The doctor brought out a fresh roll of gauze and a stack of sterile pads. "The one where you don't need skin grafts. You're a very lucky woman. The burns don't extend past the dermis. You'll be back up to speed in about a month, with only minor scaring."

My mind's eye envisioned something akin to the phantom of the opera. "Will I have to wear a mask and go lurching around underground sewers?"

"Not unless you really want to." She secured the wrap and smiled. I'll be back in a few hours.

Neil sighed and flopped into the chair beside my bed.

"I'm so sorry...," I began but he held up a hand.

"I think we should move."

"What?" I tried to sit up, a huge mistake as my battered body protested vehemently. "Why?"

He patted the air, urging me to lie still. "No good has come from us being in Hudson. You hate the winter, and I hate seeing you like this."

Panic tightened my vocal cords. "Think this through, love. Winter's almost over. We can't sell the house in this economy and the boys, and Marty's mess. And I promised Sylvia we'd make a go at the joint Shui Cleaning thing. And Leo's going to be off his game for a while, after Richard. He'll need us close by. It just isn't the right time. It was one madman, Neil. One guy caused all this misery. And the police are gonna get him, right?"

"We already have him in custody." Detective Capri entered, her hard cop eyes assessing my condition. "He's in interrogation with the feds right now, spilling every detail, going over every nuance of his," she made air quotes with her fingers "grand master plan.' It seems Candie was the linchpin, she agreed to stage the kidnapping in order to punish Valentino. She told him how to access the house security system, where to plant bugs after the FBI had swept for them, so he was always one step ahead.

From what I could discern, he made a pass at Candie, but she announced she was through with men and he lost whatever cool reason he'd ever possessed, hacked her into pieces, and set up Sloan as a convenient scapegoat. So don't worry about Garner. He'll be locked away for the rest of his life, I guarantee it. Valentino's closing down shop too, since his shoddy ethics have been put under a microscope. He'll probably start over in some other state, but without the financial backing of Candie's family."

She turned to Neil. "Don't let him chase you away, don't let him win."

Neil was on his feet before I could blink. "Maybe if you did your job, she wouldn't be in this mess." He stabbed a finger at the bed. "Maybe if you actually protected the people you're sworn to serve, I might feel comfortable staying put."

Unfair. I opened my mouth to speak but coughed violently instead, returning my husband's focus to me. He poured some water into a plastic cup and inserted a straw into my mouth. "Calm yourself,

Uncle Scrooge. You don't have to make any decisions right now."

The water was cool going down, soothing my parched throat. "Not her fault." I croaked. The statement brought forth a new coughing jag.

"I'll leave. I just wanted to tell you that the City Council voted to honor you at the spring festival next month. We're all grateful for your...," I could practically see her swallowing her pride, "Sacrifices."

Neil's gaze bore into the back of her head as she left. "Cold comfort. A citizen's award, just ducky."

"I never received an award before," I whispered. "To you it's no big deal, but to me...."

Neil sighed and I smiled, glad to know I'd won this round. We'd stay, at least until spring. Warmth, hope, a new start. That reminded me...,

"After I'm back on my feet, let's get a dog for Kenny. And we promised to set Josh up in his own room."

He shook his head. "We don't have the space right now, what with Marty and Penny—"

"Yeah, I've got an idea about them, too."

"Oh sweet Jesus," Neil gazed heavenward and flopped back into the chair.

~The End~

Want more Maggie and Neil? Join them in the zany mystery series

The Misadventures of the Laundry Hag: Swept Under the Rug

Narrated by Suzanne Cerreta

Now available on Audiobook

Audible

Amazon

iTunes

Book 1: The Misadventures of the Laundry Hag: Skeletons in the Closet

Maggie Phillips hasn't had it easy. As the wife of retired Navy SEAL, and the adoptive mother of two little hellions, Maggie is constantly looking for ways to improve her family's financial situation. She accepts a cleaning position for her new neighbors (who redefine the term 'eccentric'), never imagining she will end up as the sole alibi for a man with a fascination for medieval torture devices when he is brought up on murder charges.

While Maggie struggles to prove the man's innocence, her deadbeat brother arrives, determined to sell Maggie and Neil on his next great scheme and to mooch with a vengeance. If that isn't bad enough, her in-laws, (the cut-throat corporate attorneys) descend on the house, armed with disapproval and condemnation, for the family's annual Thanksgiving celebration.

As the police investigation intensifies, Maggie searches for the killer among the upper echelon of Hudson, Massachusetts in the only way she can— by scrubbing their thrones.

Of the porcelain variety, that is...

ISBN-13: 978-1511761826   ISBN-10: 1511761822

Available in print, ebook and audiobook narrated by Suzanne Cerreta.

Book 3: The Misadventures of the Laundry Hag: All Washed Up

Maggie Phillips is fine—just ask her. So what if two psychos tried to do her in and her business is all but dead, she never wanted to be the laundry hag to begin with, so why should she mourn her tattered reputation? With spring comes a fresh start, garage sale season and the birth of her brother's first child. Life goes on even if cleaning has lost its luster and the sight of her scarred hands brings back horrific memories.

Help is on the way, whether she wants it or not. When Maggie's mother-in-law asks her to assist with renovations to their project house in upstate New York, she smells a rat. Matters become murkier when Laura casually tells the former laundry hag to "see to that pesky ghost," like the phantom is ring around the bathtub. But both Neil and Sylvia are eager to undertake the zany task and really, what else does she have to do?

How about solve a two decade old murder, find a few long lost relatives, fix her mental hang-ups and reconnect with the husband she's pushed away. And if she has any time to spare, maybe she can even survive a pissed-off apparition and keep it from finishing the job the last two killers started Third time's the charm...right?

ISBN-13: 978-1511811798   ISBN-10: 151181179X

Available in print, on ebook or for audiobook narrated by Suzanne Cerreta.

And before she was the laundry hag, Maggie Sampson was just a girl looking for a hero. And a clue.

Cue Neil.

Who Needs A Hero?

A romantic comedy available now.

A Heroine in Distress....

In the span of one afternoon, Maggie Sampson lost everything—her job, her fiancé and her inheritance. The thing she'll miss most though is her mind. What else could explain her vision of the handsome and enigmatic stranger who retrieved her engagement ring when she hurled the rock into the Atlantic Ocean? Normal people just don't do things like that. Sometimes fantasy is better than reality.

A Hero Who Needs Saving....

To the rest of the world, Neil Phillips is a decorated war hero, a Navy SEAL who has what it takes to get the job done. In private he is a walking raw wound with two boys, a broken marriage and a nasty case of PTSD. Despite his personal struggles he helped Maggie when she needed it most. Now, Maggie is on a mission and she's not going anywhere until she returns the favor—with interest.

Who Needs A Hero?

A warrior with a wounded heart, a woman with

nothing to lose—there are no victims here, only courageous souls, both in need of rescue.

ISBN-13: 978-1463620967   ISBN-10: 1463620969

Now available in print, ebook and audiobook narrated by Suzanne Cerreta.

Audible

Amazon

iTunes

About the Author

Jennifer L. Hart knows that surviving as military spouse takes persistence, comfort food and a stellar sense of humor. Her books often focus on people who've lived the military lifestyle and zany antics of neurotic heroines, who like to eat, drink and have fun. Her works include the Misadventures of the Laundry Hag mystery series, the Damaged Goods mystery series and the Southern Pasta Shop mysteries. Follow her on social media using the hashtag ***#mysterieswithhart*** or visit her on the web at *www.jenniferlhart.com* or *www.laundryhag.com*

Made in the USA
Middletown, DE
26 April 2016